PLAYING WITH FIRE

"What did you wish to say?" Annis asked Don Alonzo with a show of indifference.

Sparks flashed from his dark eyes. "Do not toy with me, Lady Burham. And do not prose on about your English proprieties. They should never stand in the way of a man and a woman in love."

Before Annis could speak, he seized her, kissed her. "Let me go!" she demanded.

He smiled the same superbly confident smile that always irritated her so. "Protest if you wish, but I know deep down that you could not prefer a tame English squire to me. You need excitement in your life, and passion."

"I shall scream," Annis told him.

"It is kind of you to warn me," he said, and bent his head to hers again . . .

CAROL PRO... ...Harlingen, Texas. She attended the College of ... and Mary in Virginia, where she received her B.A. in English with a minor in European History. She obtained her Master's degree in Scriptwriting from the University of Texas in Austin. After working in broadcasting in various parts of Texas, she married and now has a young son. Her favorite pastimes include gardening, fishing, and music.

A Dashing Widow

by

Carol Proctor

A SIGNET BOOK

With thanks to all the lawyers in my family,
this book is dedicated, with love,
to Mom and Dad

SIGNET
Published by the Penguin Group
Penguin Books USA Inc., 375 Hudson Street,
New York, New York, 10014, U.S.A.
Penguin Books Ltd, 27 Wrights Lane, London W8 5TZ, England
Penguin Books Australia Ltd, Ringwood, Victoria, Australia
Penguin Books Canada Ltd, 10 Alcorn Avenue, Toronto, Ontario, Canada M4V 3B2
Penguin Books (N.Z.) Ltd, 182-190 Wairau Road,
Auckland 10, New Zealand

Penguin Books Ltd, Registered Offices:
Harmondsworth, Middlesex, England

First published by Signet, an imprint of New American Library,
a division of Penguin Books USA Inc.

First Printing, September, 1991

10 9 8 7 6 5 4 3 2 1

PUBLISHER'S NOTE
This is a work of fiction. Names, characters, places, and incidents either are the product of the author's imagination or are used fictitiously, and any resemblance to actual persons, living or dead, events, or locales is entirely coincidental.

. . . I leaped headlong into the Sea, and thereby have become better acquainted with the Soundings, the quicksands, & the rocks, than if I had stayed upon the green shore, and piped a silly pipe, and took tea & comfortable advice.

—*John Keats, 1818*

1

THE air was thick and hot. The high winds which had made midday bearable had slackened with the afternoon, denying any promise of respite from the heat. The damp, warm air was a wearying and almost insufferable blanket, making every movement an effort.

A dejected little figure in black sat facing out the window, her chin sunk in her hands, an expression of resigned melancholy upon her face. She was watching, with no particular interest, a dark-skinned native who was preparing to divest a nearby palm of its coconuts. As he grappled with the narrow trunk and began to inch his way up it, she evinced no admiration for his acrobatic daring. As the top of the tree began to sway with the man's exertions, a small black shape dislodged itself and began to career in confused and ever-widening circles. Her languor vanished instantly. Leaping to her feet, she took hold of the heavy shutters and hurriedly closed them, leaving the room in semidarkness.

A dark-haired young woman, whose beauty was marred only slightly by the pair of spectacles upon her nose, gave a sigh and looked up from her sewing.

"Really, Annis! How do you expect me to get this work done when I haven't any light?"

The other made no move to reopen the jalousies. "It was a bat," she said with a shudder.

Sitting in a corner, an open-faced youth who had apparently been nursing a grievance came to life with a snort. "Women! As if that little thing could hurt you. A fine spectacle you made of yourself the other day, shrieking and rushing about the room as if there were a mad bull after you—"

A sharp glance from a pair of bespectacled blue eyes halted him in the midst of his tirade.

7

"That disgusting creature made straight for me when I opened the door to the room—you saw it!"

As her half-brother made a scornful noise somewhere deep in his throat, her sister, Elizabeth, leapt in hurriedly. "Now, you know they said that it was by the unlikeliest mischance that it found its way into our room."

Annis shuddered again. "It was horrible—and this whole island is covered with those repulsive creatures. No one seemed to think it was anything out of the ordinary to be attacked by a—"

Her brother, Laurie, his youthful patience exhausted, rose and addressed her. "Give over, Annis. This poor bat's undoubtedly gone by now, and it's sweltering in here." His wilted shirt points gave testimony to the truth of his statement.

Annis' head snapped around at the mention of this fresh affliction. "It's *always* sweltering on this accursed island—so miserably hot in the midst of winter—and so wet! I hate crawling between the sheets at night because they are always damp!"

Elizabeth, who had put down the lawn handkerchief she was carefully edging with black thread, now folded it and placed it in her workbasket. "Well, we won't have to suffer it much longer now. The ship leaves for England tomorrow, after all."

Her soothing words had the unhappy effect of reminding Laurie once again of the unjust blow he had been dealt. "Yes, and I still don't see what harm it would have caused for me to have gone down to watch them load it. I'm old enough to take care of myself, after all." He anticipated Elizabeth's response and cut her off before she had a chance to begin. "And you needn't feed me all that rot again about Annis needing my support and all. What good am I doing shut up in the room here? Just because she's in mourning, I don't see why none of the rest of us can go anywhere or do anything either—"

He was interrupted by Elizabeth, whose own stock of equanimity was growing rather short. "Oh, do be quiet, Laurie."

Surprisingly, it was Annis who burst in, "No, he is right. What are any of us doing here, after all? To spend months traveling across the ocean, in constant sickness from the motion, in order to land on this blasted island with the heat, the bats, and the insects. And all for nothing!" Her anger increasing, she tore off her widow's cap and flung in on the floor. "I hate it! I hate this miserable island and I hate these wretched clothes, and it's all Richard's fault!" Another female might then have indulged herself with a fit of weeping, but Annis was made of sterner stuff.

Laurie was startled into silence by this display, but Elizabeth merely directed a significant glance at him before responding mildly, "It seems a little unfair to blame Richard for our predicament. As I recall, he was more than willing to wait. You were the one who insisted upon an immediate wedding." She might have added that Richard himself had hardly chosen to be lost at sea. Some urgent business had taken him from Jamaica to Honduras before their arrival, and during the return voyage the ship had encountered a terrible storm and had sunk, taking all hands down with it. The weeks of hoping in the face of ever-increasing doubt had taken their toll on her sister. When the certain news of Richard's death had reached them, Annis had closeted herself for a day, then reemerged as she was now, fiercely angry and determined not to shed a tear.

Annis was about to speak, but Elizabeth forestalled her by saying smoothly, "Laurie, would you be kind enough to fetch us some lemonade? Yes, I know that the servants might do it, but I would like you to bring it to us yourself."

As the door closed behind him, Annis rounded on her sister. "You know very well that I would have preferred to marry Richard before he left England." She scowled at the memory. "But he had to go and sail off for the other side of the world again, without even saying good-bye to me first!"

"He did write a letter to explain why he had to leave so suddenly," Elizabeth pointed out in a fair-minded way. Taking advantage of her sister's preoccupation, she rose and crossed the room to reopen the shutters.

"If that wasn't just like Richard, too!" Annis stamped her foot in rage at the thought. "Leaving without any sort of apology—just a lot of idiotic nonsense about business affairs. He simply assumed that I would be happy to sit there buried in the country until he deigned to return."

"Richard always was a trifle high-handed," admitted her sister.

"A trifle!" Annis' wrath almost kept her from speaking.

"Look at our engagement. Did he ever ask me to marry him? No!" She snorted in disgust. "He simply *informed* me that he had settled everything with Cousin Ambrose, as if I should be pleased to hear it."

"It seemed to me that you *were* pleased to hear it," her sister said with a flagrant disregard for danger. Ignoring Annis' tirade, she had seated herself once more and resumed her sewing.

"Well . . ." Annis was at a loss for words for a moment. "That is not to the point at all. He never even considered my feelings in the matter, which is all of a piece with his treatment of me. He has always shown the most blatant disregard for my wishes."

"I wish you would keep your voice down," Elizabeth remarked with an air of futility. "I can't help but think that everyone in the street might not wish to be privy to these family matters."

Annis rounded on her. "I suppose you think I should be sitting here in the corner sobbing over Richard, simply because he's dead. Well, I won't!" She added with vehemence, "I won't be such a hypocrite. Why should I pretend to mourn a man who did his best to vex me and thwart me when he was alive? Why, if he could see the pickle we are in now, he'd probably laugh, just the way he always . . ." She stopped in the midst of what she was about to say, her lower lip trembling suspiciously.

"Unconvincing, sister," Elizabeth muttered under her breath, but aloud she said, "I do not see that we are any worse off than before. We are merely inconvenienced for the present."

Annis would have responded hotly, but she was forestalled by Elizabeth, who waved a finger at her before gathering up her sewing and rising once again. "I am afraid that I shall have to find a room where there is some peace and quiet if I am ever to finish this handkerchief, not that you will need it, of course." She smiled rather sadly at her sister. "If being angry at Richard helps you forget your grief, then I do not care what others may think either. You may tell Laurie that I am in the next room." She turned and left, closing the door softly behind her.

It would have been entirely understandable if Annis had thereupon flung herself down on a chair and indulged herself in tears, but she scorned such theatrics. She shook her glossy black ringlets and drew herself to her entire five-foot-two-inch height.

She pulled her lips together tautly in order to regain some semblance of self-control. "I mustn't think about him now," she murmured to herself, "I must devise some way out of this predicament." Elizabeth could afford to be calm. She didn't know the full extent of their problems.

Broodingly, Annis once again assumed her former position by the window. She was not to enjoy more than a few minutes of solitary contemplation, however.

Without preamble, the door opened and Laurie entered, awkwardly balancing a tray that held a pitcher of lemonade and several glasses. He looked about him with an obvious sense of grievance.

"If that isn't Lizzie all over! She sends me down to get this stupid lemonade and then she disappears before I bring it."

"You had better put it down before you drop it," Annis advised him. "She said to tell you she'd be in the next room."

Taking her advice, Laurie set the tray on the table emphatically, so that the glasses tinkled together and the lemonade splashed about dangerously.

"Well, if she thinks I'm carrying it to her, she's wrong. It was all an excuse to be rid of me anyway." His sense of ill-usage did not prevent him from pouring a generous glass of lemonade and downing it.

"No, thank you. I do not care for any," Annis said irritably.

Her remark apparently went unheeded by Laurie, for he poured another glass and flung himself down in an armchair. There was little about him which proclaimed that he shared the same father as Annis and Elizabeth. He was as fair as they were dark, and seemed to have inherited all the characteristics of his Scottish mother's family, from his sunny temper to the lavish dusting of freckles across his nose. Although just sixteen, he took seriously his responsibility as his sisters' male protector, a fact which often made him seem less a boy than he actually was.

"Haven't told her about Ambrose yet, have you?" he remarked noncommittally.

Annis had the grace to look ashamed. "No, how could I? Particularly when she doesn't seem to have any suspicions herself."

"Well, you've made things deuced awkward, haven't you?

Can't imagine that the slimy fellow intends to welcome us back with open arms.''

"How on earth was I to know that Richard was to go and get himself killed? He seemed the unlikeliest person in the world to . . .'' A disobedient tear escaped one eye and she dabbed at it angrily. "Anyway, I would have had control of my money by now, and Richard would have seen to it that Ambrose dealt honestly with Elizabeth's portion.''

"It's not that I really blame Ambrose,'' Laurie said philosophically, between sips of lemonade. "Not with that shrew he's married to. Can't understand why fellows want to get married anyway.'' He shook his head sorrowfully at the thought.

"He fell in love with a pretty face,'' Annis remarked scornfully. "But he should have had better sense than to marry so expensive a wife.'' She heaved a sudden sigh. "But it does no good to discuss that now. The question is, what are we going to do?''

A dejected silence met her question. She shook her head. "I have made a muddle of things, haven't I?''

To see Annis downhearted was an unusual sight. Laurie did his best to respond. He put down his lemonade, rose, and crossed the room to pat her awkwardly on the shoulder. "That's all right. If you hadn't said something, I probably would have. Remember, he'd been dipping into my funds too. When we discovered that Ambrose had been paying that tutor only half of what he said he was, I was ready to go to Sir Ralph. Perhaps I should have,'' he added thoughtfully.

"No, Sir Ralph was too ill. And Ambrose would have had some excuse ready anyway. He's clever enough for that.'' She reached over to pat the hand resting on her shoulder. "It's sweet of you to try to take some of the blame, but it's all my fault, as usual. I simply don't think before I do things. Oh, how could I be so stupid!'' She sank her face into her hands.

Laurie was not unusually perceptive, but even he could see that Annis was leaving part of her worries unspoken, and he addressed her with a sudden sharpness. "Look here, you're not imaging that Ambrose would try to do anything desperate, are you? Why, he wouldn't be such a fool!'' He saw his words were not having the desired effect, so he added a trifle anxiously,

"Besides, you have me to protect you. I'm not a child any longer, after all."

Touched by these brave words, Annis raised her head, doing her best to conceal the worry in her eyes.

"I'm sure you're right," she said without conviction, "Ambrose is hardly the violent sort, after all. It's just that . . . Oh, how I wish I hadn't said anything to him about the trust!"

"Well, you couldn't have known what would happen," Laurie said practically. Deciding that he had done enough to restore his sister's equilibrium, he returned to his chair and his lemonade. "It was a deuced silly way for your grandfather to set up a trust, after all," he commented. "Putting all your money into Ambrose's hands until you married."

Annis gave a most unladylike snort. "If that wasn't just like Grandfather. I know you never knew him very well, but he was a complete old tyrant. It must have galled him to leave his money to 'a pair of rubbishy females,' as he would have said." She lifted one shoulder and let it fall. "Of course, Grandfather had no idea that Ambrose wasn't completely trustworthy. Neither did I."

The two fell into a brooding silence once more. Laurie finished his glass and poured himself another. After a few more moments he cleared his throat. Annis looked at him questioningly. "You could always marry someone else," he offered.

"Someone else?"

"Well, you would have control of your own money, after all." He blushed beneath her skeptical gaze. "I mean, well, dash it, you're not such a bad-looking girl, and I daresay most fellows would be happy to—"

She gave him a half-bow filled with irony. "As flattered as I am by your description, it seems most unlikely that I should meet with success by rushing down into the street and searching for a bridegroom today."

"Well, there's always the boat," Laurie said hopefully. At his sister's look, his face fell. "That's right, you spent the whole crossing being sick, didn't you?"

Annis, who disliked being reminded of her weaknesses, remarked with some asperity, "The whole idea is ridiculous. Let's not discuss it further."

"Well, at least it was an idea," Laurie said resentfully.

Annis could not remain seated any longer. She sprang up from her chair and resumed her pacing. "I am desperate enough to try almost anything," she admitted frankly. "Our situation is bad enough, but what of Elizabeth? She deserves a Season in London—and Ambrose will never agree to that."

Laurie wrinkled his forehead thoughtfully. "Think that's what Lizzie would like? Funny, seems to me—"

Annis cut him off impatiently. "Oh, that shyness is just because she has such a hard time telling who anyone is without her spectacles. Even you have to admit, Laurie, that our sister is a beauty. And what hope will she ever have of finding a husband, since Ambrose keeps us buried in the country?"

"True, but . . . Perhaps it's just that I'm used to them, but she doesn't look so terrible to me in those peepers. Seems to me she'd be better off wearing them and knowing whom she's talking to."

Annis gave him an incredulous look and he shrugged. "She scares away enough fellows by being the bluestocking that she is."

"Laurie, how can you say that of our sister? Why, she's not a bluestocking," Annis burst out indignantly, "she's just . . . she's just clever, that's all. Anyway," she added crossly, "this discussion is doing us no good. We can't change what's happened."

His thoughts turning in a new direction, Laurie did not even hear Annis' reponse. "I've another idea," he said abruptly.

"What is it?" she asked without much hope.

His face glowing with excitement, Laurie began, "You said it yourself. Everything would be all right if Richard were alive. Well, why can't we pretend that he is?" Glancing at his sister's face, he added hurriedly, "We can say that Jamaica didn't agree with your constitution, which is the truth anyway, and Richard could not leave because of some pressing business."

Annis shook her head. He deflated instantly. "No, I suppose you're right. It wouldn't work."

"Richard's business associates know of his death," she reminded him. She glanced at her mourning weeds distastefully. "It would be easier to pretend that I am his widow. After all, I'm dressed for the part."

There was a pregnant pause as the two digested her words. His eyes round with excitement, Laurie shouted, "Annis! What did you say?"

She was thinking furiously to herself and began muttering aloud. "It might work. It might well work. It's not as if we'd invited guests to the wedding. Thank goodness Richard wanted the thing done quietly and quickly."

"We've hardly met a soul since we've been here," Laurie pointed out helpfully. "We've all had to stay cooped up in this place, since Lizzie didn't want to leave you by yourself."

"Of course, Richard had already left Jamiaca for Honduras before we arrived," Annis said in the same manner as before, "but who's to know that? We might have been married before that business arose. He wouldn't have wished to take me along with him, since I'd been so ill on the crossing."

"And we can confirm the whole thing. Say we were witnesses at the wedding and all that. Only, Lizzie . . ."

Their eyes met. "I'll talk Elizabeth round," Annis said forcefully. She hesitated. "But all the same, perhaps we shouldn't mention the business about Ambrose to her. It will upset her unnecessarily."

"Whatever you say. Shall I go fetch her now?"

"Was it I you were coming to fetch?" Elizabeth remarked blandly as she entered the room, forestalling Laurie's response. "Oh, Laurie, you did bring the lemonade after all. I declare I am parched."

He had no choice but to pour her out a glass as she seated herself calmly. He brought it to her and she thanked him while Annis regarded her in a speculative way.

After taking a sip or two of the lemonade, Elizabeth addressed her sister. "I do wish you wouldn't look at me like that. It's most unnerving. You'd better tell me what it is directly, although perhaps I'd better find my vinaigrette first." She began to feel about her for the item in a vague and mindless way.

"It may please you to make light of us, but the truth is—" Annis began.

"That you and Laurie have hatched some elaborate scheme between yourselves. I knew it would happen. Well, it looks as if I shall have to do without my vinaigrette after all. I shall try to be strong." She fixed her sister with an unwavering gaze.

Annis was beginning to be irritated. "I wish you would stop making it sound as if we were embarking on some childish plot. It is a very simple matter, after all. We do not require anything great of you."

"That is certainly a relief." She saw that Annis' temper was beginning to rise in earnest and gave a slight smile. "There, I won't tease you any more. You tell me what I'm to do and I doubtless will agree to do it." She permitted herself a small sigh. "Though sometimes I do wish I were less persuadable."

"Oh, stop babbling on, Lizzie," Laurie said impatiently, "and let Annis talk."

Despite her disclaimer, an hour's worth of argument by her sister and half-brother still had not convinced Elizabeth to fall in with their plan. Laurie had given up trying to contribute to the discussion, and instead had retired to the window seat, leaving Annis to handle her sister alone.

"But, my dear, can't you see how very wrong it would all be?"

Annis shook her head. "No, I'm afraid that I can't. It's *our* money after all, not Ambrose's. It's not as if we were trying to deprive him of his own." Before Elizabeth could respond, she added abruptly, "And what chance do you think we'll have of ever finding husbands in Kent? There isn't an eligible gentleman anywhere in our neighborhood. And Ambrose has made it clear that he won't allow us to go to London."

"Well, Richard did offer for you, after all."

Annis looked her sister in the eye. "You know as well as I do that Richard's offer was pure luck. If he hadn't happened to come home, and if he hadn't happened to become Laurie's trustee at his father's death, and if he hadn't happened to have needed a wife at that point—"

"Annis, you can't believe that," Elizabeth said gently.

"He felt sorry for us, and it was convenient for him," Annis said, her chin held defiantly high. She took her sister's hand and gripped it tightly. "I knew Richard practically from his cradle. There is no one else who will come by and offer marriage to either of us. Don't you understand? Richard was our one hope. We shall grow to be spinsters, living in Ambrose's house, for that is what suits him, and we haven't the means to do otherwise.''

Elizabeth's face was pained and Annis relaxed her grip slightly. "Besides, there is Laurie," she added in an undertone. "Father meant for him to go away to school. You know it was Ambrose who persuaded his great-uncle and Sir Ralph to let him remain with us and hire tutors instead." She scowled. "And you know how worthless they have been."

Elizabeth's face was troubled. "I still cannot like it," she said finally.

It was the first sign that she was about to succumb. Annis pressed her case eagerly. "It is not so great a deception, after all. Richard and I were to be married. We would have been married, had not circumstances prevented—"

Elizabeth threw up her hands in a gesture of surrender. "I cannot approve this scheme. It is the most foolhardly start you have ever engaged upon, Annis, and I speak as one who knows you well. It is clear, however, that I shall not be able to dissuade you, so . . ."

Annis gave her sister an enthusiastic hug. "It will work out for the best, you'll see."

Attracted by the commotion, Laurie came up to clap Annis on the back. "Well done, by Jove."

Rendered breathless by their enthusiasm, Elizabeth managed to gasp, "Haven't you forgotten something?"

The two turned to regard her quizzically.

"What about Louisa?"

"Oh, Louisa, pooh!" Laurie dismissed this worry with a snap of his fingers.

"I cannot think that she will approve of such falsehood," Elizabeth stated flatly.

"I will fetch her and we shall see," Annis said confidently. She returned a few minutes later with the lady in tow. Rather on the wrong side of thirty, Louisa was tall, though her figure could not be called elegant. Her simple dress of black bombazine was well-used and her coiffure was sadly behind the fashion, consisting a short crop of frizzed curls, which became her ill. Her features, too, were plain, although this was relieved somewhat by a pair of piercing and surprisingly beautiful gray eyes. Her appearance proclaimed her profession. She was the young ladies' companion.

She listened quietly enough to Annis' explanation and made no comment, looking startled when Elizabeth asked if she had any objections.

"Objections! How should I have any objections?"

"I thought that as a clergyman's daughter, you would be opposed to such deception."

Louisa considered the matter for a moment before replying calmly, "It is perhaps that very fact which has taught me to make the best of whatever situation in which I find myself."

Elizabeth blushed slightly. Louisa's father, while he had never actually left the Church of England, had harbored sentiments so unpopular as to make it difficult for him to find a living. Because of that circumstance, coupled with his unworldly generosity, he had died practically penniless, leaving his spinster daughter in a most awkward position. The trip to Jamaica had come at a most providential time, enabling the girls to offer a position to one who was a close friend despite her superiority in years.

"The matter is settled, then," Annis said, cutting the awkward moment short. "Good." A queer kind of smile lit her eyes. "Do you know, come to think of it, I shall make rather a dashing widow, shan't I? I wonder what Richard would have thought of our scheme?"

"I have commented several times that of course the circumstances are most unfortunate, but still, it is true that you do look most charming in black. Naturally, since you must remain veiled in public, the effect is somewhat—"

A knock on the door interrupted Louisa's well-intentioned speech. Annis went to open it and discovered a tanned gentleman of seafaring aspect without. He gave her a low bow.

"The captain sends his compliments, miss, and he wishes to advise you and your party that the ship will weigh anchor at daybreak." As he straightened himself, he became conscious of an air of confusion in the room. "I beg pardon, miss. Have I the honor of addressing Miss Thurstan?"

Annis smiled at him sweetly. "No, my good man, though your mistake is a natural one. I was Miss Thurstan until quite recently, but now I am Lady Burham."

As he executed another, even lower bow in acknowledgment of Annis' statement, Elizabeth could not help giving her head a little shake. "Lord help us," she murmured, "We're in for it now."

"She has the bit between her teeth, that's for certain," Laurie responded in a low voice.

"Ssssh," went Louisa, mindful of their visitor.

The return voyage was a particularly rough one, and both Annis and Louisa were confined to their bunks the entire time. One unfortunate result of Annis' protracted illness was that it prevented her usually nimble brain from devising strategies for their return and gave her no chance at all to discuss her ideas with the others. Upon embarking at Portsmouth, they obtained rooms at the George. Elizabeth saw to it that Annis and Louisa both were made comfortable before returning downstairs to partake of a hearty dinner in Laurie's company. Between the two of them, they were quite well able to do justice to a fine meal of crimped cod, roast mutton, and a marrow pudding. After the sea fare, the food seemed particularly delicious, and Elizabeth was conscious of an uncomfortable feeling of fullness as she broached the subject of their predicament.

"As I see it, our best plan is to remain here at the inn for several days, until Annis and Louisa recover their strength. It will also give us the opportunity to see whether Annis is serious about carrying on this mad deception—"

"Lizzie—" said Laurie uncomfortably.

"Please, let me continue. As I was about to say, then we may hire a post chaise and make our way to the Briars, where—"

"But we're not going to the Briars." The voice was tired and weakened, but no one who knew her could mistake that note of determination. Elizabeth looked over her shoulder to see that Annis had entered the private parlor.

"My dear! You should be resting. You are still much too ill—"

"We haven't the time," Annis said as she wearily took a seat beside them. A half-eaten slice of mutton reposed on a plate in front of her and she pushed it away with a grimace of distaste. She shook her head at Laurie's offer to share the remains of the marrow pudding, but she did accept a glass of wine from her sister's hand.

"Whatever are you talking about?" Elizabeth asked, clearly bent upon humoring the lunatic.

Annis took a sip of wine, then sighed. "We can't waste any time," she explained. "Laurie must go to hire the post chaise at once. If Ambrose were to hear of our landing, he might try to intercept us."

"We will still have to meet him when we return to the Briars," Elizabeth reminded her gently.

Annis fortified herself with another sip of wine. "But we're not going to the Briars," she said once more. She lifted her head and met her siblings' gazes frankly. "I intend for us to take up residence in Thurstan House."

"I say, what a dashed marvelous notion," Laurie said enthusiastically.

"But . . . but you can't!" Elizabeth sputtered. She looked up to see that odd gleam in her sister's eyes and was unnerved once more.

"Oh, yes I can," Annis said quietly.

2

To return to a country house that has been uninhabited for five years and to take up residence again without making any arrangements in advance might well daunt all but the most lionhearted. Annis refused to be intimidated, overriding all her sister's objections; and so it was that within two days the entire party found themselves installed, for better or worse, at Thurstan House.

Once settled, there could be no opportunity for regrets. It was gratifying to be living once again in their family home, and the amount of work to be done left little time for wondering whether the decision had been the right one. Each member of the party was quick to perceive a need and take it upon his or her shoulders.

Laurie placed himself in charge of the stables, and soon was to be found driving a borrowed gig about the countryside, scouring it for suitable animals to provide them with transportation at least temporarily. Annis had taken upon herself the arduous task of hiring a full staff. This chore was rendered slightly easier by the fact that many of the servants who had been dismissed when the house was closed had been reduced to shifting for themselves in the farms and villages nearby. Restoration to their former positions of prestige came as a windfall to them. Combined with their feelings of loyalty to the Thurstan family, this fact made them among the most willing workers that had ever been hired. Elizabeth, with Louisa's help, busied herself by deciding which apartments must be opened and in which order.

This particular morning they were looking over the furniture in the parlor when they were interrupted by a loud pounding on the front door. Elizabeth turned in that direction, surprised that the noise should carry so far. "Now, where are the servants?"

The knocking persisted unabated. She heaved a sigh. "I suppose Annis has Mrs. Eastry and everyone else working upon some project or another. I'll have to get it myself."

"I'll be happy to get it for you," Louisa offered.

"Thank you. I *would* like to have a look at those curtains."

The sheer force of the knocks should have warned Louisa that something was amiss. When she opened the door, however, and was confronted by the large, angry figure of Ambrose, she could not help taking a step backward and uttering a squeak of alarm.

Ambrose strode in, his handsome florid countenance made even darker by his warmth. "I have come to see Miss Thurstan, and by gad, none of you can prevent me!"

"I . . . No, that is . . ." Louisa involuntarily retreated a bit farther.

"What nonsense." Louisa turned at the sound of the sharp voice behind her and was greatly relieved to see that Elizabeth had come to her rescue.

"The servants are simply out upon one errand or another and Louisa and I were back in the parlor and did not hear you until now. I am profoundly thankful there are none about at the moment. How ridiculous you are being, Ambrose. As if we should try to prevent you from seeing her."

Her calm tone produced a marked effect upon their visitor, Louisa observed with satisfaction. Though Ambrose was still red-faced, he was no longer breathing so heavily.

"My business is with your sister," he told Elizabeth curtly. "I know very well that this mad scheme was none of your idea."

Louisa tried not to look conscious at these last words, but Elizabeth only lifted an eyebrow and remarked, "As I have no idea what it is that you're referring to, I can take neither the blame nor the credit. I have no idea where Annis is at the moment, but perhaps Louisa will be kind enough to find her for us. In the meantime, though we are still in the process of uncovering it, I think it would be best if we withdrew to the parlor. I will see if I can't find Mrs. Eastry and procure some sort of refreshment for you."

He made no move to doff either his hat or his heavily frogged coat. "You needn't bother. Your time would be better spent packing." He scowled at Louisa. "You may tell her that I'm waiting for her in the hall." Still taken aback, she was slow to respond to his command. He gave a snort of disgust. "Well, go, then."

She could not keep from giving another little start, but she turned and fled obediently down the passage. Luckily it was not many minutes before she found Annis in her father's study, deep in contemplation of a fat ledger.

Not taking the time to knock, Louisa burst into the room. "Your cousin is here and he seems very angry. He told Elizabeth to pack, and he's waiting for you in the hall."

Annis' heart sank within her like a stone. She rose out of her chair and took a half-step forward. Abruptly she halted. So this was how Ambrose expected to see her. Like some penitent schoolgirl caught in the act of wrongdoing. Well, she was going to disappoint him. Were she truly Sir Richard's widow, she would give him his packing-penny without hesitation. She glanced about her, taking some courage from the familiar books and paintings. How many happy hours she had spent with her father in this very study. She drew herself suddenly erect. She would face Ambrose from this position of strength.

She stepped back to her desk and smiled at the confounded Louisa. "You may tell my cousin that I will see him here." She sat down once again and deliberately opened her ledger.

Her strategy proved effective, for when a furious Ambrose entered a few moments later, he halted on the threshold, momentarily startled by the sight that confronted him. Perhaps it was the serviceable dress of black bombazine or the cap she now wore, both of which proclaimed her widowhood. Perhaps it was the way her pen scratched unhurriedly across the paper, as if she were unaware of his presence. Perhaps it was her face, which was both thinner and paler from the long ocean voyage, leaving the fine bones to stand out with a more mature prominence underneath the translucent skin. In any case, he received the uncomfortable impression that this was not the light-minded young miss he had expected to encounter, but a grown woman who was fully capable of taking care of her own affairs.

In those few seconds Ambrose came to a decision. With a lightning swiftness he quickly mastered his anger, planted a sorrowful smile upon his face, and strode forward with an outstretched hand.

"My dear, dear Annis. What a boor I've been! When I heard of this sudden return, I naturally assumed that for some reason you had decided to cry off from the match. I never dreamt that Sir Richard had . . ." He disliked saying the ugly word, and Annis offered him no help. Abruptly aware of his transgression in maintaining his tall beaver hat upon his head, he swept it off and stood before her, crimping the brim somewhat nervously.

"That is . . . you have my every sympathy, my dear. Sir Richard was such a fine man . . ."

He might be saying the words of anyone, Annis thought cynically. She could no longer bear to look at that fleshy face surmounted by the carefully arranged curls, which owing to a lavish use of pomade, had survived the drive intact. She allowed her gaze to drop to his top boots, their shining perfection betraying Ambrose's pretensions to dandyism.

" . . . Of course, Maria will be devastated when she learns of your loss." An admonitory tone began to creep into his voice. "My dear child, I know I must make allowances for the present disturbed state of your mind, but did it never occur to you that your proper place at such a sad time is with your family? You need not mourn in isolation, for your grief is ours. I have hired a post chaise, which is waiting at this moment to convey you and Elizabeth and Laurie back home to the Briars with me."

She judged that she had retained silence long enough, and raising her eyes to his, addressed him in a low, even tone of voice. "What you say is very true, cousin. I do consider that home is the best place for me to be at this time. That is why I decided that we should return to Thurstan Hall. We have imposed upon your good nature far too long already. We could not dream of doing so further."

Ambrose's face, which had assumed a normal color during his opening remarks, now began to pinken with anger again. "You are mistaken in believing that you could impose—"

Annis cut him off with a brusque wave of the hand. "You are too good, but I am afraid we must insist."

His breath was coming faster as he struggled to keep his temper. "I don't believe that you could have considered this matter carefully, cousin. Two young unmarried ladies can hardly live alone, after all—"

"You forget that I am now Lady Burham." She had decided that the time to dissemble had passed, and the steel showed in her voice. "I am perfectly free to set up my establishment wheresoever I choose." She tried to soften her tone a little. "With regard to the proprieties, you must remember that we have Louisa here to bear us company, after all."

His face was red with anger. "I won't have it, do you hear? You're nothing more than a chit of a girl, and this arrangement is unsuitable in every way—"

"Your opinions do not concern me. I have made my decision and it is final."

"It is laughable," he replied. The determination in her tone had convinced him that further argument was useless. He stood glaring at her for a moment; then his expression gradually changed to one of cunning.

"Very well. As you point out, I cannot compel you to come with me. However, I do not intend to leave without Laurie, and I doubt very much that his guardian will care to put control of his estate into the hands of a schoolgirl."

This was the point which Annis had secretly dreaded, but she maintained an appearance of calm. "I am sorry to disappoint you once again, cousin, but I do not think that Laurie wishes to go with you."

"By Jove, I'll say I don't," a heartfelt voice boomed. Annis felt almost overpowered by a sensation of relief as Laurie bounded into the room, his coat and boots liberally splashed with mud. "Hullo, Ambrose. Found a nice little lady's mare today, Annis. Fifteen hands, sweet-tempered, and smooth action too. Wouldn't want to take her hunting, but on the other hand, you're not likely to do much of—"

"Get a servant to pack your bags," Ambrose said icily, cutting him off. "We're leaving for the Briars immediately."

Laurie looked more annoyed than worried, bless him, thought Annis. "Look here, old fellow, don't mean to seem rude and all, but I'd rather remain here. Take care of the ladies and all that."

"You're a mere boy and your wishes have nothing to do with the matter," Ambrose informed him. "You were left to my care and I shall do as I think best for you."

"No," Annis was beginning, but Laurie interrupted. "Hate to stand on points with you, but the truth is that it was Sir Ralph who left me in your care temporarily—"

"So he could be with his sisters," Annis flashed.

"And when his son, Sir Richard, succeeded him as my guardian, he took me into his own care," Laurie continued.

"And I am Sir Richard's widow!"

"Which does not make you Laurie's guardian."

Laurie coughed in order to catch their attention. "Sorry to interrupt and all that, but the fact of the matter is that Annis and I have already written for Great-Uncle's consent in order that I may be left in her care. Can't see why the old gentleman should have any objection. We should be hearing from him any day now. Her claim is a little better than yours, after all, since she is a blood relation."

Thwarted, Ambrose turned nearly purple in his fury. It took a moment or two before he was able to find his voice. "By gad, you think you're clever, but I'll tear apart this childish scheme. If your guardian has even a particle of sense he will not entrust your estate to a twenty-three-year-old girl with no knowledge of—"

Laurie yawned unconcernedly. "As to that, you needn't worry. I daresay we'll be happy to leave it all in the agent's hands, just as it's been for—"

"I shudder to think how quickly the females of your family will squander your inheritance. Why, I'll go see your great-uncle, if need be, to tell him not to give you a penny until you are of age—"

"You needn't worry about Elizabeth's and my squandering Laurie's inheritance," Annis said with sudden blandness. "After all, our mother's father provided for us quite well, all on his own."

As he realized that she was telling him that she intended to take control of her fortune, Ambrose's face contorted with rage. He stood before her, breathing heavily, and for a few seconds she wondered whether he might strike her. After a moment or two more he apparently regained some measure of self-control, for he whirled abruptly and, clapping his hat on his head, left the room without a word. As the stamping sound of his boots faded off down the hall, Annis' eyes met Laurie's.

"Phew," he commented, rolling his. "Bore it well, didn't he, for a man who's had two purses snatched from him in one day."

Annis lifted her shoulders slightly and dropped them again. "He had to know sometime. Besides, I need to get at that money soon, if we mean to pay these servants."

Laurie wrinkled his nose thoughtfully. "What, is it low tide with us already?" Abruptly he straightened, his mind recalled by more important matters. "Almost forgot with all this fuss. Do you want to see the new mare or not?"

The nagging problem of money was one that was always in the back of Annis' mind. Although they had managed to conserve a reasonable sum from their Jamaican trip, it could not begin to defray the cost of operating their household. She would have had to admit defeat were it not for the fact that all the village tradesmen seemed quite eager to extend credit to the new Lady Burham in hopes of assuring her future custom.

This particular morning, with a quiet week having passed since Ambrose's visit and the promise of a beautiful day before her, she decided to thrust the problem from her thoughts and walk over the grounds with the gardener. The day had dawned bright and glorious, filled with the promise of the Kentish spring. It made enjoyable even the tedious task of deciding what might be salvaged from the gardens and where entire replanting would be required. Louisa had offered to accompany her and had made herself useful by revealing a surprising wealth of information on horticultural topics. Annis, shamed by her own ignorance, could not fail to be impressed, and quickly allowed herself to be guided by her friend's advice as well as the gardener's suggestions. They finished their task in record time but, comfortable in their warm pelisses, decided to prolong their walk on this most pleasant day.

By unspoken mutual agreement, they changed directions and headed for the orchards, where blossom-laden branches waved invitingly in the breeze. The combination of the sunshine and the fresh, crisp air was invigorating, and Annis gratefully drew in a deep breath and expelled it. With such beauty all about her, it was possible to forget her own somber black garb for a few moments and imagine that she was once again a carefree child.

"The trees, at least, never change."

Louisa, perceiving that Annis was in a nostalgic mood, merely smiled by way of reply. They reached a corner of the orchard and Annis halted, lost in thought.

"That is where I fell and sprained my wrist."

Louisa murmured a question. Annis responded without taking her eyes off the tree, an odd little smile on her face. "It was just beginning to be autumn and the apples were not quite ripe yet. I told Richard so, but he insisted that some at the top looked ready to him. Naturally, he climbed the tree and then made a great show of picking and enjoying one. "I was hungry . . ."" She frowned slightly with the effort of remembering. "Oh, yes, we had been fishing that morning, and we hadn't thought to bring any food with us. In any case, I asked him to throw me one, and of course he said I'd have to climb up and get my own."

Louisa had met Sir Richard but infrequently, and it was quite impossible for her to picture that coolly self-possessed young man as a mischievous boy.

Annis was smiling again faintly at the memory. "I never was one to refuse his challenges. I started up the tree. He was sitting above, with that ridiculous smirk on his face. I made it to the first branch without too much difficulty. I was about halfway up the tree when my dress caught on a limb and I fell."

Louisa gasped.

"I landed with my arm underneath me. I know I must have been crying, in spite of myself, for it hurt abominably."

"And Sir Richard?"

"He practically leapt down from the tree himself. He was ashen-faced. Of course he had never imagined that I might fall. I kept telling him that I was all right, but he insisted upon taking me back to the house himself." Annis' eyes held a faraway expression. "He actually carried me all the way, which was unnecessary, since it was my wrist that was hurt."

"Quite a long walk," the pragmatic Louisa commented.

"Well . . . I must have been about nine or so, which would have made him thirteen, I suppose. He was always large for his age. I guess that I wasn't too heavy a burden for him." Annis' face clouded suddenly. "There isn't any sense in dwelling upon the past. There is still much to do at the house."

Without warning, she turned on her heel and started briskly off in the direction of the house, leaving her bemused companion staring after her.

Louisa's surprise was profound. She long ago had accepted Annis' assurances that her marriage was simply an arranged one. Louisa's slight acquaintance with Sir Richard had not led her to believe that he was the sort of man to inspire a grand passion. He was certainly tall, and powerfully built, but his features were more distinguished than handsome. This fault was not remedied by his expression, which habitually bordered on the arrogant. In fact, to Louisa he seemed the last sort of person for whom Annis would cherish warm sentiments. This brief conversation now made her realize that she had been entirely wrong. She gave her head a little shake to dispel the shock of her discovery, and set off after Annis' fast-retreating figure.

They had almost reached the house when Laurie came stalking out to meet them. "Where have you been? I've been searching all over for you," he complained.

"Out in the gardens." Louisa took the trouble to reply for them both.

As they entered through the rear door, Laurie inclined his head toward the parlor. "Old Fishwick's here. Lizzie's been entertaining him for the better part of an hour already."

Annis made an inarticulate noise somewhere deep in her throat, causing Louisa to look at her anxiously.

"He is . . . was Richard's lawyer and ours. It was he who drew up the marriage settlements," Annis whispered huskily.

Louisa let out a groan of comprehension, but Annis was already busy untying her black silk bonnet. "Do you think . . . that is, did he seem as if anything were amiss?" she asked Laurie in a low voice.

"Dashed if I know," he replied cheerily enough.

Annis nodded as if she could not have expected a better report than this from Laurie, and she lifted her chin determinedly. "It will not do to keep him waiting longer, in any case," she said. She smoothed her gown, made a minor adjustment to her cap, and sailed into the parlor.

The elderly gentleman in the sober black tailcoat and old-fashioned knee breeches rose rather creakily at her entrance, intending to sweep her a bow. "Miss . . . Lady Burham," he said, correcting himself.

Annis' heart, which had stopped for a moment, resumed its beating at a slightly more rapid pace. She strode forward and prevented his bow by holding her hand out to him with the ease of one who had known him since childhood. "Mr. Fishwick, how good of you to come."

Elizabeth had risen at her entrance also, and now with a smile that also hid relief, she excused herself, saying, "I know that Mr. Fishwick has business he wishes to discuss with you, and as he has been kept waiting so long already, I would not delay you both further."

As the door closed behind her sister, Annis found her hand grasped with a fervor that was more than polite.

"My lady, I cannot begin to express my . . . my grief at your loss. I have always had the very highest opinion of both Sir Richard and yourself, and . . ." His eyes were beginning to fill.

For the first time since Richard's death, Annis felt as if she herself might break down. She tilted her chin upward to keep the incipient tears from spilling out of her eyes. With a squeeze of understanding she released his hand. Taking a seat herself, she indicated with a gesture that he should resume his former one.

He sat down again, not disdaining to extract a handkerchief from his waistcoat and apply it to his eyes. "I beg your pardon, my lady, I am afraid that my age makes me susceptible to such frailities."

"Oh, Mr. Fishwick . . ."

He shook his head and then wiped his nose resolutely. "No, I do not intend to add to your burden. It was just that the loss was so sudden, so unexpected, and Sir Richard was such an excellent young man. I wished to express my sincere sympathy to you."

"It was very kind of you to come all the way from London," Annis said softly, hardly daring to trust her voice.

He shook his head once more while replacing the handkerchief. "I am sorry that I lacked the time to write and advise you that I should call, but I felt it was best to waste as little time as possible. I should be the last one to wish to intrude upon your grief at this time, but unfortunately, circumstances forced me to do so."

Annis' heart sank at these words, but by an effort she managed to preserve an unaltered countenance. "Someone who has served both our families so long and so well could never be considered an intruder," she replied gently.

He heaved a sigh and then abruptly became businesslike. "Well, I shall take up as little of your time as possible today." He met her gaze squarely. "There will be a great many things for you to think over, my lady. For example, you will have to decide whether you wish to remain in residence here or remove to Harden Park."

"Harden," Annis stammered, beginning to pale despite herself. "But I hadn't even considered . . ."

He nodded at her. "I've no doubt of that, but these matters will have to be attended to sometime. You are, after all, Sir Richard's widow and his only heir. I myself understand that your first thought would be to return to your childhood home. Others will consider—and perhaps upon reflection you may agree—that Harden Park is the more fitting residence for Lady Burham." He saw her genuine look of distress and added in a softer tone, "I am not advocating your immediate removal, my lady. I am aware that there must be a great many memories associated with Harden which would be most painful to you now. It is always wise to look to the future, though."

Annis' mind was racing. She never had thought out fully the consequences of being Richard's widow. Every feeling revolted against her touching even a penny of his money. "Surely there are some formalities that must be taken care of first," she managed to stammer.

"There are, of course." Mr. Fishwick hesitated, dropping his gaze for a moment while he gathered his thoughts. "Sir Richard was gifted with unusual foresight for so young a

gentleman. When he asked me to draw up the marriage
settlements, he asked me to make out a new will at the same
time.'' He looked up to meet her eyes again. ''I thought it an
unnecessary precaution at the time, but he asked me to name
you as his sole beneficiary from that moment on. I tried to
dissuade him, but his mind was apparently set. 'No, Fishwick,'
he said, 'if anything should happen to me, I should feel better
for knowing that Taggy should have no difficulties.' ''

Taggy. Even the odious nickname sounded dear to Annis'
ears now.

''I reminded him, of course, that you have quite a considerable
fortune of your own and that it was not customary to name a
fiancée as beneficiary.''

''What did he say?'' Annis could not help asking the question.

The ghost of a smile lit the lawyer's eyes. ''Oh, he simply
looked down his nose at me in that way he always had and said,
'Humor me in this, Fishwick.' ''

How like Richard that was. She could easily picture him saying that. Tears were stinging her eyes now. How like Richard
it also was to be so sweet when one least expected it. Though
she had been given no opportunity to share her suspicions about
her cousin with him, it had been clear that he had harbored some
doubts of his own. But how thoughtful it had been of him to
take such measures in the midst of all that confusion, with the
additional burden of his business affairs pressing upon him! She
could almost believe that he truly had loved her.

She took her black-edged handkerchief and pressed it to her
cheek to entrap an escaping tear. What an elaborate fabrication
she was weaving because of one simple action. She had been
listening to Elizabeth too much. No, she knew that Richard had
never loved her. He never once had said the words. He merely
had decided that he should marry upon his father's death, and
lacking time to cast about for a wife, had settled on her for
expedience's sake. He had never once considered her feelings.
She gave her head a weary little toss. What did it matter now,
anyway?

The lawyer, ignorant of her thoughts, was continuing, ''No,
there are no obstacles to your taking control of Sir Richard's
property. There will be a great deal to discuss, of course.'' He
gave her a kindly look and added, '' . . . but we may do that

at some future date. There is one matter of business, however, which is so pressing that I could not delay in coming to see you."

Annis by now was too preoccupied with her own thoughts to feel a sense of foreboding.

Mr. Fichwick had dropped his eyes again, with the appearance of being uncomfortable. "It's about the trust. I . . . well, your cousin is a fine man, but quite a stickler for form, which is good, of course, but . . ."

He had Annis' full attention now.

"It is not that your cousin doubts your word in any way, of course, it's simply that he wishes everything to be executed correctly. He has always taken his position as your trustee very seriously, for which I cannot help but commend him."

Annis lifted her chin slightly. "Is my cousin causing difficulties?" she asked frankly.

He shook his head and interjected hurriedly, "Oh, no, my lady. It is simply that . . . well, he wishes to prevent any problems or questions from arising." The lawyer heaved a small unconscious sigh. "Put simply, he wishes to see the marriage license himself to make sure that all is in order."

Annis felt as if she had been struck a physical blow, but she managed to remain outwardly calm. "I see." Her thoughts were spinning about wildly. Why, oh why, had she not been prepared for this eventuality? Should she give up the whole pretense now? She thought of Ambrose and suddenly she was overwhelmed by anger. How happy he would be to have her once again under his thumb, with her fortune under his control. Undoubtedly he would make her pay for her deception.

She made her decision instantly. There was not the slightest doubt in her mind. Elizabeth might think her scheme dishonorable, but to Annis the real dishonor would be in purchasing her freedom with Richard's money, though she was now legally entitled to it. She could not think of it as other than blood money.

She turned her eyes once again to the lawyer and saw uncertainty in his face. Why, he was afraid of offending her! It was a novel sensation. She drew herself up proudly. "You needn't be concerned, Mr. Fishwick. I fully understand that you are not to blame for my cousin's apparent wish to delay the inevitable with every means at his disposal."

He looked at her in some relief. "I can have the papers

prepared very speedily, my lady, if you would be so kind as to give me the documents."

She shrugged with a tolerable imitation of indifference. "I would be happy to oblige you, but unfortunately, I cannot."

"You cannot?" He looked shocked.

"No. You see, we passed a most uncomfortable voyage and both our companion and I were in a weakened condition by the time of our return. Elizabeth and Laurie had their hands quite full managing two invalids and . . . well, I am afraid that not enough care was taken to see that we had all our luggage when—"

The lawyer started forward, a scowl of concern upon his face. "My dear lady, please do not tell me that the documents have been lost!"

"Well, as a matter of fact . . ." Annis began with some diffidence.

Mr. Fishwick stared at her, perplexed. "But no action can be taken on the matter of the trust until we have them. I myself could do nothing without them. We should have to send to Jamaica for a sworn copy, which of course would delay the process for months."

Annis saw ruin staring her in the face. "Dear Mr. Fishwick, of course I did not mean that they had been *permanently* lost. In our haste and confusion, they were simply left behind in Portsmouth, with some other things. I daresay that we shall have them back in a few days, or at worst, a week or two."

The lawyer let out a sigh. "You have relieved my mind greatly," he admitted. He thought for a moment and appeared to come to a decision. "There are some business matters that await me in Maidstone. After I have dealt with them, it would be quite simple for me to visit Thurstan House again before returning to London."

"That won't be necessary." Annis, caught off-guard, spoke with a not entirely polite haste. She smiled at Mr. Fishwick by way of compensation. "What I meant was that I should hate for you to make an unnecessary trip, since we are not certain when they will arrive. I may easily send them on to London, after all. A few extra days can make no difference to me."

"Whatever you wish, my lady." He rose with an effort. "I

do not desire to take up any more of your time than is necessary during this difficult period.'' He bowed to her. ''I will be happy to wait upon your ladyship at your convenience and to serve you however I may.''

''Thank you, Mr. Fishwick.'' As he left the room, she sank even deeper into her chair, her mind still reeling from the shock. A feeling of doom overwhelmed her. A marriage license! What in the world was she going to do?

3

AFTER the lawyer's departure, Elizabeth and Laurie quickly crowded into the room, anxious to learn what tidings he had brought. They found Annis sunk in gloom and unresponsive to their queries. A more circumspect Louisa tapped gently on the door.

"You might as well come in," Elizabeth advised her. "We can get nothing from Annis."

Laurie had seated himself beside his elder sister, taken her hand in his, and begun patting it. "Come, now, Annis, what did Fishwick say?" he asked cajolingly.

"It's no use. We are lost."

"She persists in saying that," Elizabeth informed Louisa with a shake of her head.

"We might be able to think of something, you know," Laurie said, "but we can't do a thing unless you tell us what he said."

Annis merely shook her head hopelessly.

"Oh, for pity's sake," Laurie said rather more roughly, "I am fast losing patience with you. We're all in this together, so you'd better tell us what you know." He took her by the shoulders and gave her a little shake, which seemed to produce the desired effect of awakening her from her stupor.

"Well, really, Laurie," Annis said, irritated.

"That's more like it. Now, tell us what he said."

Annis heaved a sigh, but she replied obediently, "I am afraid the game is at an end. Ambrose wishes to see the marriage license."

Annis' despair suddenly became infectious. She looked around at the others' faces and could see nothing but sorrow and uncertainty there. She heaved a sigh. "I told you. There is nothing we can do."

Laurie was not one to give up so easily. "You could tell him that you lost it."

"I did. He said they would send to Jamaica for a copy. So I told him we had mislaid it in Portsmouth instead."

"That's good." Laurie was quick to seize upon this ray of hope. "Then we have a few days to try to devise a plan."

Annis raised her eyes with a look of scorn. "What plan?" She shook her head and rose wearily. "No, I suppose we had better start packing. I am sorry that I landed us all in the basket."

"Oh, Annis." Elizabeth put an arm around her sister and hugged her. "It was worth a try. Ambrose will be angry of course, but . . ." She straightened her shoulders. "He's angry at us half the time anyway." She adjusted her skirts and prepared to leave the room. "I suppose I had best go inform the servants. I'm sure Ambrose would be willing to compensate them for the time they have spent here."

Louisa had remained mute since entering the room, but now she startled the company by speaking abruptly. "Wait!" She turned to Annis. "You did not actually tell Mr. Fishwick about the deception?"

"No, I couldn't. He is such an upright gentleman that—"

"Then all may not be lost." Six eager eyes turned upon Louisa at these words. She swallowed painfully. "I do have one idea." It was hardly more than a whisper, but it produced an expectant silence.

Laurie was the first to break it. "Well, tell us," he demanded.

"I don't know, perhaps it is not—"

"We can hardly be in a worse spot than we are in now," Annis reminded her.

Louisa appeared uncertain. Annis gestured at her and she sank into a chair. The rest of the company followed suit. Elizabeth adjusted the spectacles resting upon her classically perfect nose and said encouragingly, "You might as well tell us, you know. Annis is bound to worm it out of you sooner or later."

Louisa shook her head. "I must confess, I am ashamed to have thought of it at all."

Laurie gave a snort, causing Louisa to look up and read his impatience, which was reflected in the faces of the two girls. She heaved a sigh. "Very well," she said. "You all knew my papa and doubtless were aware that in his view . . . well, you know that many of our difficulties arose from the fact that . . . of course, he never abandoned the Church of England, but it was felt that he inclined too much toward—''

Annis cut her off. ''He had too much sympathy for the Evangelicals.''

''Exactly.'' She paused for a few seconds, struggling to bring her words into a coherent order. ''As you know, he felt himself called to help the misfortunate, the impoverished, the destitute. It was a most worthy cause, but during our time in London''— here she frowned—''it meant that he . . . well, that he was forced to associate with, or at least to be familiar with, the criminal element.'' She fell silent.

Annis, who had made the connection quickly, leaned forward with a delighted smile upon her face. ''Louisa,'' she breathed, ''do you mean that you actually are acquainted with a forger?''

Elizabeth could not prevent a horrified gasp from escaping her lips.

''Well, I'll be dashed,'' Laurie said admiringly.

Louisa drew herself up stiffly. ''Certainly not! He had ceased that . . . that occupation before Papa ever met him. His right hand had been ruined in an accident and he had been reduced to begging in the streets.''

''Then I don't see how he can be useful to us,'' Laurie commented with some disappointment.

Louisa directed a frosty look at him. ''As I was *about* to explain, this gentleman, Mr. Williams by name, was entirely won over by my father and renounced all his former wickedness. He was one of Papa's more pronounced successes. Papa managed to find him opportunities for honest industry, and since he possessed certain advantages in his upbringing as well as those of mind and will, he eventually earned enough to purchase a small but entirely respectable inn in a village not far from—''

''I still don't see why this is of any help to us,'' Laurie muttered unhelpfully.

''Mr. Williams, so thankful for his own escape,'' Louisa said, ignoring the interruption, ''decided that he would devote his energies and resources to saving other poor wretches from the evils he himself had fallen prey to—''

"You think he might know a forger?" Annis asked.

Louisa held up her hands, a troubled expression upon her face. "I do not know. Even if I did, I am not sure that he would consent to aid us in our scheme. He is a scrupulously honest person and—"

Elizabeth had paled during this discussion, but now she rose and addressed her sister forcefully. "No, Annis. You must not consider this mad idea, even for a moment. This is no bending of the truth, but an outright, purposeful breaking of the law. Surely you must see that it is infamous!"

Annis rose also, her eyes flashing. "So, it is infamous? Well, is it any more infamous than Ambrose's having control of our money for the rest of our lives? He means to have us die spinsters, or haven't you seen that? Is it so right, then, for him to keep Laurie from going to school? Or for him to provide Laurie instead with incompetent tutors, clearly hired for the meagerness of the wages they are willing to accept?"

"I admit our cousin is close-fisted, but—" began Elizabeth weakly.

"Well, I won't have it!" Annis was beginning to fly into a passion.

"If you would just be patient, we could talk to—" Elizabeth tried a soothing tone.

"I have been patient, and I have tried reasoning with Ambrose for these past five years and more!" Annis exclaimed. "He is happy to pay lip service to all our complaints, but he never has shown the slightest sign of doing other than what he has intended all along. I rue the day that Grandfather left our fortune in his control. But I do not intend to let our one opportunity for escape slip by. If we are caught, then it may all fall upon my head, and welcome."

She crossed her arms defiantly, rather intimidating Louisa by the ferocity of her looks.

Laurie gave a cough. "Have to say, I cast my vote with Annis," he said somewhat apologetically.

"But the low company you should have to encounter . . ." Elizabeth shuddered at the idea.

"She'll have me to protect her," Laurie said in a pugnacious manner.

Annis gave a grimace of exasperation. "Well, *you* certainly don't have to go, Elizabeth, if you're afraid."

Stung, Elizabeth replied, "I am more than ready to go. It is the whole idea to which I object." She gave a disdainful sniff. "But I see that *my* opinions are clearly of no importance, so I will leave you to *your* plans." With that, she turned and exited the room haughtily.

"Elizabeth," Annis called after her, without producing any response. She turned to see Louisa's eyes, wide with distress, fixed upon her. "Oh, she'll come round, you needn't worry."

"But she *is* right." The words burst from Louisa. "Even Mr. Williams, though he is a fine Christian now, is hardly the sort of person that a gently bred young lady would associate with."

"Pish," Annis said, with a dismissive wave of her hand. "Let us decide what is to be done. Now, where exactly did you say this inn is to be found?"

It was in the early morning some two days later that a post chaise departed Thurstan House, headed in the direction of London. Elizabeth, afraid that her valor might be called into question, had insisted upon accompanying them. To her secret relief, Annis had overridden her, maintaining that Elizabeth needed to remain at home in order to allay Cousin Ambrose's suspicions, particularly if he arrived for another unannounced visit. "And there's no use saying that you should go instead of one of the rest of us," Annis told her frankly, "You're the only one who's clever enough to think up a story that will fool Ambrose."

It was afternoon by the time they reached the inn. The sight caused Annis to heave a sigh of relief. Far from the main coaching road, the establishment clearly made no pretensions toward catering to the upper echelon of society, but the white-washed walls were clean and it projected an overall appearance of neatness and comfort. Annis' lightened spirits were to be lowered again by the approach of the ostler, a bent, one-eyed man who welcomed them with a toothless grin as he took charge of the horses. Annis was conscious of a feeling of hesitation, but apparently Louisa was not afflicted by it. She fairly bounded out of the carriage as soon as the door was opened, exclaiming, "Oh, I do hope that he is here and that we have not made this journey for nothing."

She was not to be disappointed, for as Annis and Laurie were descending in a gingerly fashion, a tall man in an old-fashioned frock coat of broadcloth came out the door. He seemed to be headed for some destination of his own, but at the sight of Louisa he stopped dead for a moment, then came hurrying over to her.

"Miss Louisa!" he called, gladness in his voice.

"Mr. Williams," she returned, a smile on her face.

He removed his hat with his left hand, and Annis noted that his right hung stiff and unmoving. He was a big man, approaching middle age, although his freckled face and candid blue eyes lent him a boyish appearance. Not the sort of man one would take for a criminal, mused Annis, but her thoughts were interrupted as Louisa made introductions. Williams made a quite creditable bow, surprising Annis once again. He professed his delight at meeting them and apologized gracefully for the simplicity of the hospitality he would be able to offer.

Louisa quieted him, telling him that they had a serious purpose in coming. He lifted his eyebrows in surprise, but promptly escorted the company into the inn's deserted public room. He called at once for refreshment, earning him Laurie's approval. Williams would have remained standing, but Louisa indicated that he should join them, " . . . for it is a most important matter that we have to discuss with you."

Having by unspoken unanimous consent assumed charge of the expedition, Louisa proceeded to broach their dilemma to him in the most delicate way imaginable, making the most of the injustices done to the Thurstans by their cousin, and pausing in her narrative only when a serving maid entered the room with a tray of victuals.

Williams, frowning, also preserved his silence as the girl set down a pigeon pie, some fried smelts, and a cold roast joint. Laurie thoughtlessly made an immediate assault upon the food, but his female companions, more apprehensive, merely stared anxiously at Williams.

As soon as the serving girl had left the room, he gave his verdict by shaking his head. "Miss Louisa," he said without heat, "I can't for the life of me see why you should think I would wish to be mixed up in such an evil scheme."

Annis' shoulders fell in dejection, but Louisa gamely refused to surrender. "But, Mr. Williams, haven't you heard what I have been telling you? Miss Thurstan's cousin will not let her or her sister touch a penny of their money—and it is theirs, after all, not his. And he means to prevent them from ever being able to claim it, either."

Williams shook his head again. "I don't deny that it's unjust, but we cannot expect justice in this world." He raised his eyes reverently upward. "Only in that to come."

Louisa still persisted. "I am not asking you this lightly. I would not have come at all if there were another way out of our difficulties."

"Miss Louisa, you do not know what you ask."

"You need not have anything to do with our scheme directly. All we ask is that you point us to a person who could be helpful."

"That wouldn't make it any less wrong."

Becoming desperate, Louisa pulled out her ace. "If you retain any feelings of affection for my late father and me, you will give us the help we need."

This appeal seemed to carry some weight with him, for he dropped his eyes and stared at the ground consideringly for a moment. Annis allowed her spirits to rise ever so slightly, but they were to be dashed in the next instant.

"I am sorry, I cannot do it," he said determinedly. "I had too much respect for your father to allow his daughter to be mixed up in such doings."

Judging from the look of dismay upon Louisa's face, she had run out of arguments. Annis judged it to be the time to make an effort of her own.

"Miss Utterly need not be involved in this transaction in any way," she informed him. "Indeed, I would have preferred coming here without her, but she generously insisted upon aiding us in any way she could. This scheme does not affect her at all, but rather my family and me."

He had crossed his arms and assumed a stubborn look, leading Annis to realize that she was making no impression whatsoever upon him. She gave a sigh and began again.

"Louisa," she said, abandoning all pretense of formality, "is not in possession of quite all of the facts. The truth is that my brother and I suspect—actually, we *know*—that my cousin has been bleeding the trust for his own purposes."

Was it her imagination, or had his scowl deepened just a trace? She continued, "Up until Rich . . . my fiancé's death, my cousin was not in control of my brother's fortune, but without the document we seek, he very probably will be."

"Aye, he's clever enough for that," Laurie muttered between mouthfuls of pigeon pie.

"He has shown that he is quite as happy to appropriate my brother's fortune as my own." Annis saw the headshake coming and held up her hand to stay it.

"Wait, I have not told you the worst yet." Seeing that she had his attention, she went on. "With my engagement I became foolishly overconfident. I told my cousin that I was aware of his wrongdoing and that my future husband would deal with him soon enough." She lowered her gaze ashamedly. "I cannot assume that he intends us merely to take up where we left off, with my knowing what I do. I have placed my brother and my sister in jeopardy, and all through my own foolish pride."

A silence followed her words. She looked up dejectedly and saw that his eyes were still fixed on the floor. She heaved a sigh and rose to her feet. "I am sorry that we troubled you for nothing. Let us go."

"Wait!" It was an anxious Laurie who spoke. "Dash it, no sense in leaving halfway through my meal. These smelts are excellent, if you care to try one, and I haven't even had a chance to sample the joint yet."

"Oh, very well," Annis said, plopping back into her chair resignedly, "though I don't care for anything myself."

Williams lifted his eyes, fixing Annis with a shrewd stare. "Might I ask you one question, miss?"

She nodded.

"If anything were to happen to you, where would your fortune go?"

"To my sister."

"And if anything should happen to her also?"

"It would go to my cousin."

"Ah!" He seemed to reach a decision, for he straightened

himself and leaned forward in the chair. "I was thinking that it was a matter for lawyers, but if what you say is true, you might be in some danger even now, and the lawyers would take far too long. I've plenty of experience of fellows such as your cousin, and I don't doubt that he'd be likely to take desperate steps once his back is to the wall."

"Then you'll help us?" Annis was filled with a mixture of joy and disbelief. Louisa was flutteringly grateful. Laurie could not help but leap up from the table and shake Williams' hand warmly.

With this little matter of cooperation settled, Laurie now felt himself, as the gentleman in the party, to be in control of the expedition. He settled back down at the table and regarded Williams with a knowing eye.

"We are greatly obliged to you. All you need tell us is whom we must meet and where."

Williams could not prevent a grin from slipping onto his face. "I'm afraid it's not quite as easy as that, young master," he replied easily. "My work here has kept me from the Lord's business lately." He leaned back in his chair to call to the serving maid in the other room. "Bess, will you send Harry in?" He addressed them again. "I've sent him as my deputy, since he was rescued from a life of crime, same as me."

Annis watched with some trepidation as the door swung open and the one-eyed ostler approached. He gave them his amiable grin and nodded jerkily at them several times.

Williams briefly laid their problem before this rather unattractive ally, but concluded with a warning that the matter must be kept secret. The ostler nodded gravely, brushing his nose with his forefinger and remarking that "Old Harry was never one to conk," which Annis took to mean agreement.

The two men then entered into a discussion, of which the greater part was to prove unintelligible to the Thurstans, though Louisa seemed to have no trouble following it.

"What about Phineas Brown?" Williams was asking.

"Ain't clapped me ogles on him for over a year," Henry returned apologetically, "and it ain't no use asking about young Higgins neither."

Williams questioned him with a look.

"In quod," Harry said succinctly.

"That's prison, most likely Newgate." Louisa had seen the puzzlement on her friends' faces and taken on the role of interpreter for them.

Williams thought for a moment. "Well, there's always Bingley." His henchman looked troubled. "Well, what is it?" Williams demanded.

"Max."

"Gin," Louisa said quietly.

"Think he'd be unreliable."

"You've nicked the matter there. Ain't seen him without 'e 'as 'is fambles about a flash of lightning nowadays, and spends most of 'is time in his dab." Harry made a face of unconscious felonious regret. "An' a pretty talent 'e 'ad, too. 'E'll end it as a cadger or a prig."

"A begger or a common thief," Louisa whispered.

Williams sighed. "Well, who else is there?"

"There's old Solomon. They tell me 'is queer screens 'ud fool the lord treasurer 'imself. What's more, 'e's as flash a cove as there is, and 'e ain't leaky neither."

"Apparently this gentleman's speciality is banknotes, but he is thought to be very knowing, and not at all talkative," Louisa explained judiciously.

"Well, he would seem to be our man, then. Is he at the same, er, address?"

"Last I heard of 'e was."

"Very well." Williams turned to his auditors. "There you have it."

The ostler's face had assumed a look of shocked disbelief. "Lord save us, guv'nor, you don't mean to be sending these gentry-morts to old Solomon—"

"No, of course not. I'll go myself."

These words, naturally enough, provoked a long and somewhat tedious discussion during which Williams had the presence of mind to dismiss the ostler from the room. Annis, who had given little previous thought to their current under-taking, now felt her eyes to have been fully opened by Old Harry's conversational style. All of Elizabeth's pleadings and arguments came back to her and she was forced to admit the good sense of what her sister had been saying. She had half a mind to give up the entire scheme without further ado, but was prevented by two circumstances. One was the very present danger that Ambrose posed to them. The other was Louisa's foolhardy but generous insistence upon going to London and negotiating the entire transaction herself. She was deaf to Annis' pleas that she herself should be the one to go, since she was the only one concerned.

"But, my dear Annis," Louisa said gently, as if humoring a child, "you probably won't even understand half of what he says to you."

"You're both being ridiculous," Laurie interrupted her ruthlessly. "I've said it before and I'll say it again. It's a man's job and it's up to me to do it."

Williams was about to make another protest, arguing his own superiority for the task, but Annis shushed them all. "Enough," she said wearily. "Since none of us can agree on which of us is to go, we shall *all* go."

"Beggin' your pardon, Miss Annis," Williams said, with all the force of his convictions, "but the lot of us simply cannot all go trooping into Solomon's. Why, we'd flush him out the back door of his panny just like a fox from his lair." He had a regettable tendency to lapse into cant when excited, Annis had noticed.

"You are quite right, of course, Louisa and Laurie will accompany us to London, where we will find a hotel or inn of some sort. We will pay the postboys off and you and I will take a—what did you call it?—a rattler to where we must transact our business." There were various exclamations of disagreement, but Annis faced them all with a look that brooked no further discussion.

"I would prefer not to involve anyone else at all in this, but clearly I need Mr. Williams' aid."

"But I must be there to chaperone you," Louisa could not help exclaiming.

"Fortunately, since I am in mourning, I will be veiled. You had best busy yourself with thinking of lodgings where there is no possibility of our being recognized. Ambrose certainly would be able to put two and two together and become suspicious, at the very least."

* * *

The rest of that day and the next took on a nightmarish quality for Annis. First there were the twenty anxious miles to London. Her nerves had begun to affect her stomach, making her prey to motion sickness. It apparently was a contagious disease, for Louisa also succumbed. Though she was too selfless to moan or complain, her closed eyes, pallor, and hiccups told the tale.

Then there was the small and unfashionable inn to which they were driven. This destination evidently awoke the postboys' curiosity, for there were some searching looks, though they refrained from making any comments. Inside it, Annis learned what she had already suspected, that the inn was not quite as clean as it might be. At least, judging from the clientele, they were in no danger whatsoever of encountering any of their acquaintances here.

In a different mood, she might have derived some entertainment from Williams' professional chagrin at being forced to put up at such an indifferent establishment. She observed that he more than once was forced to bite his tongue when dealing with the lackadaisical staff. She was persuaded that it was only his desire not to call attention to their party which prevented him from exclaiming aloud when he was served a pair of cutlets that were both scorched and cold. He could not keep from muttering darkly, as he ate, that he would not care to wager from what type of animal the cutlets had derived.

She felt oddly bereft when he informed them that he must leave them to call upon Solomon. With a shake of his head he dismissed her offer to accompany him. "Why, you didn't imagine, did you, Miss, that such a matter could be taken care of in a few minutes? We'll be fortunate if he can have it ready for us in a day."

Annis realized more than ever now how ignorant she had been when she had decided upon this course. "But Mr. Wi—" she began, cutting off the word. All had agreed not to use names, for discretion's sake. This precaution had proved wise, as Annis was all too aware of more than one pair of sharp and interested eyes and ears about them. "But dusk is falling. Surely it would be better to visit the gentleman in the morning instead."

Williams ducked his head, not quite repressing a grin while Louisa whispered, "Just think for a moment, my dear. We are much better off transacting our business in the dark.''

Williams then departed while the rest of their group made their way upstairs. Annis spent the better part of the night tossing and listening to the din from the public room below. Her companion apparently was untroubled by the racket, enabling Annis to make the unwelcome discovery that Louisa snored.

Annis lay gazing up at the ceiling while various reproachful thoughts crowded into her mind. How easy it would have been if Richard had lived to marry her. All of her difficulties would have been solved. She realized now how lucky she would have been. Even if Richard didn't love her, he was a decent person and would have treated her well enough. Moreover, he had, at least, a sense of duty to her, and with time perhaps it might have grown into affection, particularly given her own feelings toward him. In her mind's eye she could see his face, wearing the smile that transformed it and made it boyish. She shut her eyes as if to shut out the thought. She had promised herself not to remember him like that, for it was simply too painful to bear. Her eyes fell open again as there was a particularly loud eruption from her companion. She never would have appreciated the good fortune of her situation, for she never had imagined the turn her life would take. This adventure was making her realize that it might even be far, far worse. She shuddered, then resolutely shut such dismal ideas from her mind.

If ever I find another decent, honorable gentleman to offer me his hand, she thought, I will value it as I ought and dismiss all these romantic schoolgirl ideas that I harbored for so long.

On this positive note she finally fell asleep, but her dreams were haunted by prisons and wretches begging in the streets, and toothless, one-eyed persons of menacing aspect.

4

UNAWARE of the extent of her sister's sufferings, Elizabeth was quite preoccupied with problems of her own. It was true that Ambrose had not put in a return appearance, but at least she would have been prepared for that eventuality.

Her difficulties began the morning of Annis' departure. She had seen them off, then turned to some of the many tasks that awaited her attention. She had enlisted the housekeeper, one of the maids, and a footman to aid her in clearing some of the flotsam and jetsam which the tides of previous generations had spread generously throughout the house.

They were at work in one of the upstairs bedrooms, where she was fingering what undoubtedly had once been a lovely rococo porcelain shepherdess. Unfortunately, the figurine had at some point suffered decapitation, leaving simply a headless figure, crook in arm, making a delicate curtsy.

"Really," Elizabeth exclaimed, "I can see why Stepmama hesitated to clear out some of this rubbish, but I can't imagine why Mother did not do so when she had the opportunity."

It was doubtful that she was actually soliciting an opinion of any of the company. In any case, they had no time to reply to her, for the elderly butler, Hickeringill, having been deprived of his footman, came puffing into the room and made a breathless bow.

"Miss Elizabeth," he said between gasps, "there is a caller downstairs."

A frown creased Elizabeth's marble brow. "Did you explain to him that we were in mourning?"

"Yes, Miss Elizabeth, but he seemed quite determined to remain." He held a card out to her. She read it. Don Alonzo Rodríquez y Vega. The name meant nothing to her.

She looked up and correctly interpreted the expression on the butler's face. Foreigners were uncivilized and therefore not to be held accountable for their actions.

"Very well, I shall go see him, Hickeringill."

She had the foresight to remove the offending spectacles before she entered the parlor, but even without them she had a feeling that their visitor was an attractive man.

A tall dark-haired gentleman stood and bowed deeply as she entered the room. When she introduced herself, he pronounced himself charmed and bowed over her hand and kissed it. Even she could catch a glimpse of dazzlingly white teeth when he smiled.

"Miss Thurstan, I am so sorry to trouble your household at this time, but my business is of the most urgent." His English was very good and his accent was rather appealing.

"So our butler told me. Please, won't you be seated?" She gestured in the direction of what she hoped was a chair as she sank into one herself.

He waited for her before seating himself. When he spoke, there was a question in his voice. "I apologize if I have put you to unnecessary trouble. My business is with Lady Burham. I was told that she is residing here."

Dear me, who could the fellow be? Elizabeth hoped that her countenance did not reflect her unease. "My sister is from home at the moment," she replied, determined to reveal no more information than necessary. Could he possibly be some sort of spy for their cousin?

"Ah." The disappointment was evident in his voice. He paused for a moment before speaking again. "Then, if it would not cause you too much inconvenience, I should like to wait here for her return."

"I am afraid that would be impossible," Elizabeth replied hastily. "My sister will be gone for quite some time. I am afraid that I do not know when she will return."

"Ah." Again she could hear the disappointment. He cleared his throat, but then did not speak. She suspected that he was debating whether to try to force his presence on her anyway, or to surrender and leave. It was such a handicap not to be able to read his face. She said nothing, and eventually he addressed her again.

"In that case, I will take my leave of your most charming presence. When she returns, would you please present my card to her with my compliments and ask if she will do me the honor of allowing me to wait upon her tomorrow. My business is urgent and it may be to the utmost benefit of both of us."

These last words were ominous. "I regret to say that I do not know whether my sister will have returned by tomorrow." Annis had packed a small trunk and Elizabeth doubted that she would return that day, unless their mission met with no success.

"Ah, well, I shall call tomorrow anyway, in hopes of finding her here."

Hickeringill no doubt would have found that statement indecorous, but Elizabeth did not know how to discourage the foreign gentleman any more than she already had.

"It was most delightful to make your acquaintance. Thank you again for seeing me. I can show myself out."

He proceeded to do so, leaving Elizabeth to wonder about manners that were both unusual and autocratic. Her curiosity got the better of her, and putting on her spectacles, she ran to the front windows to see their visitor walking to his carriage.

He was dressed with great elegance and formality in a black tailcoat and pantaloons of a foreign cut. He wore a tall beaver on his head, and his greatcoat, which he wore carelessly open, looked both expensive and new. He conferred for a moment with the postboys, then turned and entered the carriage. Elizabeth thus was permitted a glimpse of quite the most handsome visage she had ever seen. The heavy-lidded dark eyes, the aristocratic nose, the thin-lipped and rather cruel mouth proclaimed that he belonged to a certain social class even if she hadn't already seen the evidence of his clothing to support it. As the carriage drove away, Elizabeth found herself shaking her head. What on earth could this attractive and insolent foreigner want with Annis? Well, she might puzzle her head about it all day, but she was not likely to find an answer. She sighed and began to make her way thoughtfully upstairs once more.

The next day arrived with no sign of Annis or her companions. Don Alonzo presented himself promptly, according to his promise. If he felt any irritation at Annis' continued absence, he concealed it well, spending quite three-quarters of an hour with Elizabeth in charming small talk. Though he professed himself to be entranced by her beauty, Elizabeth could not help but suspect that he was merely delaying his departure in hopes that Annis might arrive. It was striking, too, that although he was full of questions himself, he revealed nothing about his own background or his purposes in coming there. The situation made Elizabeth most uneasy, and though she had expected it, she could not prevent a twinge of dread when he said he would call again on the morrow.

She fully expected than Annis would return that day, but as dusk fell, she saw that it was not to be. If Ambrose was behind these visits, he must be growing more and more suspicious. Elizabeth said a quick prayer that her sister soon would arrive and put an end to the nerve-racking situation.

On the following morning, though he was quite as charming as before, it was clear that Don Alonzo was also beginning to tire of this game. Despite his politeness, it was obvious that he did not quite believe her repeated assurances that she did not know when her sister might be expected. It was also clear that he did not intend to decamp meekly as he had done the two previous days.

"Miss Thurstan, I hope that you will indulge me. I am sure that this beautiful house must boast a magnificent library. Books are my particular weakness, you see, and I would count myself as most privileged to be allowed to examine yours. And perhaps if Lady Burham returns meanwhile, I may be allowed to present myself to her."

There was no request in his tone. It was an out-and-out command. Elizabeth didn't quite know what to do. Her strong-minded sister would probably have sent him to the rightabout without delay, but Elizabeth was not sure how to accomplish this. Besides, if he did come from Ambrose, dismissing him might cause them trouble.

"Hickeringill will show it to you, then," she said emotionlessly as she pulled the bell rope to summon the butler. But I won't offer him anything to eat, she thought by way of compensating herself for a certain feeling of spinelessness.

* * *

In the background, a waltz was playing. It was a warm night and she was fanning herself. She was watching the dancers, silk dresses and black tailcoats twirling gaily about the room, while she listened idly to the gossip of those about her. For an instant it was as if everything stopped, though of course it hadn't. From the moment she saw Richard enter the doorway she was caught up by a queer detached feeling, as if he and she were the only people in the world. To her, he was the most handsome man in the room, but then, she supposed that was a part of having loved him her entire life. All she knew was that other men seemed to pale beside him.

It was so odd. She had not seen him for such a long period of time, and yet he appeared exactly the same as he had in her dreams. He turned and saw her, and she knew in that instant that the feelings she had always hoped to inspire were there. He made his way over to her, not pausing, not even acknowledging the acquaintances delighted by his unexpected return. He strode directly up to her and took her hand. "Annis," he said quietly.

"Richard," she breathed.

Without another word, he led her to the floor. He was holding her in his arms, and the joy in her heart was almost too much to bear.

"Annis . . . Annis . . ." It was not Richard's voice calling her name now, and that irritated her. She wanted nothing more than to return to him.

Someone was slapping her hand now. "Annis." Why couldn't she be left alone? Richard was waiting for their dance to continue. He still held her other hand.

"Annis." She was recalled to the present with a vengeance. She pushed the malodorous object away from her nose, choking, coughing, and feeling sick to her stomach. "No," she insisted weakly.

As her eyes were forced open, she made the unhappy discovery that she was in excruciating pain. Louisa's and Laurie's faces were hovering anxiously over hers. Seeing them, she realized the awful truth that her mind had been trying to evade.

"Richard is dead," she said quite clearly, as large and silent tears began to slip out of the corners of her eyes.

"I am sorry, my dear. Yes." Louisa was patting her hand now, but she exchanged a glance with Laurie. Heaven help them if Annis' wits were affected!

Annis put her hand to her head, which seemed to be the central source of pain. "What happened?"

Laurie took the initiative now. "Our chaise was ditched by some devil-may-care driving the stage. You got a nasty knock on the head and Louisa just this moment succeeded in bringing you round with her vinaigrette."

"Oh." Annis' exploring fingers had located a large tender knot on the back of her skull. That explained the pain. For a moment she could not think of what she should do or say.

"Luckily, it looks as if the chaise is still in one piece, and by a miracle, the horses don't seem to have taken any harm," Laurie volunteered helpfully. "The postboys are walking them up the road right now to make certain of that."

Annis' brain had decided upon a first course of action, which was to stand. Unfortunately, lifting her head was enough to prove this decision foolish, and it fell back down as she groaned.

"Here, old girl, there's nothing else wrong with you, is there?" Laurie was beginning to be anxious. She was dreadfully pale and he had no memory of ever having seen his sister cry.

"Perhaps she simply needs to lie here a little longer," Louisa said in an indecisive voice.

Odd, unconnected thoughts were turning about in Annis' head. She saw a tall freckled man grimacing as he tasted some soup in a dirty inn. She remembered a hackney ride and the ever stronger, ever more offensive odor of filth and refuse and decay. There was a thin ragged woman sitting on some steps, nursing a baby and drinking from a bottle of gin. She spat in their direction as they passed. Then, dimly, through a heavy veil, she could see a handsome room, in fantastic contrast to the world outside. There was some conversation with a well-dressed, hard-eyed man. She could remember signing her name to a document in the flickering candlelight, her hand surprising her by its steadiness and—

Annis' eyes snapped open. "Where is it? Is it still there?" She began her attempt once again. This time, ignoring the pain and gritting her teeth, she managed to raise herself to a sitting position.

For a moment her auditors were blank. Louisa shot Laurie an anguished glance. It was as they had feared. Annis' mind was wandering. "I think perhaps you had better lie down a little longer, my dear. Lawrence, I noticed a windmill just a short distance back. Perhaps you might go and ask the miller's wife if she would be kind enough to receive an invalid for—"

"Be quiet." Annis' head was pounding but she shoved Louisa's helpful arm away, determined to maintain her hard-won position. "I must get up. I must see," she said, and made an effort to gather her legs underneath her, though she was greatly hampered by her tangled skirts.

"My dear Annis, you must not!" Louisa was making a vain attempt to counter these efforts, but Annis brushed her away.

"Laurie, help me," she commanded. Accustomed to obedience when addressed in that tone, he complied. Their combined efforts managed to raise Annis to her feet, though it made her stomach turn over most unpleasantly. She nearly collapsed against Laurie, but with his help she was able to maintain her precarious balance.

"She shouldn't be doing that," Louisa said disapprovingly.

Laurie, who had an instinctive kind of faith in Annis when in an autocratic mood, said eagerly, "No, I think she's going to be all right."

Still leaning on him, Annis took a first tottering step toward the road. "Where . . . is . . . it?" she hissed, enunciating each word as plainly as possible. They continued to hear her in silence and she realized she was going to have to be more specific. "Where is my trunk?" she repeated in the same manner as before, though speaking cost her a great effort.

Laurie gave Louisa a look which told her plainly that he had known best all along. "She's thinking about the papers," he explained. He patted her sister's arm. "Needn't worry. The trunk's tied up in back of the carriage, same as it was when we left. No one's touched it since."

They had reached the side of the road and Annis did not yet

feel equal to the climb. She struggled to get another word out. "Ambrose."

Louisa was the first to catch the significance of it. She paled. "Good heavens, do you think that he is responsible for our accident?"

"Nonsense," Laurie said firmly. "He couldn't have known we'd be traveling this road. Just some bosky blade at the reins. Bribed the coachman to trade places with him. The postboys said this sort of thing happens more often than you'd think."

Her suspicions aroused, Louisa could not be soothed so easily. "If that were the case, then why didn't they stop when they saw they'd forced us from the road?"

Laurie glanced at her sharply, but replied, "I suppose they saw we were in no real danger. Coachman would stand to lose his job if we reported the incident, after all."

Louisa was far from satisfied, but she understood his unspoken message.

"Here comes the chaise now," Laurie exclaimed in some relief. "Think I'll go get one of the postboys to help—that is, if you feel well enough to continue on," he said, addressing his sister solicitously.

"Yes," Annis lied faintly. She felt nothing short of awful, but she suddenly was aware of the vulnerability of their position. They must return to Thurstan House without delay. "Louisa," she said softly, trying not to think about the pain, "tell Laurie to question the postboys about the accident, to see whether they noticed who was driving and whether it was a regular stage."

Louisa nodded her comprehension as one of the men, in his traditional yellow jacket and beaver hat, came scrambling down the bank toward them with Laurie close behind.

If Annis had thought her sea voyage to be the ultimate in agony, she now realized that the scope of her imagination was far too limited. Though this journey could not compete in terms of length, it far overshadowed the other in terms of suffering. Every part of her body was in revolt and she had to use all of her failing strength to keep Louisa from using the odoriferous vinaigrette again. Though the chaise was well-sprung, and the postboys had been advised to travel at little more than a crawl, every jolt was torture to her aching head and uneasy stomach.

Every bit as painful was the sense of remorse she now felt. Despite Laurie's assurances, she had to believe that Ambrose was at the bottom of it all. It was her own foolish, intemperate tongue that had landed them all in this danger. Why had she needed to confront Ambrose before she left England? To show how clever she was? She had thought herself entirely safe as she boarded the ship and left him staring openmouthed behind. She just hadn't been able to resist the chance to have the upper hand, after suffering all of Ambrose's dictates for the past five years. What a child she had been!

Annis shook her head mentally, for it would have hurt too much to actually move it. Though it was only months ago, she felt years older now. Of course, then she had not lost her fiancé either. Well, there was no sense in repining now. She had no other option than to pursue the course she had chosen.

Though it seemed like years later that they arrived home, the remainder of the trip actually was mercifully brief. It was with a sense of relief that Annis felt the carriage stop and Laurie announce that they had reached Thurstan Hall at last. Their arrival did not go unobserved. Laurie was helping Annis from the chaise when Elizabeth came rushing up to them in a whirl of black skirts.

"Annis, I'm so glad you've returned," she exclaimed breathlessly. "We have had the strangest visitor—"

She stopped as she saw the warning look on Laurie's face and at the same time noticed that her sister was in difficulties. "What is it?"

"We've had an accident," Laurie said shortly. "Will you call a footman to help me get her upstairs?"

"Lord, I'll help you, guv'nor," exclaimed the waiting postboy who had aided him before. At Laurie's nod, he dismounted and crossed over to Annis' other side.

"An accident . . . ?" Elizabeth was beginning in some alarm, but again she encountered the unexpected glance from Laurie.

"We'll tell you about it later." He departed with his burden, leaving Elizabeth to stare helplessly at Louisa.

Mindful of the servants, these two accompanied each other

in silence into the parlor. "Is she seriously hurt?" Elizabeth asked as soon as the door was shut.

"She apparently bumped her head rather badly, but it doesn't seem to have addled her wits. What were you saying about a strange visitor?"

"A foreigner—he has been here the last three days," Elizabeth replied distractedly. "He is gone now. Dear me, I think I should send for the apothecary."

Louisa nodded. "That would be wise. I will go and make a hot posset. Perhaps it will make her feel better."

Her mind in a whirl, Elizabeth mechanically attended to everything she had to do. She wrote a brief urgent message to the apothecary and dispatched it with their groom. She went outside to see that the chaise had finished being unloaded. She would have gone to settle with the postboys herself, but she saw that Laurie had assumed this task. She gave orders to see that the unpacking would be accomplished and, with her heart in her mouth, she made her way to her sister's bedroom.

She entered to find Annis in bed with the curtains drawn. Louisa was seated beside her, the apparently neglected posset resting on a side table. Louisa indicated with a gesture that Annis had fallen asleep. Elizabeth drew near to the bed and was taken aback once again by her sister's paleness. She did not like Annis' stillness, though she was reassured by her regular breathing.

She met Louisa's eyes. "I will stay here with her," Louisa whispered.

Elizabeth was reluctant to go, but there was obviously no point in remaining. She felt she must discover what had happened. She nodded at Louisa and left to go find Laurie.

She found him outside, bidding farewell to the postboys, with whom he apparently had established a most cordial relationship. She felt like screaming her anxiety at him, but instead she waited woodenly as he bade farewell to these new cohorts. However, as soon as he turned back to the house, she seized his arm and whispered desperately in his ear, "Laurie, I must speak with you now!"

"Certainly. What do you say we have tea in the study?"

His expression revealed nothing, for he was well aware of the need for discretion in front of the servants. She was beside herself with impatience by the time they reached the study. He had chosen the location wisely, for it was unlikely that they could be overheard here.

"Tell me what happened," she demanded as soon as the door was closed.

He sank casually into a leather-covered wing chair. "We were forced off the road by another carriage, coming the opposite direction."

"Another carriage? Who was driving it?"

"It was the stage, and we didn't discover who was driving it, for it did not stop."

"You cannot be serious!"

Laurie shrugged. "There was some young fellow driving who was three sheets to the wind, at least that's what the postboys report. They said he was sitting up beside the coachman on his box. Apparently it's rather common sport to take the reins for a while and try tooling the stage."

"But how peculiar not even to stop."

Laurie's eyes shifted from her face as he repeated the assurances he had given Louisa.

Elizabeth, ever observant, began to be suspicious. "Laurie, what is wrong? What aren't you telling me?"

He set his chin resolutely, but still did not look her in the eye. "Told you everything. Postboys said the accident wasn't out-of-the-ordinary. Sort of thing that happens more often than you'd think."

Behind the spectacles, Elizabeth's blue eyes narrowed thoughtfully for a moment; then she suddenly relaxed her shoulders. "That's all right, Laurie. You needn't tell me your secret at this moment. Just bear in mind that I will worm it out of you sooner or later, and probably when you least expect it."

Laurie turned an indignant face to her. "Dash it, Lizzie, it's not fair for you to use your brain on me for this sort of thing."

"I think it entirely fair when your secret involves an accident that has hurt my sister and might easily have killed both of you," Elizabeth replied coolly, watching him.

"Oh, it wouldn't have *killed* us," Laurie replied with an admirable carelessness. He caught his sister's expression and frowned. "Here, stop looking at me like that. I'd tell you if

I could, I suppose, but it's not my secret—it's Annis'."

Elizabeth could not quite contain an exasperated sigh. "Well, since Annis is at this moment lying upstairs asleep as she attempts to recover from what might have been a *serious* injury, don't you think it would be wisest of you to confide in me? Or would you prefer that I go upstairs and wake her and demand to know what has happened? I doubt she has the energy to argue at the moment," Elizabeth added sweetly while looking at Laurie with a satisfied expression.

"Lizzie, you wouldn't."

By way of reply, she rose.

He looked at her for a moment, then frowned. "I should have known you'd take an unfair advantage of me."

Recognizing capitulation, she seated herself again.

He gave a heavy sigh. "Annis has a notion that Ambrose means to do away with us."

In spite of herself, a laugh escaped Elizabeth. "Oh, Laurie, you can't be serious. What a flight of fancy!" She had to giggle as a fresh thought struck her. "Oh, dear, what do you suppose Ambrose would say if he knew? He cares more for propriety than anyone else in the world."

She looked up at Laurie, her eyes brimming with laughter, and was surprised to see a grave expression there. She shook her head, still smiling. "Please don't tell me that she's managed to convince you, too."

His expression had not altered. "As to whether he was behind this accident, I can't say. It would have been dashed difficult for him to know which road we would be traveling and when. Doesn't seem clever enough for Ambrose, either. If he'd wanted to dispatch us, he might have done a more thorough job."

Seeing that he was serious, Elizabeth had lost her smile.

"Annis has her reasons for believing Ambrose might attempt something." He sighed again. "She'll be so angry when she discovers I've told you about it."

"She might not have to know," Elizabeth said quietly.

There was a knock on the library door. It was a footman with the tea tray.

Annis opened her eyes slowly. The pain in her head told her

that yesterday was not merely a bad dream, as she had hoped. She raised herself to a sitting position with a groan. Her mind was definitely fuzzy this morning. She supposed she had the apothecary to thank for that; she vaguely remembered his poking and prodding her before forcing some vile sort of draft down her throat. She felt the need to clear her head, and so rose, not without a struggle, and made her way over to the window and opened the curtains.

Almost immediately, Elizabeth appeared in her room. "Annis, you're awake! I thought I heard you moving about in here."

Her sister blinked at her bemusedly.

Elizabeth addressed her in a hurried manner. "Annis, he's here again. He insisted upon seeing you. I told him of your accident, but he is determined to stay . . ."

Nothing Elizabeth was saying was making sense. Annis put a hand up to her aching head. "Who is here?" she asked. "Ambrose?"

"No, no . . . oh, I forgot that you don't know. A foreign gentleman. He has been here the past three days demanding to see you. He won't say what his business is."

The hand on Annis' head was busy exploring the site of her contusion. There it was, a sizable and painful knot. She winced.

"I'm sorry, I didn't even ask how you are feeling this morning. Are you all right? The apothecary seemed to think that your injury was not dangerous."

Annis was spared having to reply by the appearance of a maid. "Ah, Rose," she remarked in some relief, "would you please be kind enough to draw me a bath?"

Annis turned to her sister. "And if you would be good enough, please have a tray sent up? The gentleman can wait, whoever he is."

"What would you like?" Elizabeth inquired solicitously. "We had some kippers and some excellent bacon this morning."

Annis put up a hand to stay her, not quite repressing the shudder that ran through her. "Tea and toast will be sufficient, thank you."

It was just over an hour later that Annis made her slow way

downstairs. The bath had gone a long way toward making her feel more the thing, but her head was still hurting, as it undoubtedly would for the next several days. She had caught the anxiety in Elizabeth's voice, but she was surprisingly indifferent to it. She supposed that after spending her last few days consorting with criminals and surviving an attempt on her life, she was not likely to be daunted by whatever danger this stranger posed.

With this sense of confidence she entered the room, only to be frozen in shock for a moment. Just before Annis had come downstairs, Elizabeth had returned to tell her sister what she knew about the foreign gentleman. She had described him as handsome, but the adjective was inadequate. He was gazing out the window as she came into the room, so that she was afforded a view of his faultless profile. Fortunately, she was able to recover as he turned and smiled, flashing rows of perfect white teeth at her.

"Lady Burham, I think?" He crossed the room quickly, bent low over her hand, and kissed it. "How enchanted I am to meet you."

His manners certainly were odd, but then, he was a foreigner. Annis withdrew her hand from his and sank into a waiting *fauteuil*. With a gesture, she indicated another chair. "Please be seated Mr. . . ."

"Don Alonzo Rodríguez y Vega, at your service," he replied with another flourishing bow before seating himself.

"It would seem, rather, that I am at yours," Annis responded bluntly.

The dark eyes narrowed for an instant before he opened them again with a smile. "Bravo! I see that you are an advocate of plain speaking, as you English say. I will therefore be brief."

"Please do," Annis said, not uncordially.

"Very well." His expression was immediately serious, and Annis thought that despite the man's obvious attractiveness, she could not like the lightning manner in which he changed moods.

"I am very sorry to intrude upon you at such a sad time, and especially since you had such an unfortunate accident, but my business with you is of the most urgent," he was saying. Did Annis imagine it, or was he quietly studying her to see whether or not she was properly dazzled by him? Just the thought made her bristle, though she gave no outward indication of it.

"I suppose I should begin by saying that Rodríguez y Vega is an old and noble name in Spain. My father is an *hidalgo*, though of course that will not mean anything to you." He hesitated for a moment, and again Annis had the impression that she was being assessed. Did he expect her to swoon at his feet? Well, he was going to be disappointed.

"Please continue," she said coldly, grateful for the air of dignity that her widow's weeds lent her.

"My father is old and very ill. It is my greatest wish to give him happiness before his death." He struggled for words for a moment, before starting from another direction. "Your country and mine, though allies in this last terrible war, have not always been so friendly. In the Americas, particularly, there have been disputes . . ."

Annis refused to help him.

He shrugged a shoulder. "My family has owned land in Honduras for almost two hundred and fifty years. It was deeded to us by our King Carlos Quinto, or as you would know him, Charles the First. The English dispossessed us of much of our property." Anger flared in his voice for a second, but he quickly suppressed it and continued on in an emotionless voice.

"The land itself is useless—mostly swamp. But it has always been my father's dream to regain the holdings of our family." He gave her a calculating look. "Your late husband, Sir Richard Burham, held some of these lands."

Annis was now mystified, but she did her best not to show it.

"I corresponded with him, and explained my reasons for wanting to purchase the land. Sir Richard most kindly consented to sell them back to me. I was having the papers prepared when I learned of his death."

He cleared his throat delicately. "I came to England hoping to meet his heir and so fulfill this dream of my father's before his death. I learned upon my arrival that you inherited his estate."

He lifted his chin and addressed her with an air of command. "I am prepared to pay double the value of the land. I have the papers with me. All we will require are two witnesses to your signature. I assume that you are willing to fulfull your late husband's promise to me?"

* * *

"A touching story," Elizabeth remarked as Annis recounted it to all of them after dinner that night. "I take it you signed the papers?"

"I almost might have," Annis admitted, "if it were not for that imperious manner of his at the end. He seemed to assume that I would follow his orders without question." She tilted her head consideringly. "Besides which, I could not help but be suspicious. If this land were so worthless, why would he go to such trouble to reclaim it? The tale about his dying father didn't ring quite true to me."

"Seemed rather a determined fellow," Laurie said casually. "Surprising he'd take no for an answer."

Annis put a hand to her still-pounding head. "Oh, as to that, I told him that I could not make such a decision at this time, that our own affairs were not in order. He seemed to realize that it would do him no good to argue and he said that he intends to remain in England for some time."

Louisa broke in anxiously, "I understand your hesitation, my dear, but have you considered the matter fully? What if he should investigate the matter further and discover the truth?"

"I don't see how he could," Annis said thoughtfully, "now that we have taken care of everything. I had better write to Mr. Fishwick immediately."

Elizabeth spoke her thoughts aloud. "Well, at least we can be glad that this is not all some scheme of Ambrose's to discover our secret, or at least that it does not seem to be."

The rest of the group made various sounds of assent, though more than one expression was pensive and more than one brow troubled.

5

THE next several weeks were untroubled by visits from either mysterious strangers or threatening relatives. Spring was beginning to turn into summer, and Annis started to feel hopeful that their troubles were now all behind them. Mr. Fishwick had arrived promptly in answer to her summons. She had held her breath while he examined the papers, but he seemed to find nothing amiss. He simply folded them up and told her that he would begin work on the dissolution of the trust immediately. It meant that he would have to confront Ambrose, of course. Annis was glad that she did not have to be present at that scene.

They were almost finished bringing the house in order, and the staff was sufficient to their needs, so she was free to day-dream about the future. She went to the window and gazed out. It looked as if the world were in bloom.

At this time next year, she thought, my mourning period will be over, we will be established in London, and Elizabeth will have her Season. It was a delightful thought and one that was dear to her heart. Her own life was behind her now, Annis felt, but she could take a vicarious joy in seeing her sister take the town by storm. With her beauty and wit, how could Elizabeth fail to do so? It would be worth all the deception and trouble to see Elizabeth creditably established, with a home and family of her own.

A wistful sigh escaped Annis, surprising her. She was forced to read herself a little lecture. After all, she, more than anyone else, knew that her life with Richard would have been no idyll. There was the possibility for happiness, of course, but that was all it would have been, a possibility. A noise from the direction of the stables attracted her attention and she was glad to turn her thoughts to a happier direction.

Laurie apparently had finished his lessons with the new tutor they had hired. Annis would have preferred him to be at school, but he hardly could have entered in the midst of the term anyway. The new tutor was proving excellent, which was yet another reason to be glad they were no longer subject to Ambrose's domination.

Laurie was spending the greater part of his free time exercising the horseflesh they had acquired. To Annis, their stables seemed more than sufficient, though Laurie was certain they would need to make other purchases when they went to London.

His great-uncle had turned over the management of Laurie's allowance to Annis. She was surprised by the amount of money that it entailed. Though she was firm about not squandering it, she had not been able to resist when Laurie had asked her pleadingly whether his funds were sufficient for him to be allowed to buy a gig.

She looked down at the scene below her. Laurie's pride in his acquisition was evident. He had chosen a lively animal to pull his carriage. Annis could not quite like it, but when appealed to had admitted that there could be no question that a sluggish horse would have been unacceptable. Richard had been just the same when he was Laurie's age.

She well could remember her first ride in the gig, the very day that Richard had acquired it. How excited she had been when he appeared in their drive one cool spring day, and how thrilled when she learned she was to be his first passenger. She naturally had assigned it a significance that would have surprised Richard very much had he known.

She had not even bothered to change into driving clothes, but instead had rushed out impetuously in her childish white muslin dress and demanded to be taken up immediately. Since her gentle stepmother was generally afraid to curb her, Annis got her wish, with unhappy results.

She would have been frightened of the far-from-docile animal, which plunged and danced between the shafts, had it not been for her absolute faith in Richard. To drive alone with him was a heady sensation, made the more so by his attempts to demonstrate his skill to her. She was properly impressed by his dexterous use of the whip, used to signal the horse, without ever touching it. The speed at which they traveled was intoxicating, but after a few moments she also found it to be chilling.

She hugged her arms about herself and would not have dreamt of complaining, but even her self-absorbed companion could not fail to notice that her flow of admiring remarks had ceased. He glanced at her and was dismayed to see that her lips were purple, while her complexion was assuming a bluish tinge.

He scolded her on her lack of foresight in not providing herself with a wrap, but he also slowed the carriage, finally pulling the horse to a stop. He then took off his own jacket and threw it carelessly about her shoulders, despite her protests that he would take a chill himself. He laughed scornfully at this suggestion, gave the reins a shake, and continued with their drive. If she suspected that he soon shortened their excusion because he also was beginning to be cool, she was at least diplomatic enough not to say so.

When they returned to Thurstan House, she had thanked him prettily for the ride and returned his coat to him. However, when she changed her dress that evening, she found that it still retained a scent of him, left by his jacket. She had caught it to her and pressed her face into it, then tucked it into a corner of her clothes press. How disappointed she had been when the maid found it and washed it. The thought brought a frown to her face. How foolish one could be at thirteen.

She closed her eyes for a moment. She must learn to banish Richard from her thoughts if she were ever to live without pain. Perhaps it would be easier in London, where there weren't any memories.

She opened her eyes again to see that Laurie had spotted her at the window. He gave her an inviting wave. She realized abruptly that he had no one about to impress with his driving skill. She motioned to him that she was coming downstairs. At least this time she would be wise enough to wear her cloak and bonnet.

When at last she appeared outside, Laurie had spent several minutes grumbling about how long she had taken and how he had been forced to let the groom walk the horse the entire time. Underneath this surly pose, however, Annis thought that she could detect a secret pleasure in her company. So she accepted a place in his gig without demur and settled her cloak about her, ready for the drive.

Within a minute or two of leaving, Laurie was restored to good humor, and soon Annis found herself obliged to listen to a list of all the finer points of the Stanhope gig, and how different it was from the ordinary sort of vehicle that a farmer might drive. From the topic of the gig, it was quite easy to proceed to a description of the virtues of his horse. The latter seemed to Annis to be an ill-favored and nasty-tempered brute, for she had seen it attempt to bite the groom that was leading it about. She forbore mentioning this to her brother, though as they traveled, she had to admit to herself that the animal was certainly swift enough, at least.

Only a great sisterly love prevented her from gasping aloud as Laurie swept around a bend without checking his horse and carelessly brushed some bushes on the wrong side of the road. When he only narrowly avoided collision with a farmer's cart passing in the opposite direction, she could hold her tongue no longer.

"Laurie, you must slow down."

He glanced at her and saw that she was serious. It was a shame that she was so poor-spirited, but it was only to be expected, he supposed. He drew in on the reins, a command to which the horse took instant exception.

An alarmed Annis noted that their speed, instead of decreasing, actually seemed to be increasing. "Laurie, please slow down," she implored.

He hauled on the reins more firmly, but without success. "Blasted animal has the bit between his teeth," he commented with unconcern.

The horse indeed seemed impervious to suggestion from its owner. Another bend was coming up in the road. Annis paled. "Laurie, pull him up now!"

Responding gallantly, Laurie half-stood in his seat, leaning back and hauling on the reins with all his strength. For a moment it seemed as if the horse must yield. Then suddenly there was a loud snap and the left-hand rein went flying uselessly up in the air.

"Well, that's torn it," Laurie remarked aptly as Annis

covered her face and the carriage rushed headlong into the bend.

It was some two and a half hours later that the gig returned to Thurstan House, being driven by Laurie, who had repaired the rein by the simple expedient of knotting it. He was having no trouble controlling a tired and foam-flecked horse, but Annis was still shaking from the experience. As they reached the house, Elizabeth and Louisa came running out to meet them.

"My dears, whatever has happened?" Louisa, first out the door, reached them soonest.

"Rein snapped," Laurie said hoarsely. "Had to let the horse run it out. Fortunate he stuck to the road."

Annis only moaned by way of verbal contribution. Elizabeth had come up to them now too, as Laurie pulled the exhausted horse to a stop.

"Must say," Laurie remarked critically as he handed the reins to a groom and hopped out of the carriage lightly, "thought the nag would last a little longer than it did. Perhaps I need to get one that's more of a stayer."

"Oh, Laurie," Annis exclaimed in a weak and reproachful voice. The footman was assisting her down now, and she nearly fell into his arms as her knees gave way. Had it not been for the gravity of the situation, Elizabeth would have yielded to an inappropriate desire to giggle. As it was, she addressed Laurie with some severity.

"I don't see why you should have another, when you obviously cannot handle this one. It looks as if you have given Annis the fright of her life, and you're not even sorry."

"Well, I like that!" Incensed, Laurie could not help but respond to this unjustified attack. "As if I could help it that the rein broke. Here I probably saved our lives, and *you* don't seem in the least bit grateful."

Annis interrupted this dispute. Free of the footman's arm now, she leaned on her sister's to whisper, "There is something I must tell you concerning Ambrose—"

"Sssh." Elizabeth shot a warning glance at the stables. Following her sister's gaze, Annis saw a modern and elegant dark green barouche, which was picked out in gold. "He arrived here this morning," Elizabeth told her.

So much for her hopes of that morning. Annis halted with a sudden thought. She addressed Laurie. "Tell the groom that I want him to go over every bit of harness, every saddle and bridle in the stable. Tell him that everyone in the stable must work on it, if necessary.

Laurie was skeptical. "Really, Annis, it was an old rein, after all."

"Then let us dispose of any tackle that is too old. I don't want anyone using any of it until it has been thoroughly checked. I don't want there to be any more accidents."

He was about to argue with her, but at the look upon her face, he heaved a sigh. "Very well," he said somewhat ungraciously, "I suppose it can't hurt anyway."

"Thank you," Annis said in some irritation; then she turned to go confront Ambrose.

She discovered Ambrose in the parlor, accompanied by Mr. Fishwick. Her cousin greeted her with an uncharacteristic solicitude before she turned to the laywer. The latter looked as if he were relieved by her arrival. "I am sorry to have burst in upon you like this, Lady Burham. I went to visit your cousin, Mr. Parry here, to ask him to sign the papers. He seemed to think it was easiest to bring them over here immediately to settle everything."

Annis could read between the lines of this forlorn little speech, so she gave Fishwick a reassuring smile. "Are the papers prepared?"

The actual signing went much better than she had expected. It was odd how she could have looked forward to and dreaded the event so much at the same time. Ambrose was forced to maintain an appearance of civility at least, in front of Mr. Fishwick. It was with a great sense of release that Annis finally signed the last of the papers and realized that her money was now her own at last, to do with as she chose. She looked up at the lawyer expectantly. "Shall I call Elizabeth in now, to sign her documents also?"

The lawyer was frowning at her. "My dear Lady Burham, I believe you may be laboring under a misapprehension."

There was a sick feeling in her stomach, but she tried not to let it show in her face. "What do you mean?"

"I thought you understood. Your marriage dissolves the trust, yes, but by the provisions of your grandfather's will, a new one is then set up for Elizabeth until her marriage."

Annis tried not to reveal the force of the blow she had been dealt. Her mouth was dry. "And her trustee is . . . ?"

"Your cousin, Mr. Parry, of course."

Ambrose turned his face away, but not before she saw the expression of triumph in his eyes. A part of her exclaimed mournfully that all was lost, but she refused to give in to such feelings. She had her fortune. Ambrose could not prevent her from taking Elizabeth to London and finding her a husband. And once Elizabeth married, then she, too, would be free of him.

When she awoke in the morning, Annis was glad that she had lacked the opportunity to admit what she had done and to inform Elizabeth of her suspicions. Now that matters were settled, Ambrose would seem to have no reason to take any desperate measures against them. Even though it was a smaller amount, he still had Elizabeth's fortune to siphon from discreetly. He must have gambled that their continued silence meant that she had not confided in Elizabeth. He certainly knew her well enough to guess that she would be reluctant to do so.

No, he would probably be content at the moment with controlling Elizabeth's fortune. The danger would arise when they went to London, most specifically when Elizabeth became engaged. Annis shuddered to think of Ambrose's reaction to that piece of news. By then, she hoped it would be too late for him to do anything. It was clear to her, as it was to everyone else, that they could do nothing else but bide their time until her mourning period was over. It was not to be expected that there would be no clouds to shadow their landscape.

One such was Don Alonzo, who, impervious to hints, called upon them whenever he "happened to be in the vicinity." Since it had become apparent that there was no connection between him and Ambrose, his presence was tolerated if not welcomed. His visits, which began by being brief, extended gradually until he had insinuated himself into a place at their dinner table whenever he called.

Annis lamented this development as she sat sewing with
Louisa one damp morning. "I am afraid where it will all end.
Doubtless we will have him staying with us before long. And
of course we will want him here with us at the holidays and—"

"It pleases you to be facetious, but I see nothing to object
to regarding his presence here. He is a most attractive and
charming gentleman."

"Yes, I am aware that you have succumbed to his good looks,
but doesn't it at least seem odd to you that he so often should
happen to find himself in this neighborhood?"

Louisa had her own opinions on that. Though he scarcely
could court a lady who was in mourning, his attentions to Annis
spoke volumes. She wisely kept her thoughts to herself and said
instead, "Well, we are not so very far from London, after all,
and I'm sure that he does have a great many friends to visit.
He certainly has won Laurie's heart, and you cannot deny that
his influence has been all to the good."

Annis could hardly return a negative to this observation. It
was only to be expected that, having spent the past five years
under Ambrose's repressive thumb, Laurie should find his
newfound freedom intoxicating. Nor was it remarkable that he
should have made the acquaintance of a young sporting blood
in the neighborhood. Anchitel Shernden Luffincott, known to
his intimates as "Luffy," was some two years senior to Laurie
in age and moreover possessed a great deal of worldly
knowledge not gained at university, which made him appear
to Laurie in the light of a modern Delphic oracle. His condescen-
sion in taking up Laurie as an acquaintance was almost too
magnanimous to be believed, though Annis privately thought
it might have a good deal to do with the fact that there were
no other young gentlemen in the immediate neighborhood.

It was inevitable that Laurie should spend a great deal of time
in this person's company, to the resultant neglect of his lessons.
Neither the tutor's nor Annis' remonstrances recalled him to
his duty more than temporarily. He began to affect about his
neck a spotted Belcher handkerchief, an item which his sisters
could not help but dislike, and also to introduce many sporting
expressions into his speech. Though they were generally
incomprehensible to Annis, they offended her, for they seemed

so dreadfully common and they secretly worried her, because of the unsavory pastimes they hinted at.

He had demanded to be given a part of his allowance, explaining that in the circles he now moved in a fellow had to be able to "sport the ready." She had seen, of course, that he could not be a charity case for his friend and had given the money to him with some reluctance. She was quite afraid that most of it was being squandered on betting on mills, cockfights, and perhaps worse. She began to think that Ambrose's accusations were not so ill-founded after all. It occurred to her more than once that Richard would have been able to curb Laurie easily, but of course Richard was gone. It did no good for her thoughts to turn in that direction, and she wished vainly that she could stop.

At this juncture Don Alonzo's reappearance did seem almost a welcome gift. He apparently had decided to remain in England for some time, despite his father's reputed age and illness. The foreigner had procured a dashing curricle and a handsome pair of blacks to draw it. Such an equipage could not fail to catch Laurie's eye. It was evident that the Spaniard was possessed of a fine pair of prads, and moreover, that he was handy with the ribbons.

Don Alonzo refrained from dampening the fires of Laurie's youthful enthusiasm, and even kindly invited him to take a turn if he wished. Laurie, almost overwhelmed by this generous inviation, leapt into the curricle without delay. Don Alonzo would have sent him on his way with only the groom for company, but he caught a pleading expression in Annis' eyes. He lifted a dark eyebrow for a moment to indicate that her message had been seen and understood, and stepped back up into the carriage himself.

"They may be quite a handful, for I am afraid that they are still rather fresh," he remarked gently to Laurie, but the latter already had taken the reins in his hands and commanded the groom to "let 'em go." He gave the reins a shake and the curricle started off in what Laurie would have termed "prime style."

Annis had a hard time hiding her smile at Don Alonzo's expression of astonishment as he was nearly jolted out of his seat. It served him right for being so insinuating, she thought, though she did allow herself to hope that Laurie wouldn't ditch them.

It was with some astonishment, therefore, that she viewed their return, well over an hour later. Laurie was still driving, but in a modest and far less dangerous style. Even more remarkably, he still seemed to be on friendly terms with Don Alonzo. He eased the carriage to a gentle halt, received some words from his companion with a pleased expression, and descended from the curricle with a lighthearted hop.

Annis could scarcely believe the transformation. From an effervescent Laurie she learned that Don Alonzo was a "first-rate fiddler" and that his eye was "precision itself." Apparently their trip had taken the form of a lesson, for Don Alonzo had taken the ribbons himself and given several carriages "the go-by" while "driving to an inch." Laurie also confided that Don Alonzo had observed in himself the makings of a crack driver and had ventured to give him a few hints. Whatever the method employed, and suspicious as she might be of the gentleman's motives, Annis could not but be glad of the results.

Whenever Don Alonzo arrived, Laurie's plans to call upon Luffy were subject to immediate cancellation. It was certainly an improvement, and Annis wished she could be easy in her own mind about it. Don Alonzo had hardly mentioned the property since his original visit, a circumstance which in itself was enough to raise her suspicions. Then of course there was the matter of his elderly father, whom he sometimes mentioned, but never with the news that he was leaving to visit him. His manner to her was always correct, but sometimes Annis fancied that she could see a warm look in those dark eyes that made her uneasy. She was in mourning, after all. It was far too soon to be thinking of marriage with another gentleman. She told herself that those were her reasons for feeling uncomfortable about the foreigner, and not that the memory of Richard was a constant intrusion upon her thoughts. She consoled herself with the knowledge that they would be leaving for London in only a matter of months, after all, and that it was not likely that Don Alonzo would continue to haunt them there.

London had begun to take up more and more of her ideas

and energy. She realized that this was one part of her campaign that she could not leave at all to chance. For Elizabeth to have an opportunity for success, the correct launching would be necessary. She hated to admit it, but she knew she would need the help of her Aunt Berinthea.

This formidable lady was actually her mother's aunt. She had made an excellent marriage, and had risen to a position of prominence, being recognized as one of London's premier hostesses. Childless herself, she had always taken a keen, if remote, interest in her nieces. Unfortunately, since this interest manifested itself in mandates about their conduct, deportment, and dress, a clash of wills with her equally strong-minded niece was inevitable. Their correspondence had been only desultory throughout the succeedng years, and Annis would have been more than content to leave it so. For Elizabeth, however, she would make the supreme sacrifice. She swallowed her pride and wrote a humble letter to her aunt, confiding her plans for Elizabeth and begging her advice on which part of town would be most suitable for them to occupy.

Her aunt's reply was both succinct and pointed. She would be happy to aid them in launching Elizabeth socially and seeing that she was creditably established. She could not imagine why her niece should *look* for a house in town when there could be none more suitable than Burham House. She considered that matter settled and she looked forward to seeing her nieces in town at the earliest opportunity.

Yet another unforeseen eventuality. Annis couldn't quite accept it, but there it was. Her aunt was undoubtedly right. To live anywhere but in Richard's family's town house would cause comment. Ambrose could not help but become suspicious. Its location in North Audley Street was unexceptionable, it was unoccupied, and it would confer an air of dignity that their cortege needed desperately. It was also Richard's, and in spite of the will, she felt she had no title to it. Even worse, it would be full of his presence. She could not escape him even for an instant. She closed her eyes, her brows furrowed. When would this pain ever stop?

Elizabeth found her, the letter clenched tightly in one fist. "Is it bad news?" she asked anxiously.

Silently Annis handed her the crumpled missive. Elizabeth smoothed it and, adjusting her spectacles, read. "Why, this is good news," she commented. "Aunt Berinthea intends to cooperate . . ." She fell abruptly silent as she finished reading. "Oh."

She looked at Annis sympathetically. "Burham House. Will it bother you very much to live there?"

Annis faced her sister squarely. "You were right all along, weren't you, Elizabeth? It all has been very wrong and now we are in it so deeply that there is no turning back."

Seeing that her sister was sincerely troubled, Elizabeth put her arm around her and gave her a squeeze. "You did it for the best, after all. Not for yourself, but for Laurie and me—and both of us realize it."

Annis made no reply, so Elizabeth stroked her hair lovingly. "He wanted you to have it—all of it—otherwise he would not have left it to you as he did."

Annis shook he head. "If I were truly his widow it would be another matter." She expelled an angry and sorrowful breath. "I cannot bear to have benefited from his death—can you understand that? To be wealthier in the world's eyes because . . ." Overcome, she could not continue.

Elizabeth gave her a silent hug. She proffered a handkerchief, but Annis refused it with a fierce shake of the head. "I think it would do you some good to cry," Elizabeth said wistfully, but she did not force the issue. She was quiet for another moment; then she pressed her sister's hand and released it. "I don't believe that Richard would have had any objection to your living in Burham House." Something glittered in Elizabeth's eyes for a moment, and she dropped her face to conceal it. "And of everyone I know, Richard would be the one most likely to approve your madcap scheme."

There was a pause. "Thank you." Annis turned to look her sister in the eye.

"What next, then?" Elizabeth asked with the ghost of a smile.

"There is so much to do. We will have to go over the house, there will be servants to hire, and if Laurie is right, horses and a carriage to buy." She gave a little sigh. "Mr. Fishwick has been asking me for some time now to come to London and meet with Richard's man of business in order to settle the estate. I suppose I had better do so.''

"To London, then.''

They were interrupted by Laurie, who had come bursting impetuously into the room at the sound of their words. "What, are we going to London, then? Capital! Luffy's promised to introduce me to the Champion of England when we go.''

He flung himself down in a chair and regarded his sisters with a complacent smile.

"I have the distinct impression,'' Elizabeth muttered sotto voce, "that our troubles are only beginning.''

6

In vain did Annis protest to Laurie that their visit to London was to be a short one, strictly dealing with matters of business. He did not appear to be troubled by the suggestion that town might be uncomfortably warm this time of year, nor by the fact that they were certain to find it thin of company. Luffy had decided that life in the country was rather flat and had made a sojourn to London to visit his cronies, and this was the idea that had fixed itself in Laurie's brain. He found an unexpected ally in Elizabeth.

"After all," she commented, "if we are both going, we must take Louisa too, so Laurie might as well come along. Besides, we shall be grateful for a gentleman's protection on our journey."

Annis could not but admit the justice of her sister's first observation, though she appeared rather incredulous at the second.

Considering the matter settled, Laurie bounded up from his chair, remarking, "I'll be dashed if I can't find someone in London to repair the old squirrel gun."

His sisters had no time to reprove him for his language, since he had already disappeared through the doorway. Annis turned to Elizabeth, a question in her eyes.

"It is better that we keep an eye on him anyway, to see that he keeps out of trouble," Elizabeth suggested.

Annis had to agree. A fear which she could not voice had arisen in her mind. So far, her sanguine expectations concerning Ambrose had seemed sound. There had been no more accidents, and she had begun to breathe easier. It was possible, however, that he might be spurred into action when he learned that they were planning to settle in London for the Season and had actually gone there to make arrangements. There might be some safety in numbers.

Accordingly, missives were dispatched to both Aunt Berinthea and to the lawyer, informing them of the family's impending arrival, and advising them that they would be putting up at Gordon's Hotel. This last decision had necessitated an inordinate amount of discussion, with certain factions arguing in favor of economy, while to others the need for presenting a proper appearance was uppermost in consideration. As usual, it was Annis who cast the deciding vote. The memory of their last journey to London was still vivid in her mind and she firmly rejected any suggestion that they make do with any sort of inferior accommodation.

"Besides," she commented, "part of our reason in journeying there is to ask Aunt Berinthea for her aid. Can you imagine what she would say if she learned that we were staying at the White Horse Cellar or some other coaching inn?"

Laurie, whose dislike of this august female was rather greater even than Annis' remarked gloomily that Lady Downage was bound to kick up a dust anyway if they dared stay anywhere other than the Clarendon.

True to their expectations, Annis found her first interview with this lady rather trying. Two days after their arrival, she went to call upon Lady Downage at what Annis considered the rather advanced hour of ten in the morning. Though Elizabeth had offered to accompany her, Annis decided to run the gauntlet of this first meeting alone. She had seen the wistful glances that Elizabeth had directed at a lending library that they happened to drive by the previous day. So it was settled that Elizabeth and Louisa should visit the library while Annis took the maid with her to Lady Downage's. Laurie had made no self-sacrificing offer himself. He had staged a joyful reunion with Luffy the first evening that they were in town, and quickly had fallen in with a group of what Annis considered rather rackety young fellows. She could not be positive about them, of course, since she had hardly seen Laurie since their arrival in town. All she knew was that he spent most of his mornings asleep, since his nocturnal activities kept him up until the wee hours.

If Annis felt somewhat daunted by the prospect of visiting her aunt alone, her fears were not allayed by her encounter with her ladyship's butler. This formidable individual, while not actually disrespectful, managed to imply surprise that Annis should have come to call upon Lady Downage at that hour of the morning, and without saying so, appeared to doubt that Annis was actually a relation.

"You'd think I hadn't written to say I was coming to call this morning," Annis muttered angrily under her breath, but she had to admit to herself that she was stung by the butler's disapprobation. The black gowns she had purchased while in Jamaica had excited no comment on their visit to the East End, but she was well aware that she had been the object of several less-than-discreet stares and giggles in the past two days. She knew that her dresses were sadly behind the fashion, but she told herself that it didn't matter since she was in mourning. There would be time to buy new apparel when they returned.

After a half-hour of waiting, she was escorted to Lady Downage's chamber. She found her aunt in dishabille, seated at her dressing table, while her abigail put the finishing touches on her coiffure. As Annis entered, Lady Downage dismissed the woman and gestured her niece to a chair. With the exception of a few more lines in her face, she was much the same as Annis remembered her. There were the imperious nose, the pronounced chin, and the commanding eyes, which always seemed to see a little too much. Annis was hard put not to blush as her aunt took in every detail of her outmoded gown and bonnet. Annis greeted Lady Downage and began to apologize for not calling upon her sooner. Affairs of business had been most pressing, so she had driven into the City the day before.

"You did what!" The outrage in the authoritative voice was unmistakable. Lady Downage's eagle eyes were fixed upon Annis with an expression of the utmost horror.

Annis felt an instinctive need to shelter herself from that glare, but with admirable resolution she kept her seat on the gilt-and-embroidered chair. "The hotel did not seem a suitable place to conduct business, to me, so I thought it better to call upon Richard's man of affairs myself."

"You went into the City by yourself . . ." Lady Downage looked as if she could not quite believe the words that were coming out of her own mouth.

Annis raised her chin a fraction of an inch. "No, of course not. I had our companion, Miss Utterly, and our lawyer, Mr.

Fishwick, with me." Perhaps she would have done better to have listened to Mr. Fishwick, after all. He had advised her most strongly against the journey, preferring to have Mr. Robbins call upon her at her hotel instead.

"That does not alter the impropriety of it. Oh, that a niece of mine could be so blind to it. I hardly know what to say."

Annis judged that it was time to show a little steel. She held herself proudly erect in the fragile chair. "As far as I am concerned, the less said, the better, Aunt. I am much obliged that you are willing to help launch Elizabeth, but my business affairs concern no one but myself."

Lady Downage stared at her for a full minute without speaking. Annis could feel the color beginning to rise to her cheeks, but she did not drop her eyes. When her aunt finally addressed her, it was evident that she had chosen her words with care.

"If Elizabeth is to make her come-out under *my* auspices, then everything that you say or do *must* reflect upon me. If you expect me to lend you countenance, you must give up these hoydenish tricks of yours. I make every allowance for your want of a mother's influence, but this is not Kent, you know."

The knowledge that this criticism was justified did not in any way make it easier for Annis to bear. Still, there were Elizabeth's interests to be considered. She dropped her gaze and murmured woodenly that she would try to be more circumspect in the future.

Apparently considering this point settled, Lady Downage turned her attack in a new direction. Still studying her niece with a disparaging eye, she remarked that the first order of business would be to get her to a dressmaker without delay.

"I thank you for your concern, ma'am, but I am in mourning, as you know," Annis replied stolidly.

"There is no need for you to set up your back in that way," Lady Downage remarked. "You will not be in mourning forever, after all. Though I certainly would not advocate choosing colors, I think you might well wear gray or even lavender gowns next year. In the meantime, though you may wear what you wish in the country, I am not about to have it said that my niece is a positive dowd. Come here."

Almost involuntarily Annis started from her chair and crossed the room to allow her aunt a closer inspection.

"Turn around. Hmmmm."

Annis obeyed, trying to stifle a feeling of resentment at this dictatorial manner, but as she turned about to meet her aunt's eyes once again, she was surprised to see a faint smile there.

"Well, it is not a situation that cannot be remedied, after all. I think that when you are properly dressed you will appear to advantage, my dear."

Annis looked at her in frank dismay. "But it is Elizabeth that concerns me. I have no ambition to marry again myself."

Her aunt looked at her in some surprise. "I certainly hope that you would not be foolish enough to refuse to make a suitable match should the occasion arise. You are but a young woman, after all." Annis would have spoken, but her aunt prevented her. "I must say how pleased I was with your marriage to Sir Richard. It was a most eligible connection in every way. He was a young man of character, wealth, and breeding and I was quite surprised that you had done so well for yourself, buried in the country as you were."

Again Annis was given no opportunity to interrupt the flow of words. "But with your mourning period over, there should be no impediment to making another marriage. Your good sense must admit that it is so. I was happy to see that you are not one of those females who must carry a sodden handkerchief about with her, wiping her eyes, red in the nose, and generally making everyone else uncomfortable. You are much too sound to indulge in such an excessive display of emotion."

She hesitated for a moment, and oddly enough, Annis found herself waiting silently for the next thought. "It does no good to dwell on the past, my dear. We must always look to the present and the future. It is my belief that a female is always happiest in the married state, provided she chooses her husband wisely, of course."

Lady Downage pressed her lips firmly together as she finished speaking. Annis regarded her with some curiosity. She remembered Lord Downage only vaguely as a kindly and humorous sort of gentleman, who stood in the sharpest sort of contrast to his wife's forceful personality. He had been gone these fifteen

years or more. Her aunt had never shed a tear while in Annis'
presence, and indeed always had avoided mentioning her late
husband's name. Was it possible that there was an unsuspected
depth of grief concealed beneath that stern exterior? For the
first time in her life, she experienced an odd sort of harmony
with her aunt.

Lady Downage was not one to dwell overlong on such a
lachrymose topic. "Since Elizabeth most likely is dressed no
better than you," she observed with a downward curl of the
lip, "I think that we will make a trip to the modiste's first of
all. Then we may turn our attention to other matters."

Annis lifted her chin, her momentary sympathy for her aunt
gone. Lady Downage certainly was knowledgeable in matters
of dress, but if she imagined that she would be placed in charge
of every aspect of her nieces' lives, she was sadly mistaken.

Annis had been given a real taste of power when she had gone
to visit Richard's man of business the previous day. Like Mr.
Fishwick, he had been surprised that she should call upon him
at his office in the City. Sir Richard had been a shrewd man
of affairs, but it seemed patent that his wife would not be the
sort to take the same kind of interest in such matters. Mr.
Robbins began to delineate the most pressing problems with no
real expectation that she would wish to, or even be able to
comprehend such matters.

Given her upbringing, it perhaps was understandable that she
should easily grasp the need for expenditures advised by the
estate agent. The draining of the west field was approved
quickly, as was an outlay for new roofs for some of the cottages.
In fact, she quite startled Mr. Robbins by expressing remorse
that it had taken her so long to tend to affairs.

"I do wish that Mr. Charles had ridden over to inform me
of this," she said, quite conscience-stricken. "To think of those
poor people needing new roofs all this time." He did his best
to reassure her. "Sir Richard was a most scrupulous landlord,
as you no doubt know, my lady. He left the estate in very good
repair. These are merely routine matters which arise from time
to time."

She looked up and saw his hesitation. "What else is there,
Mr. Robbins?"

Thus encouraged, he began, "As you may know, Harden Park constitutes only a small portion of Sir Richard's estate. There are other matters to be discussed, but perhaps you might prefer to do so at a later time," he added doubtfully.

"My object in coming to London was to take care of as much of this business as I might, particularly since I have neglected it shamefully for so long. Therefore I am at your disposal, though of course I would be happy to return another day if you must tend to other, more pressing business."

This unlooked-for consideration and her interest made Robbins prey to a sudden feeling of hope. With great eagerness he began to explain about a most promising new company that was forming, a generous offer that had been made for mining interests in Sir Richard's Central American property, and excessive problems they were having with a certain shipping company, which consistently delivered short goods.

To his astonishment, a very simple discourse enabled her to have an understanding of each of these concerns. She allowed herself to be guided by his judgment in everything, except that she did not wish to sell the mining interests. He pressed the matter once, but she refused to change her mind, though she tempered her decision with a charming smile.

By the end of the discussion, both the man of business and his client were able to take leave of each other in a most happy frame of mind, each being well pleased with the other. Annis was confident that Richard's affairs were in good hands. Robbins, who had expected a spoiled and mindless young aristocrat, could not quite believe his good fortune.

It was Fishwick who cleared up the mystery for him some days later. Robbins was expressing his surprise at his new client's capabilities, when the lawyer raised his eyebrows in some surprise.

"Did you not know who her grandfather was, then?"

Robbins shook his head.

"Why, John Powell—he was one of the warmest men in the City. If she's long-headed, she comes by it naturally, I'll be bound."

It was this newfound sense of self-assurance that had enabled

Annis to speak as she did to Lady Downage, when the temptation was either to quail before her or lose her temper instead. After partaking of a light luncheon, she and her aunt had agreed to meet the following day in order to go to the dressmaker. This left the rest of the afternoon free for whatever she wished.

Inspired by this fresh sense of confidence, she boldly decided to undertake a visit she had been dreading for days. She would see whether Louisa and Elizabeth had returned to the hotel yet, and muster their support in accompanying her to Burham House.

It was marvelous to feel that she was finally in control of her own affairs. She sailed into the hotel, full of enthusiasm for the expedition before her. She was only slightly daunted to find that Louisa and Elizabeth were not in their rooms. It might be that they had left a message with Laurie as to their whereabouts. She would try his room and see.

She tapped on his door, but received no reply. It was possible of course, that Laurie had gone out himself, but it was worth another try. She knocked more loudly this time, and announced herself. There was what sounded like a stifled curse, and she heard a weak voice respond, ''Come in.''

She entered to find the room in darkness, the bed still unmade. Laurie was just finishing struggling into a sumptuous dressing gown of a blue floral brocade on a cream background. Annis' brain leapt to the logical conclusion. Stepping inside the room hesitantly, she asked, ''Laurie, are you ill?''

He was mumbling a negative when his new and efficient valet entered the room and began opening the curtains. As the first wave of sunlight washed into the room, Laurie put a hand up to his eyes. ''Johnson, I think that is enough light for the moment.''

His servant bowed in obedience and asked if there were anything else he required. Laurie commented in a fretful voice that he would be glad of some tea and toast, and Johnson left to see that it was provided.

''Oh, but you *are* ill,'' Annis said sympathetically as she seated herself. ''You should have told me and I would not have bothered you.''

''Nothing of the sort,'' Laurie muttered crossly. ''Rather late night, that's all.''

"But I can see that your head is hurting," she continued in the same vein as before. "Would you like me to burn some feathers or—"

A spasm of revulsion crossed his features. His stomach evidently was bothering him too. A memory tugged at the corner of Annis' mind. Her eyes opened wide in shock. "Laurie! Have you been drinking?"

His hand went up to his head again. "Not so loud," he complained. He glanced at her and read her expression. "It's not so bad as that," he protested. "Just shared a bowl or two of punch with the fellows at Cribb's parlor last night. Met the Champion of England," he added with some pride.

"You were drunk!"

He winced at her carrying tones. "Just a trifle on the go. Nothing so bad as you think." His face assumed an expression of disapproval. "Now, Freddy was completely castaway. Not at all the thing, I promise you. Luffy said you'd think he hadn't been on the town for more than a month, which he has, of course. Said I seemed at home to a peg, yet I've been here only two days," he added with a complacent smile.

Annis could have dispensed with Luffy's tribute. "Oh, Laurie, can't you see how wrong this is?" She gazed at the pale, red-eyed, stubble-faced youth before her with dissatisfaction. "To see you this morning, anyone would think you were an old profligate and not a healthy boy of sixteen."

Sudden hope dawned in Laurie's face. "I say, do you think so?" He rose quickly as his head would permit and went over to study the mirror. "I do look older, don't I?" he added with pleasure.

Annis could see that this line of reasoning was not likely to aid her cause, so she hastily changed her tack. "I know that deep inside you there is too much good sense to wish to pursue this way of life."

Laurie had ceased admiring his dissolute appearance and was in the process of returning to his chair. "Know what, Annis?" he asked as he plopped down casually in it. "You're beginning to sound exactly like Lizzie."

Annis' sense of powerlessness stood in sharp contrast to what she had felt upon arriving at the hotel. She gave a sigh, admitted defeat, and turned the subject. "Speaking of Elizabeth, I had hoped to find her and Louisa back here at the hotel, for I plan to visit Burham House this afternoon and shall want their advice. I don't suppose you would wish to accompany me?" She could tell from Laurie's expression that he thought this expedition sounded rather flat, but he replied to her question politely enough.

"Sorry, I've a previous engagement. Luffy offered to take me to Tattersall's and help me find a good riding horse."

Irritated, Annis could not help replying, "Surely that can wait until we return to town."

Laurie shook his head. "Can always use a good riding horse—besides, wouldn't want to miss any bargains. Luffy tells me that the price of a prad goes up considerably when town's less thin of company." He added, on what was obviously intended to be a conciliatory note, "Besides, I'll be looking at carriages and horses for you, too. Daresay you'd like a smart new barouche for driving about town and in the park at five."

"Had you thought how much all of this will cost?"

"That reminds me." He leaned forward in his chair, his expression confiding. "I'll need another advance against my allowance. Town's so dashed expensive, you know. Don't want to impose on my friends—"

Annis was suddenly suspicious. "Where did you get that dressing gown?"

He leaned back in his chair again, gratified by her interest. "Handsome, isn't it? Saw the apparel-furbisher yesterday. Luffy was kind enough to give me the name. A new fellow, but had a nice touch, don't you know. Couldn't go about town looking like a shab-rag, after all. Needn't concern yourself about that, though. Fellow was only too happy to let me go on tick."

Annis was struggling against outrage. "Do you mean that this unfortunate tradesman was willing to extend you credit, when you're not even of age, and that you accepted clothing from him without even paying him anything!"

Laurie looked shocked. "Really, Annis, not a tradesman. Almost a gentleman—practically, anyway. And Luffy says it's not at all the thing to pay your tailor or anyone else right away. Why, the best sort of people do it. Why, look at Brummell."

Annis pressed her lips together tightly in order to keep mastery of herself. When she spoke, it was in a tightly controlled voice. "I never met Mr. Brummell and I well know that you never did. I have been told, however, that he was forced to leave the country in order to escape debtors' prison."

Laurie looked at her wide-eyed. "See—just what I was telling you. Why, they say that even the Prince Regent himself is—"

Mercifully, Annis was spared the rest of this explanation as another tap sounded on the door.

"Come in," Laurie said crossly, and Elizabeth entered, her eyes shining with excitement. "Oh, Annis, I was hoping that I would find you here." She crossed the room quickly to seat herself by her sister. "The lending library is the most famous place. Can you imagine—they had practically everything I wanted, and more besides, of course. I could have spent all day there, and Louisa too, I imagine. We thought we had better return, though, and see how your visit with Aunt Berinthea went."

Annis rose. "We had better continue this conversation in my room, Elizabeth, and leave Laurie to his." The object of her speech caught her eye as she was leaving. "I will see that you have some money," she said quietly.

The eroding of her self-confidence was made complete by her visit to Burham House. The edifice was not nearly as large as Aunt Berinthea's house nearby in Grosvenor Square, but it was quite sizable enough to intimidate Annis. The elderly manservant who opened the door to her knock looked quite puzzled, and without being asked, volunteered, "The master's not at home." He would have closed the door again, but Annis, grinding her teeth, stepped up and prevented him.

"Whatever is the matter with all these London servants?" she wondered under her breath, but she added aloud, "I am Lady Burham, so there is no need to tell me that the master isn't at home."

A vague sort of spark lit in the dim old eyes as he repeated helpfully, "That's right, miss, he's not at home."

Annis saw that there was no help to be gained from this quarter, so she shoved her way in past him rudely, then turned back to her companions. "Elizabeth, Louisa, do come in."

As they hesitated, the servant tried once again, frowning at her severely now. "I told you, miss. The master isn't at home."

Annis was beginning to lose her temper. "I suppose there was no point in my writing to this address," she said bitterly. "It doesn't seem to have made any impression."

Fearing an outburst at any minute from Annis, Louisa stepped up and charitably began to explain, "This is Lady Burham, my good man. She is Sir Richard's widow and your new mistress. She has come to take possession of Burham House, so will you please show us inside?"

"Sir Richard is away," the servant said, quite loudly as his scowl deepened.

"Louisa, Lizzie, come inside this minute," Annis ordered, her own voice rising.

The altercation was beginning to attract the notice of some passersby, who had stopped to discuss and observe the outcome. Beneath her dark veil, Annis could feel her face pinken. "For goodness sake, Lizzie, come in. People are starting to stare."

"That's right, Lizzie, go in," a raffish young fellow called out. From his state of disarray, he seemed to have had a glass too many already this day. A shout of laughter from the watchers made Elizabeth join her sister in blushing, and she also began to push her way past the servant. For some reason, these additional arrivals seemed to awaken some long-buried protective instinct, and he began to grapple with Elizabeth in an attempt to thrust her back outside. The crowd was enjoying itself hugely by now, and Annis began to pray that the ground would open up and swallow them.

Rescue arrived unexpectedly in the form of a broad-shouldered gentleman who mounted the stairs rapidly. A pair of gray eyes fixed themselves upon the old servant. "Greenlaw," an imperious voice commanded, "please have the goodness to let these ladies come inside."

A smile of recognition transformed the servant's face. "Mr. Walter . . . why, certainly, sir." He began bowing and making welcoming gestures. "Any friends of Mr. Walter's are welcome of course, though . . ." He turned to the stranger with a frown.

"I did tell them the master is not here, sir, but they would come in anyway."

The ladies entered and the commanding gentleman shut the door to shield them from the crowd's gaze. "And you did very well, Greenlaw, though I feel sure that Sir Richard would wish you to show these ladies every consideration possible. And I hope that you will, for my sake, anyway."

"Of course, sir." The old servant bowed stiffly once again.

The gentleman bowed to the ladies and would have turned to go, but a word from Annis halted him. "Wait!" she said desperately. "May we not even thank you, sir?" Here she glanced at the servant and added in a low voice, "For your most welcome intrusion."

He smiled at her, and if he was not as handsome as Don Alonzo, Annis liked his countenance better for its openness. "I am pleased to have been of service." He hesitated for a moment. "I take it that I have the honor of addressing Lady Burham?" At her nod, he continued, "If you will allow me to present myself, I am Walter Ulverstone and I am, or rather was, one of your husband's closest friends. I cannot tell you how deeply sorry I am for your loss."

Annis thanked him and proceeded to present her companions. He looked at her keenly. "I take it you mean to settle in town, then."

She replied in the affirmative.

He frowned slightly and told her in an undertone. "You will have to forgive old Greenlaw. He has been with the family so many years that Richard could not bear to turn him off. I think that you will find him most loyal, though his powers are undoubtedly failing. It seems to me, however—"

He was interrupted by the arrival of a stout lady liberally dusted with flour, who was wiping her hands on a cloth as she entered. "What's all this botheration?" She saw the assembled party and dropped a hasty curtsy. "Mr. Walter," she exclaimed. She turned her attention to Annis and her party and curtsied again. "And you must be Lady Burham, who wrote that you would be paying us a visit." She looked chagrined. "I am sorry that I was not here to greet you, my lady, but I was in the midst of making a pie." She looked with some uncertainty at Greenlaw. "I hope that there was no trouble, my lady."

Annis inclined her head. "Mr. Ulverstone was kind enough to procure our admission and also to explain matters to me." At the second part of the sentence the housekeeper's brow cleared.

"May I say how welcome you are, my lady," she said, with another curtsy, which was graceful despite her bulk.

Mr. Ulverstone gave a slight smile. "Well, I see that you are now in good hands with Mrs. Cherry here. I will not intrude upon you any longer." He bowed to them. "If there is any way I may be of service, please call upon me."

"Thank you," Annis said. After his departure, she turned to Mrs. Cherry and introduced her sister and Louisa. "And now, if you will be kind enough to show us over the house, we will be obliged to you."

Mrs. Cherry gave a little chuckle. "I will be happy to, my lady. It's been many years since Burham House boasted a mistress, and there's certainly a great deal that wants doing here."

She began by leading them upstairs. Annis took the opportunity to whisper in Elizabeth's ear. "What an attractive gentleman—I wonder who his family is."

"He certainly seemed very kind," Elizabeth responded, "but you know that I could not see his face."

"A pity," Louisa interjected with a sigh, overhearing this discussion.

7

A closer inspection of Burham House did not render it any less daunting. Under the holland covers lay some magnificent furniture, but Annis could not quite accept that she soon would be making her home among such imposing formal pieces. The other half of the problem was that the house loudly proclaimed its want of any feminine influence. It was not that the furbishings were in poor repair so much as that they lacked the warmth and the little touches that might have rendered it a thousand times more habitable.

By far the most painful part of the tour was when Mrs. Cherry opened a door and announced that it was the master's chamber. Louisa had looked at Annis anxiously and Elizabeth had murmured that she need not enter it just yet, but Annis had shaken her head. It would not become any easier as time went along, of that she was sure. She stepped into the room and beheld with anguish that it was in readiness for Richard's return. There was not a speck of dusk anywhere. The brass screen in front of the fireplace was spotless. The silver candlestick, with fresh candles in it, gleamed. From her perspective she could see into the dressing room, where Richard's brushes and his razor lay in neat arrangement upon a mahogany table. Averting her eyes, she walked over to the great chest and opened a drawer without thinking. Inside lay Richard's cravats, neatly pressed and starched, waiting to be used. Had she been by herself, she would have caught them to her and wept. She was not alone, however. Using every ounce of willpower that she possessed, she carefully closed the drawer. "I think I have seen enough here," she told no one in particular. Only her pale face and hurried step indicated that anything was amiss as she left the room.

"It's Greenlaw," Mrs. Cherry volunteered in a low, reluctant voice. "Most of the time he does well enough, but ever since the master passed on . . . well, somehow he just won't accept it. Nothing I can say or do will convince him that the master isn't coming back.''

Elizabeth and Louisa exchanged meaningful looks. This would be difficult enough for Annis as it was. How could she bear to live here with a servant who insisted on believing that Sir Richard was still alive?

It was Elizabeth who broached the matter of the old man-servant the next day. "I do not see how anyone could object if you pensioned him off, Annis. He obviously is not capable of handling his duties.''

Annis shook her head. "I could not dismiss such an old and loyal servant of Richard's family. Besides, Mrs. Cherry did say that he is not lacking in any other respects. I believe that I may find him a less public position in the household where he will not prove an embarrassment.''

Tying her bonnet under her chin, she changed the subject deftly. "I think we had better go downstairs now, since it is close to the time that Aunt Berinthea is to call. I have a great suspicion that she would take it amiss if she were kept waiting.''

It had been agreed that the two sisters would accompany their aunt alone. Annis had pressed Louisa to go with them, but Louisa had refused. Annis had urged her again, pointing out that it was in their own self-interest to go about with a smartly dressed chaperone. Louisa had thanked her for her generosity, and seeing that Annis was not to be dissuaded, replied that considering her own skill with the needle, she would do better to make her own dresses. Annis could not be satisfied with this arrangement, but finding Louisa unyielding on this point, she had been forced to agree.

The shopping expedition was not to prove an occasion of unalloyed pleasure. It was true that Aunt Berinthea was clearly a favored customer, for the modiste and her assistants could not have been more obliging. Unfortunately, every opinion Lady Downage expressed was accepted as a dictate from on high by these helpful ladies. Annis could see that she shocked them very greatly by daring to disagree with her aunt. In general, Lady

Downage's taste was very good, but it was only to be expected that Annis should have some ideas of her own.

Having lived so many years with no opportunity to purchase fashionable dresses, Annis had developed a scorn for such matters. As she stood in the dressmaker's salon admiring shimmering fabrics and elegant fashion plates, she discovered that her scorn had been nothing more than a pose. She found she was fascinated by the attention currently placed on trimming the top of the sleeve and the hem of the skirt. She could not help but admire the smooth line given to the front of the skirt and the bodice by the new gores, as opposed to the bulky gathers to which she was accustomed.

She felt a secret envy of Elizabeth, for whom these confections were intended, but she nobly mastered it. Like Aunt Berinthea, however, she could not help offering her opinion when it came to choosing between knots of ribbons or rosettes for ornaments or whether a bodice should be vandyked or worn plain with only a frill about the neck. She did wish her aunt could refrain from her unfailing criticism of Elizabeth. Lady Downage was constantly advising Elizabeth to lift her chin or straighten her back, and her ladyship's manner did nothing to bolster Elizabeth's already weak self-confidence. Finally Annis could stand it no longer. Elizabeth was being measured for a walking dress in a spotted muslin, and Lady Downage, as usual, was finding fault.

"Stand up there, gel. You have a good figure, but no one will be able to see it if you don't carry yourself well. You should take a lesson from your sister. She's just a little slip of a thing too, but she knows how to hold herself up."

Blushing, Elizabeth half-turned to apologize, and nearly lost her balance. Her aunt's contemptuous snort added to her discomfiture.

"Really, Aunt Berinthea," Annis hissed angrily, "I have told you that she drops her head because she can't see without her spectacles. She is shy anyway, and I do not think that your comments are helping her."

"Well, she'll either have to take up wearing her spectacles or learn to look as if she *can* see without them. She's a fine-looking girl, but that's not enough to ensure success. She'll have to give up those shambling, downcast ways of hers if she hopes to attract some eligible suitors," Lady Downage said brutally.

"I should think her fortune alone would be enough to attract suitors even if she were an antidote, which she is not," Annis whispered forcefully.

Her aunt looked at her, her lip curling either from amusement or contempt. "And do you think that is the sort of match she should make, then? A marriage with some hey-go-mad fellow with his pockets to let?" She sniffed. "There are some titles for sale, if you don't care about her husband having any character."

As much as Annis might resent her aunt's manner, she could not but admit the justice of what she said. Accordingly, she preserved her silence as Elizabeth's fitting was completed.

When her own turn came, Lady Downage informed the modiste that they wished to see some silks in lavender and gray for Annis' evening gowns.

"No," Annis said, quite firmly.

Lady Downage and the dressmakers looked at her in shock. Her aunt was the first to recover. "Come, now, gel, don't be stubborn," she commanded.

"I do not intend to wear anything other than black," Annis told her simply.

"You can't expect to attract a gentleman's attention when you are dressed like a crow," Lady Downage told her in typically blunt fashion.

That was precisely Annis' plan, but she did not mean to confide it to her aunt. She intended to fill the role of the quiet chaperone, while Elizabeth could not help but shine in contrast. It was her sister who was the eligible one, and Annis did not intend to lose sight of that. "You will not change my mind," she informed her aunt coolly.

Quite naturally, an argument ensued, but Annis held firm to her resolution. Lady Downage, who was not used to having her will opposed, grew steadily angrier. The dressmakers, torn between their two clients, were beginning to be afraid that violence would result, when Lady Downage fortunately recollected something which made her submit quickly if not gracefully. Annis was suspicious of her aunt's sudden quietude, but decided to pursue the matter no further. Lady Downage had recalled that this was only the first of many shopping trips. There were several months left before the Season was to begin, and she had too much faith in her own powers of persuasion to think that Annis would not eventually yield.

From the dressmaker, a trip to the milliner must inevitably follow, and here Annis found it even harder to resist temptation. With the encouragement of her companions, she selected several small lace caps, nor could she help but buy a bonnet of black crepe in the new high-crowned fashion. This latter purchase caused Lady Downage to remark frowningly that something must be done about their hair. Happily, she added that her dresser might be relied upon to give them the latest touch.

Of course there were further purchases to be made, such as slippers, boots, gloves, fans, parasols, and reticules. By this time, both Annis and Elizabeth were beginning to be quite weary, though their indomitable aunt seemed prepared to continue on for hours. There were also corsets, petticoats, and stockings to be purchased, but her nieces flatly refused to do any more shopping that day.

"Have some pity," Elizabeth half-laughingly told Lady Downage. "Neither Annis nor I possess your constitution, Aunt."

Lady Downage seemed rather pleased than otherwise by this tribute, and consequently returned to their carriage without further protest. They began their way back to the hotel in a state of comparative harmony. Only one incident occurred to mar their tranquillity.

It was as their carriage prepared to turn into Piccadilly that Annis caught sight of a familiar black-and-yellow curricle. There were quite a few carriages jostling for position, and so they were obliged to remain where they were for a few minutes. Annis prodded her sister and asked her if the carriage didn't look familiar. She might have saved her breath, for Elizabeth, well aware that they were subject to view in an open carriage, had not donned her spectacles today. She was replying rather crossly to that effect when a tall dark-haired gentleman strode from a nearby doorway and went to exchange a word with the groom at the horse's heads.

Perhaps Annis' gaze had attracted the groom's attention, for the gentleman glanced up quickly, espied them, and removed his hat, executing a low bow in their direction. Protected as she was by her veil, Annis still could not help feeling embarrassed. She acknowledged Don Alonzo with a rather stiff nod in his direction, as their carriage began to roll forward. Her circumspection had come too late. Lady Downage had already noticed him. Her aunt had extracted a lorgnette from her reticule and was using it to study him none too discreetly as he was swept from their sight.

"That's a fine-looking gentleman," she pronounced, passing a favorable judgment. "I do not believe that I have met him. One of your admirers, Annis? Dear me, country life must be less dull than I imagined."

Annis flushed hotly, rendering her glad again for the protection of the veil. When she spoke, her voice was icy. "If you are referring to the gentleman who bowed to us just now, Aunt, he is Don Alonzo Rodríguez y Vega. He had some business dealings with . . . Sir Richard." She still could not bear to say "my husband."

Lady Downage was eyeing her with some curiosity. "It appears that he is tolerably well-acquainted with *you*. What are his birth and his fortune?"

Annis could not help but resent her aunt's prying into matters that did not concern her. "I am afraid that I cannot tell you. We believe his birth to be respectable and his fortune certainly seems adequate, but he has not confided any particulars to us." She hoped that this speech would have the effect of dampening her aunt's zeal, but she was to be disappointed.

"Pity he's a foreigner," Lady Downage said. "Still, I will make a few inquiries and see what I may learn."

Annis was beginning to be quite angry by now, but she realized that losing her temper would benefit neither Elizabeth nor herself. She decided to try turning the subject. "That reminds me, Aunt. A most well-bred gentleman assisted us yesterday at Burham House when one of the servants was reluctant to admit us. Are you acquainted with Mr. Walter Ulverstone?"

Her aunt nodded. "He is a well-bred gentleman indeed.

Pleasing manners, an agreeable appearance . . ." She sighed. "It's a pity, but he is not for either of you," she announced with finality.

Forgetting her resolve, Annis showed her exasperation. "Everything that you say would seem to recommend him to us as at least a pleasant acquaintance. Morever, he told me that he was one of Richard's closest friends."

"Oh, there's that, of course," Aunt Berinthea responded, not at all discomposed. "No, I do not say that you may not take him up as an acquaintance, my dear, but I would be careful not to let the relationship develop any further than that. He is a younger son, and his brother, the Earl of Worthington, has recently married. A respectable income, nothing more. You both can do much better."

Annis had to press her lips together to keep from venting her rage. To her relief, Elizabeth, who was well aware of her sister's tension, began to introduce a flow of inconsequential small talk. Annis was able to continue the rest of the ride in silence while her sister and her aunt discussed the theater. Lady Downage might be an expert on the fashionable world, but Annis considered that she had a false idea of the attributes a man must possess to be a good husband.

The one thing that had been made evident by their shopping trip was that they must return to London much earlier than they previously had anticipated. It was clear that weeks would have to be devoted to purchasing suitable apparel, hiring staff, and furbishing Burham House. In their discussion the next day, Laurie was quick to add that it would take some time to find the right sort of carriages and suitable prads. Annis heard him with a sinking heart. He had already announced that a gig was far too tame a vehicle to be driven in town and she understood from several broad hints that he intended to purchase a curricle. She intended to oppose him, but she knew this would precipitate a royal battle.

The return to Thurstan House was uneventful, unmarred by mysterious accidents. Though Annis was still on her guard, she and her companions had avoided the topic for several weeks.

It was more pleasant to believe that nothing would happen, and events seemed to prove this view correct.

Life in the country seemed particularly placid after their trip to London. Summer was beginning to change into fall, heralded by the arrival of several cool, damp days. To Laurie, as to any other sportsman, it signaled the beginning of hunting season. He took to disappearing every morning, despite the fact that his sisters often wondered aloud why he would wish to go out in such dirty weather. He might be envious of his friend Luffy, who was staying with relations in Leicestershire, but he was not about to deny himself the lesser sport that was to be obtained locally. Annis could not help but observe that this preoccupation boded ill for his lessons also.

Still, they managed to exist in some tranquillity, a state which was soon to be disrupted by unexpected visitors. The first, not surprisingly, was Don Alonzo. He seemed to be able to gauge to a nicety how long he would be welcome, and never overstayed his time. He cheerfully accompanied Laurie on his hunting expeditions, never complaining about the weather, and bore it well when Laurie freely characterized him as a poor shot. He was unfailingly courteous to the ladies and never lingered when he saw that their day was to be taken up with household activities. He was, in short, the perfect guest, and Annis could not quite account for her growing dislike of him.

He was handsome, he was polite, and he dressed well. He seemed the epitome of a gentleman. Yet he made her uneasy. In the limited time she spent with him, his manner had seemed far too loverlike to her. It was true that her mourning had but a few months to go, but surely a gentleman would refrain from making his intentions so clear. He had insinuated himself so well that the notion that he should not be in their household at all during this time had ceased to occur to her. She wished that it might have been Elizabeth that he was smitten with, but their relationship was quite formal, as Elizabeth's relationships with gentlemen always were. Annis shook her head. It was going to take a great deal of work to make Elizabeth abandon her shyness and the hauteur she employed to conceal it.

Oddly enough, it was Don Alonzo's presence that drew their next visitor to Thurstan House. If Annis had forgotten the impropriety of receiving a stranger there during her mourning, her cousin certainly had not.

Ambrose arrived in a post chaise one wet October morning. Though perhaps her recent visit to town had jaded Annis' eye somewhat, it seemed to her that he appeared somewhat less magnificent than formerly. Although his collar points were as high and his coats as wasp-waisted as ever, she thought she could discern that his clothes showed rather more wear than he would have permitted in the past. Well, if he was learning to retrench, it was all to the good. Ignoring the flush of anger on his face, she greeted him affably, though she refused to rise to meet him.

This little gesture was not lost on him, for his face darkened and he said frostily, "My business is not with you, but with your sister. Where is Elizabeth?"

Annis would have replied frankly that she had no notion, but she was forestalled by the entrance of Elizabeth, who hurried in, putting aside her apron as she spoke.

"Cousin Ambrose, h-how are you? The footman said you had arrived. I am sorry to be late in greeting you, but we were preserving some cherries."

He frowned. "Surely that might better be left to the servants."

"Well, it's my own special receipt." She gave him a guileless look behind her spectacles. "And I often did so when we were at your home, after all."

He chose to ignore this hit. "I will not bother to discuss trifles with you. My business is more important. I wish you to pack your bags and return with me to the Briars."

"We have been through all of this already," Annis informed him tartly.

He turned to her. "If you will permit me to mention it," he said with heavy sarcasm, "I pointed out at that time your unfitness as a guardian. The ensuing months have proved me correct."

"What do you mean?"

"I must confess that even I was surprised at the extent of your carelessness, though I suppose I should have expected it."

"Make your meaning plain."

"To receive a stranger here, nay, to permit him the run of the house when the family is in mourning . . ."

There was some justice in what he said. Annis could feel a warmth beginning to spread over her face, but she jumped to her own defense. "If you are referring to Don Alonzo, he is, or was, a business associate of Sir Richard's, and I hardly see why you—"

"So familiar already? I suppose you mean that as a recommendation, though I hardly think you would wish to receive most of Sir Richard's *business* associates here, in mourning or not."

He was right, of course, but she held on gamely. "Don Alonzo is a gentleman."

"Upon whose information is this based? I trust that you have made some inquiries into who his family is?"

Stung, Annis replied, "You may tell with ease that he is a gentleman by his manner, which, incidentally, is much better than that of some others I know."

He ignored this thrust and pursued his topic doggedly. "By his manner, then? My ignorant little cousin, has it ever occurred to you that many scoundrels in the world are quite able to ape the *manner* of a gentleman when they wish to do so?"

She could think of no reply. He saw it and pressed his advantage.

"I'm sure it never occurred to you. Your youth and inexperience make you easy prey for such traps. That is why I intend to take Elizabeth home with me, where she will be protected from such adventurers."

A frown creased Elizabeth's brow. "Cousin Ambrose, what are you saying?"

"I am saying that your sister lacks the sense to keep an out-and-out fortune-hunter from courting you, which is particularly offensive, considering that the family is in mourning."

Without warning, Elizabeth's face split into a smile. The two angry combatants stared at her, resentful and uncomprehending.

"I am afraid that you are laboring under a misapprehension. I regret that you have made such an unnecessary journey," she informed him between chuckles.

"What do you mean?"

"Don Alonzo certainly is not courting me," she informed him. "His manner has been most circumspect, it is true, as

Annis has already informed you. If he has indicated an interest, though, I am afraid that it is in my sister.''

Ambrose's mouth was open in astonishment. His lips moved, but he could not formulate the words. It was evident that his mind was racing to recover from this blow.

"Elizabeth!" Annis was at no such loss for words.

"I am sorry, Annis, but even you have to admit it." She took Ambrose by the arm. "You see, you need not be afraid for me. There have been no fortune-hunters importuning me for my hand.''

He turned to Annis. "Is this true?"

She was still ready to do battle. "I have never offered him any encouragement whatsoever!"

He blinked, still digesting the facts. "No, what I meant was, is it true that this fellow is dangling after you and not Elizabeth?"

Though still resentful, she could not help but drop her eyes. "Well, that is to say, if he displays a partiality, it probably is . . .'' She could not quite finish the sentence.

Her silence apparently convinced him. "I see." He faced Elizabeth. "Be that as it may, I do not see that this home is a proper environment for you. There could be none more suitable than mine, and Maria has often expressed to me how she longs for your company.''

Elizabeth still could not contain her amusement. "But since you so justly have pointed out the danger to us, would I not be remiss in my duty if I departed and left my sister prey to an *adventurer*?'' A laugh bubbled out of her.

"I find your mirth sadly inappropriate, miss. I consider it a mark of the gradual degradation of your character that you would find humor in the situation. However, I see that *my* opinions count for nothing.'' He regarded them haughtily. "My offer of a home is still open to you, Elizabeth. I think you are far too intelligent not to see the good sense of my arguments ultimately.''

Never wishing to deliberately offend, Elizabeth caught him by the sleeve. "No, forgive me, cousin. I know you mean well. Pray stay and have some tea with us, or a spot of nuncheon.''

"You have already made it clear that there is no purpose in my staying, so I shall go.'' He gave them both a short nod.

"Good-bye." He squared his back and strode angrily from the room.

As the door closed, Elizabeth collapsed onto the damask sofa, laughing as she did so. Annis regarded her with a frown of disapproval. "I must say, I don't often agree with Ambrose, but I do in this case. I do not see what there is to laugh about, Elizabeth."

Her sister extracted a handkerchief from her pocket and began wiping her eyes and spectacles. "Do you not? Oh, I found it so diverting! Ambrose obviously heard that an eligible gentleman had often been seen at Thurstan House, and he naturally assumed that Don Alonzo was courting me. He couldn't chance losing the last fortune he has to siphon from, so he literally came posting here with all possible speed. It is too rich a jest!" She couldn't help breaking down again. "Didn't you happen to notice how unconcerned he was about the possibility that *you* might wed a ne'er-do-well?" She had to laugh once more.

The light was slowly dawning for Annis. She looked at her sister accusingly. "Elizabeth!" she shrieked. "You know! And here I have been trying so hard to keep the truth from you. What . . . have you known all along?"

Leaping up, Elizabeth did her best to reassure her, patting her sister on the back. "No, no, of course not. I mean, I have suspected that Ambrose was helping himself to part of our fortunes all along. I would have had to be an idiot not to notice that. I really had no idea that you thought he had designs upon us until the day you and Laurie and Louisa had the carriage accident. I knew something was wrong and I forced the information from Laurie."

The two sisters sank thoughtfully onto the sofa. "I just wanted to protect you," Annis offered.

"I know." Elizabeth smiled her understanding. There was a moment of hesitation and her face became grave. "I think it will be best if we all protect each other. From his behavior today it does not appear that Ambrose would view my being courted with any equanimity."

Annis made no response. It was true that Ambrose had confirmed her suspicions today. Though there was nothing that he could do openly, there would be certain to be some kind of violent reaction when he learned that the family was to travel to London solely to launch Elizabeth into the Marriage Mart. And when and if Elizabeth became affianced . . . Annis shuddered at the thought.

Her sister noticed her slight trembling and took her hand in hers. The reassuring pressure steadied Annis' nerves. She had risked everything for this—to give her sister this one chance at happiness. No one, not Ambrose nor anyone else, should prevent it. She squeezed her sister's hand before letting loose of it, gave her a reassuring smile, and rose. ''I suppose I should let you return to your cherries,'' she said. ''And there is some unfinished business to which I must tend, also.''

8

IT was about a month later that their household, like every other in England, was shocked and saddened by the news of the death of the young Princess Charlotte. Since she had been married for only a year and a half, was the heir to the throne, and was the most popular member of the royal family, circumstances could hardly have been more tragic. Though it was not unusual for a woman to die in childbirth, it seemed almost inconceivable that England's most prominent physicians should have been unable to save either mother or child.

As the weeks passed and Christmas approached, they made plans for a rather somber celebration. Laurie might sigh rather wistfully, remembering the lavish entertainments they had sponsored in the past, but Annis had no heart for any festivity. It had been almost a year, but still the expressions of joy seemed hollow and meaningless to her. For once she was glad of the shelter her mourning afforded her. She was not required to attend gatherings with happy faces and dancing and stolen kisses under the mistletoe. There were too many memories here, memories of happy Christmases past. There was Richard at eight, cantering up to the house joyously on his new pony, and taking her up for a ride behind. Or Richard at ten, thoroughly unimpressed with her new doll and taking no pains to hide it. Or Richard at twelve, with awkward pride presenting her with her first silk scarf, and blushing and pushing her away when she kissed his cheek in thanks. She still had that scarf, though since she had been a careless child it had become stained and was torn slightly on one corner. No other would ever be half so dear to her.

It was an unproductive direction for her thoughts to take. She sighed and resumed her needlework. She must keep her thoughts directed toward the future.

* * *

As the Christmas season passed and December turned into January, Annis found herself at the end of her mourning period. She did not greatly feel the difference, for true to her resolution, she remained gowned in black. It made little difference to their social lives either, for now all their time was spent making themselves ready to journey to London. As usual, there was much to be done, and Annis, Elizabeth, and Louisa were all thoroughly wearied by the time they were ready to depart.

It was upon a cold and snowy February morning that their carriage began to make its way from Thurstan House. All the occupants were aware of a feeling of excitement, which, for some more than others, was mixed with pleasurable expectations. This at last was the culmination of Annis' plans, what they had all worked toward when they began that deception so long ago. It was true that the Season would not begin for several months, but as they had already discussed, it would take a certain amount of time to make Burham House comfortable and to establish themselves.

They arrived late that afternoon, fortunately not much delayed by the snow, and began the tiresome process of settling in. There was a great deal to be done and Annis threw herself into the monumental task with all of her energy. Furniture had to be uncovered, linens must be aired, and decisions made regarding who was to occupy which chamber. To Annis' own relief, the housekeeper, Mrs. Cherry, had prepared the room next to Richard's for her, stating that it was the one usually occupied by the mistress of the house. Annis did not think she could have endured staying in Richard's room, though perversely she welcomed the idea of being close to it.

Though Annis had decided to disturb the furbishings as little as possible, cost her what suffering it might, it was apparent that some changes could not be avoided. New draperies must be purchased for Elizabeth's bedroom, to replace the rather masculine-looking ones there. Lady Burham's room, unused for many years, inexplicably lacked many necessities, such as a dressing table. The furniture that was in it was not in good repair, as Annis discovered the first night, when the canopy over the bed collapsed upon her. Clearly some purchases were in order, despite her resolve to economize.

She had read about certain Rooms in the Strand, where one might look over and purchase furbishings in the very latest mode, and accordingly she resolved to journey there. To her surprise, neither Elizabeth nor Louisa evinced any particular interest in joining her expedition. A short talk with her sister revealed the reasons behind Elizabeth's reluctance. Annis had not taken into account what a sacrifice had been required of her sister to remain in the house, helping Annis for the week or so that they had been in town and never venturing to even one library or bookstore. Though she did not complain to Annis, it was easy for the latter to see what Elizabeth's preference was. Accordingly, it was decided that Annis should journey to the Strand with a footman to accompany her, while Elizabeth and Louisa were rewarded for their hard work by a trip to search for a few greatly desired volumes.

After some consultation, Elizabeth decided that they should first visit James Robson, the bookseller, in Bond Street. Just to enter the establishment gave her a heady sensation after such a long period of deprivation. In her eagerness to peruse the titles there, she lost her head and assumed her spectacles, quite careless of who might see her. It was Louisa, standing beside her, who saw Mr. Walter Ulverstone approach and bow as he recognized them. She poked Elizabeth sharply in the ribs, causing her to drop with a cry the book she was examining. The two ladies went scrambling on the floor to retrieve it, while Louisa advised Elizabeth in a hasty undertone just who it was that had greeted them. Elizabeth swept her glasses hastily off, concealing them behind her back, and greeted Mr. Ulverstone with a vague smile.

"I am sorry," he said, helping to raise Louisa to an upright position. "I certainly did not mean to startle you ladies. It is Miss Thurstan, is it not? And Miss Utterly?"

Not unnaturally, the awkwardness of the situation had rendered them dumb. In his well-bred way, Mr. Ulverstone took no notice of this, but searching for conversation, inquired whether they had only lately returned to town. The two nodded in response.

Unsure whether their reserve sprang from shyness or whether they disliked being interrupted, he decided to take his leave of them. "I hope that I may have the pleasure of calling upon you someday. Please present my compliments to your sister.''

Louisa, the first to recover, murmured something appropriate about how delighted Lady Burham would be to renew his acquaintance, whereupon he bowed and took his leave of them. He made his way to the front of the store to inquire of the bookseller if the volume that he had ordered was ready yet. This gave Louisa an opportunity to study him further.

"Oh, dear, what a nice gentleman he is—and most attractive too. It is such a pity that you cannot see him.''

"I don't dare put my spectacles back on now,'' Elizabeth whispered, busy inserting the offending object into her reticule. "Do you still have *Rob Roy*? Tell me when Mr. Ulverstone leaves the store, so we may go up and pay for it.''

"But what about the other books you wanted?'' Louisa asked, still admiring the broad back of Mr. Ulverstone.

"My nerves are too shattered to remain here any longer,'' Elizabeth confessed. "Imagine encountering someone that we know *here*. It is the unlikeliest mischance!''

Annis was more than a little vexed with Elizabeth. First of all, her sister had muffed an excellent opportunity to dazzle Mr. Ulverstone in the bookstore. "Really, Annis,'' Elizabeth complained, "I cannot imagine what you expected me to discuss with him.''

"You were in a bookstore,'' Annis had replied tersely. "You could have talked about books.''

When Mr. Ulverstone fulfilled his promise and came to visit, Elizabeth compounded her error by remaining stiff and silent in his company. She replied only monosyllabically to his conversational gambits. She was not impolite to him, but neither did she receive him with any warmth. Though he became a frequent caller, Elizabeth showed no signs of unbending in his company. Annis, who, despite Aunt Berinthea's negative opinion, considered Mr. Ulverstone a very eligible suitor indeed, was exasperated with her sister. "I do not understand how you ever expect to be courted if you continue to treat gentlemen in this fashion. Why, poor Mr. Ulverstone probably believes that you hate him, if he is at all guided by your manner toward him.''

Elizabeth released a long-suffering sigh. "I have told you before, Annis, how difficult it is to make conversation with a relative stranger when you cannot even see his face. The most you can hope for is to bore him with inanities and let him assume that you are bird-witted."

"Better that he should think you bird-witted rather than openly hostile," Annis retorted acerbically.

"I will never marry a man who is looking for a feeble-brained lady for a wife," Elizabeth stated unequivocally.

It was Annis' turn to sigh. How did Elizabeth expect to find a gentleman who was her intellectual equal if she refused to have anything to do with the sex? Well, further arguing was useless, she knew. Besides, if Elizabeth did not learn to overcome her shyness, she undoubtedly would be receiving a multitude of advice on the subject from Lady Downage. Annis doubted that the older woman's strictures would prove any more efficacious than her own counsel, but she could see no sense in making Elizabeth listen to lectures twice.

Neither did Elizabeth wish to discuss the matter further. It wearied her and it seemed to gain them nothing. Besides, she could not share with her sister what was in her heart. There was a deeply held conviction, born of experience, that any gentleman who met them both should instantly prefer her lively sister. Elizabeth did not underrate her own looks, but they seemed to count for nothing when combined with a shy, tongue-tied personality. She despised her own weakness, but she knew of no way to overcome it. It was easy enough for Annis to tell her what to say. Annis had never had any difficulty making conversation in her life.

There was a further secret that she could not divulge to her sister either. She had seen how Annis' eyes had brightened when she heard that Walter was coming to visit. She had heard a lightness creep into her sister's tone in her conversation with Walter, a lightness that had been missing ever since she learned that Sir Richard was dead.

It was true that the two spent a certain amount of time discussing Sir Richard, but that seemed natural enough to Elizabeth. With Walter's help, she hoped that her sister might finally go through the grieving process which she had been avoiding for so long. And when she was finished, it appeared that Walter would be only too pleased to console her.

If she had known the direction that her sister's thoughts were taking, Annis would have been unhappy indeed. Given her ignorance, she was merely irritated instead.

She had nourished some high hopes for Elizabeth's come-out ball this evening. There was no doubt that Elizabeth was exquisite in her blue silk gown, cut rather lower than she liked, but very high in the waist, with rosettes ornamenting the top of the puffed sleeves and the deep flounce of blond lace at the hem. Her hair had been caught up artfully on the top of her head, while in front it was disposed in charming ringlets. No style could have been better suited to set off those perfect classical features. Even Elizabeth had been pleased by the overall effect as she admired herself in the mirror. When the time had come to go downstairs, however, Elizabeth had quietly removed her spectacles and Annis could see her sense of confidence ebb.

She had assured her sister over and over how beautiful she looked, but it did not serve to make Elizabeth smile or even to raise that downcast face. Annis had regretted once again that her aunt had not seen fit to introduce Elizabeth in slow stages, beginning with perhaps a dinner party, instead of launching her with one of the season's first balls.

The one fortunate aspect of the event was that they had not been required to participate in the planning in any way. It was the sort of thing Lady Downage managed to perfection, and she would have resented any attempts at interference. It would have been hard to improve upon her aunt's efforts, in any case. The ballroom had been hung with festoons of silk, the orchestra was first-rate, and the few refreshments that Annis had been able to try were delectable. The admittedly enormous group of people that had been invited seemed convivial: everywhere people were flirting, gossiping, and dancing. The only soul who did not look as if she were enjoying herself was the honoree.

Lady Downage had been most efficient in making Elizabeth known to all the young gentlemen in the ballroom. Elizabeth had received many admiring glances from afar. As soon as the gentlemen drew near, however, the inevitable happened. She kept her face downcast, despite her aunt's prodding. She refused to smile at anyone and she greeted those she met in a voice that was scarcely audible.

With her forceful aunt by her side, there had been offers to dance, of course. Elizabeth had led off the figures with one of Lady Downage's husband's grandnephews, a dull but amiable gentleman who performed his part willingly enough. She then had danced with an elderly but wealthy baronet, whom Annis suspected of being one of her aunt's flirts. There was also Lord Bainbridge, who was attractive enough but who was well known to be in need of a fortune. There were other gentlemen, too, whom her aunt pressed into service, but Annis could not quite forgive them for the momentary looks of relief that escaped their faces when their duty had been discharged.

Her sister's face Annis could read quite well. Elizabeth at least had her chin up, which was a necessity if she meant to keep from barging into the other dancers. Her countenance might appear perfectly expressionless to almost everyone else in the room, but Annis knew it to be frozen in terror. Though her excellent memory enabled her to perform the dances without an error, Elizabeth was in constant fear that she would not see someone, and either bump into a person or tread on a toe. Annis observed that her sister was far too distracted to respond in more than a cursory way to the attempts at conversation that her partners offered. Often they simply refused to persevere, and with a sinking heart Annis saw at least one roll his eyes meaningfully at his friends across the floor. Elizabeth's sense of release was so great when the dances finished, too, that she would do no more than thank her partners in a perfunctory fashion, which further failed to endear her to them.

It was from Laurie that Annis learned the unflattering sobriquet that some unkind wit had bestowed on Elizabeth. Henceforth, she would be known to London society as "The Ice Maiden." How Annis wished that her sister's shyness would take a different form than this cool remoteness. Nothing could be more devastating to her chances.

Annis was filled with despair, but what could she do? Her aunt was using every spare opportunity to read Elizabeth another lecture, which made that lovely head droop even lower. Even if some brilliant idea had occurred to her, though, Annis would not have been able to help, for she had problems of her own.

She realized now that she had made a mistake in giving in to vanity and selecting the fashionable gown that she herself was wearing. The dressmaker had assured her that it was in the latest mode, and she simply had not been able to resist it. It was of black net worn over white satin. It was cut low, with a square neck, and on the shoulders were black satin epaulets, which were wired to make them fashionably prominent. It was caught very high under the best with a simple ribbon of black satin, and delicately embroidered throughout. The skirt was cut daringly short, and the double rouleaux of black crepe at the hem did nothing but call attention to the fact. Annis had felt quite matronly, being dressed in black from satin toque down to her chamois slippers. It was immediately evident, however, that she had made an error in her assumptions.

The gentlemen showed no disposition to be discouraged by her attire. She realized too late that the Princess Charlotte's death had made mourning attire very smart this year, judging from the number of black dresses about her. Now she could understand why Lady Downage suddenly had shown no disposition to argue about her wearing colors this spring, and why the dressmaker seemed to have such a large selection of sketches in black.

Her mourning attire was therefore no protection to her, even though she took her place among the matrons. Louisa was engrossed in conversation with an elderly gentleman, so she was of no help. Annis was importuned again and again by gentlemen requesting her hand for a dance. Annis refused each of them, though it was beginning to make her weary to do so. She supposed the fact that she also had inherited Richard's fortune made her a doubly attractive prospect.

Such a consideration could not influence Sir George Reeves, who was proving himself to be among both the most persistent and the most inane of her new admirers. Chief among his virtues was the great wealth he was known to have inherited. Unfortunately in Annis' eyes, that was not enough to compensate for his being a person whom even his friends apostrophized as a dressmaker's dummy. Why he had abruptly chosen to devote his attentions to her, Annis could not guess. Attempts to discourage him proved ineffective, for he was impervious to hints. In desperation she managed to rid herself of him by pretending thirst and sending him in quest of a glass of punch, then moving to a different part of the ballroom. No sooner had he departed, though, than his place was filled by other, equally insensitive suitors.

To have attention distracted from Elizabeth and focused on herself was the last thing that Annis had intended. Her aunt was not likely to be of use, as preoccupied as she was with Elizabeth. Annis was becoming desperate, and could see no way out of her predicament. Her very standoffishness seemed to awaken the gentlemen's sporting instincts, and they pursued her with even more avidity. Annis could have screamed her frustration aloud. Why, when she did her best to discourage them, did the gentlemen flock about her, and when beautiful Elizabeth was cool, they fled?

When rescue arrived, it was from a most unlikely quarter. Annis had not seen Don Alonzo enter the ballroom, but he suddenly materialized at her side. She did not recall her aunt mentioning having invited him, but she had no time to think it over. For once she was glad to see him. Even that hooded, enigmatic face was better than the multitude of unfamiliar ones about her. He drew up to her with slow grace, and executed one of his perfect bows. Upon straightening himself, he glanced over his rivals with an expression of bored hauteur. It was amazing, Annis thought, how they melted away under that frosty gaze.

When they had dispersed, he inclined his head to Annis again. "May I dare to hope that Lady Burham will favor me with a dance?"

"I do not dance, as you may already have guessed," Annis replied in some irritation.

"I beg your pardon," he replied, though he did not seem at all discomposed. Without asking for any sort of permission, he ensconced himself by her side. His eyes rolled over the assembled company. "It is a most delightful occasion," he remarked politely.

Annis' gratitude to him for her rescue did not extend beyond a few minutes. It was true that he did manage to keep the other gentlemen at bay through sheer force of personality, but she was not so very sure that it was an improvement. Surely it looked most particular to have him monopolize her in this way. She began to scheme how she might be rid of him.

The means most suited to her ends was to have him partner her sister in a dance. He was at least good-looking and well-dressed, and so should add to Elizabeth's consequence. She interrupted some courteous praise he was murmuring about her appearance and made the suggestion. He hesitated for a moment, and Annis did not like the look in his eyes. It was gone in an instant and he waved a languid hand in Elizabeth's direction. "But you see, my dear Lady Burham, she has a partner already." True enough, Elizabeth was being led onto the floor once again by Lady Downage's obedient relation.

Annis felt like grinding her teeth, but instead she smiled at him sweetly. "Well, perhaps you might dance the next with her, then. I know it would mean so much to Elizabeth to have a dance with you."

He regarded her from under drooping lids. "Lady Burham, I am at your command, as always. Should I see that she lacks for a partner, I will be all alacrity."

Annis was forced to drop her eyes. Don Alonzo knew very well that Lady Downage would see to it that Elizabeth never *appeared* to lack for a partner. How could she be rid of him? She found his proprietary air toward her most distasteful.

She looked up, and as if in answer to a prayer, there stood Walter Ulverstone. He was looking in her direction, and when he caught her imploring gaze, he responded immediately, crossing the room.

"Lady Burham, my compliments, may I say how delightful you are looking this evening?"

Straightening himself, he fell under Don Alonzo's hostile glare, which fortunately seemed to bother him not one bit. Annis made uneasy introductions.

"Your servant, sir." He bowed again, and catching Annis' eye, smiled reassuringly. "Lady Burham, I hope you will tell me if I am presuming too much, but knowing my interest in art, you once made a promise to show me the frescoed ceiling in the gold salon. If the time is not opportune . . .?" He let the question hang in the air in the most graceful way imaginable.

What a thoughtful gentleman he was, to leave her an excuse in case he had misinterpreted her look. Annis did not hesitate to pounce upon this opportunity. "Oh, dear, how remiss I have been! I know I promised to show it to you *months* ago. No, really, it would be much too rude of me to postpone your visit again."

She smiled at him as she spoke, and he willingly took her hand, tucking in comfortably in the crook of his arm. Don Alonzo remained behind, glowering at Annis and her broad-shouldered escort. He was not one to admit defeat readily. "Lady Burham, I hope that I may be allowed to escort you into dinner?"

As her escort, he would be entitled to sit with her all during dinner. Walter felt her tension and the sudden pressure of her fingers on his arm. Hoping that he was interpreting her wishes correctly, he smiled slightly at Don Alonzo. "I am afraid that Lady Burham previously has promised that singular honor to me. Your servant, sir."

There was little Don Alonzo could do. He watched them depart with smoldering eyes. Annis felt as if they were burning holes in her back. She and Walter talked of inanities until they left the ballroom and made their way into the gold salon. She turned to him, her face expressive of her gratitude.

"Thank you so much," she said. "I . . . I don't know quite what I would have done."

She presented a charming picture and the effect was not lost on Walter. "I shall be happy to rid you of any and all unwelcome suitors," he said, adding gallantly, "though it may require all my waking moments."

It was the first real compliment he had paid her, and she felt the color rise to her cheeks. By way of a distraction, she explained about Don Alonzo. "He is not actually a suitor," she confessed. "He is merely one of Richard's business associates."

A little crease appeared between Walter's brows. "A business associate of Richard's?"

"Yes."

"Am I correct in assuming that he is a *Spanish* gentleman?"

"Why, yes—is there something wrong?"

"No, of course not," he said hastily, and by way of distraction began staring at the ceiling. "It is very fine work," he remarked.

Annis glanced up at the gilt-and-frescoed ceiling with indifference and surveyed the half-clad mythical figure reposing on clouds. "Is that a fresco?" she asked. "Oh, I thought you made that up."

Walter looked at her with some shock. The frescoed ceiling in Downage House had been executed in the previous century by a French master and was quite famous throughout London. Judging from his companion's expression, she would be unlikely to be interested in that sort of information, so he swallowed his surprise and replied, "Just so."

Though Annis was to enjoy the rest of the evening now, the same could not be said for her unhappy sister. It was doubly humiliating, though, to be reminded of the fact every step of the way. Of course, the masculine attention that Annis was attracting had not escaped her aunt's notice. Elizabeth was so sick of being compared with her sister that she felt like screaming in her aunt's ear that she was a different person. Instead, she kept quiet and grew ever more miserable. How she hated London! There was nothing good about it except for the bookstores . . . and perhaps the opera . . . and the theater . . . Well, there was nothing good about these functions anyway. She felt strongly the cruelty of the fate that had decreed that she must be nearsighted. I shall perish a spinster, Elizabeth thought, and that will suit me just as well.

If Elizabeth had consulted her sister, she might have been surprised to learn that Annis was every bit as dissatisfied by the outcome of the evening as she herself was. Annis had been disappointed for her younger sister's sake, of course. She had nourished a hope or two concerning Walter and Elizabeth, since they had so much in common, but clearly it was not to be. Having accepted this fact, she had proceeded to enjoy Walter's company herself.

He was everything a gentleman should be. He dressed fashionably, but avoided the extremely high shirt points and the wasp-waisted coats which made the dandies appear so ridiculous in her eyes. He was not the sort to lavish pomade upon his hair or to spend hours perfecting the creases in a cravat. His well-cut, quiet clothing displayed his powerful figure to advantage.

In short, he was a man's man, and she could see why he had been Richard's friend.

In some ways, of course, he was not at all like Richard. He was more of an intellectual, enjoying reading, the theater, and the opera: all activities which would have made Richard blench. Well, perhaps not quite all. She imagined that Richard would have derived a great deal of pleasure from observing the shapely limbs of the opera dancers. It made her quite angry to think of how much he would have enjoyed it, and of how he would have laughed at her resentment. He never considered her opinions of any importance, and . . . She was dismayed by the direction her thoughts were taking and so turned her mind firmly back to her escort of that evening.

Walter would never do such a thing. He was the most courteous, considerate gentleman she ever had met—the sort she had always thought of as her ideal. A gentleman who paid you such agreeable compliments, who was interested to discover your opinions on various topics, who never forgot his manners in front of a lady—no, he provided the greatest contrast to Richard that could be imagined. If such a person were to court her seriously, it would be the fulfillment of all her wishes. At least, it *should* be the fulfillment of all her wishes.

It was most puzzling. Walter was the epitome of all she thought a gentleman should be, yet her thoughts remained on a careless, inconsiderate, rough-voiced, ill-mannered, stubborn, despicable man who had perished over a year ago. And yet, she could almost feel him walking about the ballroom with them, joking with Walter or making some remark to her which would make her want to box his ears. The amused way his eyes would rest on her after he said something to send her into a passion always made her suspect that he had done so deliberately.

She shook her head violently. She was becoming more and more fanciful. Richard was dead—he would trouble her no more. If a certain amount of her liking for Walter was due to the frequency with which they discussed Richard, she did not have to admit it to anyone, including herself.

She tried not to be exasperated with herself. Surely the wound would someday heal. In the meantime, she might as well enjoy getting to know Walter. He had promised to take her driving in the park the day after next.

9

THE next morning, the arrivals of various bouquets and nosegays brought home even more sharply the injustice of Elizabeth's situation. To Elizabeth's admittedly prejudiced eyes, it appeared that she had received fewer than half the flowers her "widowed" sister had, nor did the offerings she received seem nearly so grand. Annis busied herself with trying to correct this mistaken impression, but Elizabeth refused to listen.

"It is just that they think of me as a wealthy widow, Elizabeth. I daresay all of these are from gazetted fortune-hunters—"

"And who do you think sent mine, then? Lord Bainbridge, Sir John Elliot, Mr. Guy Fenshaw—"

"Oh, did he send one to you too, then?" Annis asked, temporarily diverted. "What a complete dolt! Did he think that we shouldn't compare notes?"

"Those aren't from a fortune-hunter," Elizabeth stated, pointing an accusing finger at a large and handsome bouquet.

Annis shrugged. "Sir George Reeves is an idiot," she said frankly.

Elizabeth indicated a charming nosegay of tiny pink roses, bound up handsomely with a ribbon in a deeper shade of pink. "That's a pretty posy," she said, studying her sister's face closely.

"Oh." Annis looked pleased, nothing more. "Mr. Ulverstone is a most considerate gentleman." She turned back to her sister. "But you are being ridiculous! It is not as if all of yours are from fortune-hunters." She glanced at several of the cards. "Now, see, he's not."

"Lord Wilberham is sixty if he's a day," Elizabeth said dryly. "What's more, he told our aunt he liked me because he could see that I wasn't one of those young, flighty gadabout misses that you meet with nowadays."

"Here's one from Mr. Blackthorne. You can't accuse him of being old."

"I can't accuse him of having a particle of sense either," Elizabeth said tartly.

Annis continued examining the offerings. At last she found a slim volume of poetry and held it up with a crow of triumph. "Here is one that is wealthy, attractive, young, and must have some tastes similar to yours, Elizabeth. He is obviously original too—to send you a book instead of flowers."

If possible, Elizabeth looked even slightly more glum. "Oh, yes, Lord Eversley admires me—as 'a source of aesthetic gratification,' or so he told me. He would like to have my features immortalized in sculpture as the goddess Aphrodite, in order that he may place me upon his mantelpiece."

"Elizabeth, he never said so!" Annis exclaimed, torn between fascination and horror.

Elizabeth had no opportunity to reply, for their attention was claimed by a fracas emanating from the entrance hall. The sisters looked at one another in consternation. Against all advice, Annis had retained Greenlaw as senior footman at Burham House. She was unwilling to retire him, could not bear to demote him, and besides which, was secretly impressed with his no-nonsense method of keeping out unwelcome visitors. The old retainer, though never fully accepting that Richard was dead, had seemed finally to grasp that Annis had been married to the master, and accordingly had transferred his allegiance to her instead.

From what they could hear, Greenlaw was hotly contesting someone's right to enter Burham House. The sisters ran to the entrance hall and found the elderly servant wrestling with a red-faced Cousin Ambrose.

"Here, fellow, let go of me, I'm a relation," Ambrose was exclaiming.

"Not of the master's, you aren't," Greenlaw gasped. "I never laid eyes on you before in my life."

The scene brought a smile back to Elizabeth's face, but Annis was appropriately grave. "Greenlaw, you may release him." The servant complied as she added, "Though you did very well not to let him enter."

The servant bowed in acknowledgment, though Ambrose's

face grew a shade or two darker. "What do you mean, he did well?" Ambrose asked furiously.

"I am afraid that we are not able to be so informal here as in the country," Annis told him. "One cannot be too careful in town, you know. The next time, please have the goodness to be announced first."

Ambrose was ready to tell her just what he thought of this edict. Somehow, under the dignified gaze of the old footman, he could not. He choked and muttered something inaudible instead.

"Will you join us in the drawing room?" Annis asked him politely. "It's rather early, but perhaps you might care for some tea or a spot of nuncheon?" Ambrose growled something low in his throat, which Annis took for an acquiescence, and they made their way into the drawing room.

"It is so kind of you to pay us this unexpected visit," Annis was continuing in the same vein when Ambrose cut her off.

"Unexpected. Aye, I'll wager that it is. So you thought to hide from me in London!"

Annis wrinkled her nose in perplexity as she and her sister took chairs and indicated that Ambrose should seat himself also. He did so reluctantly.

"I am sure I do not know what you are talking about, cousin," she said politely.

"I went to call on you at Thurstan House and found that you had packed up and left, without so much as a by-your-leave. It took a good long while to worm from your servants where you'd gone, too."

Annis, despite a vow to keep her temper under control, was becoming angry. They had left only the most elderly of the household servants at home, judging that the travel and the pace of city life might prove debilitating to them. The picture of Ambrose bullying them was almost more than she could bear.

"By what right, cousin, do you barge into our home and force our servants to reveal our whereabouts?"

His anger suddenly turned cold. "How soon we forget," he told her icily. "I am still Elizabeth's trustee, after all, and as such am required to know where she is. You should remember, Annis, that there are sometimes documents to sign, and other matters upon which I wish to consult her. In fact, I am not certain that your attempting to conceal her whereabouts doesn't justify my removing her from your household."

"You forget, cousin, that Elizabeth is of age and may live wherever she likes."

"Peace!" Already exasperated by the events of last night, the usually quiet Elizabeth managed to silence her companions by drowning them out in stentorian tones. As they both turned to gaze at her in surprise, she addressed them at a more normal volume.

"Have you considered that by now every servant in the house must be aware of your differences, to say nothing of passersby in the street?"

Neither Ambrose nor Annis could make any reply to that.

Seeing that they were quelled for the moment, Elizabeth addressed them both more gently. "It's all too ridiculous in any case. Ambrose, we certainly should have written to you, and I apologize for not doing so, but it must have been obvious that in May we should be in London." He began to stammer out a few angry words, but she cut him off. "Nor can I believe that you imagined that you would find us anywhere but Burham House." She directed a warning look at her sister. "Perhaps Ambrose would care for a glass of sherry while the meal is being prepared."

Her diplomacy might have saved the day had not Ambrose's eyes lighted upon the floral offerings. "Suitors!" he exclaimed with a fresh wrath. "You needn't tell me. I knew that as soon as the word was out, you would both be surrounded by all the adventurers in London."

Elizabeth tried to pass it off with a humorous touch, and so pretended insult. "Sir, though you may underrate our charms, there are gentlemen who do not!"

Ambrose refused to be distracted. "I knew what would happen—the two of you with no more experience of the world than a pair of newborn babes—"

"I really must object to your tone," Elizabeth was telling him more seriously.

"I won't stand for it! You had best remember, Elizabeth, that any match you make is subject to my approval, and I certainly do not intend you to wed any fortune-hunter."

"My word! Whatever is the matter? Have you all lost your

senses?" Lady Downage, shocked by the commotion, had decided to enter unannounced. Her appearance inspired silence, although Elizabeth did manage to stammer out introductions. Lady Downage regarded Ambrose with a look of deep dislike for a few moments. It did not help that she always had disapproved of her younger sister's marriage to a person associated with trade, even though the match was a financially advantageous one. She had refused to have anything to do with those whom she termed "a vulgar set of mushrooms," so it was not entirely surprising that she had never met Ambrose.

"My good man," she said, addressing him as if he had been a servant, "although *my* nieces are as yet quite *unspoiled* by town life, I think that I may venture to say that I have been in the world quite long enough to be able to discern an *adventurer* when I see one, and morever, to *protect* them from him."

Her meaning was too plain to be ignored. Ambrose flushed angrily, but it was clear that he was reluctant to enter into a battle of words with this imperious lady.

Satisfied that she had effectively eliminated this menace, Lady Downage turned to her nieces. "My dears, how do I find you today? Did you enjoy yourselves last night?" She too noticed the posies. "I see that your admirers have been busy already."

Just then a footman entered to announce that the meal was served.

"Aunt," Annis said briskly, "we were preparing to partake of a little refreshment. Would you care to join us?"

"Why, I . . ." She turned to stare at Ambrose, as if surprised that he could still be in the room. He flushed again, and taking the hint, said that he had other matters to attend to and that he would call upon them at another time.

"I swear I could have kissed her!" Annis later told Elizabeth appreciatively. "Did you notice the expression on Ambrose's face? And all she had to do was look at him. I wish I had the knack."

"Yes," Elizabeth replied absentmindedly. She had been as delighted as Annis by Ambrose's rout at the hands of their formidable aunt, but it had taken only a few minutes before her worry had begun. If Ambrose was willing to take desperate measures, as Annis had thought, perhaps they would have been better off conciliating him. She could have assured him quite honestly that there were no serious suitors.

She had no more time to ponder the problem, however, for her thoughts were interrupted by the arrival of Louisa. The two sisters flashed guilty glances at each other when they saw their faithful companion. With so much on their minds, they had not spared a thought for how Louisa might have passed her time at the ball. The carriage ride home was only a brief one, so there had been no opportunity for discussion.

Louisa saw the glance they exchanged and misinterpreted it. "Oh, dear, I was hoping that you hadn't missed me this morning."

The two both assured her that they had been quite busy with other matters, and Elizabeth ventured to ask her how she had enjoyed the previous evening. Louisa responded in her usual wholehearted fashion.

"Oh, I thought that the ball was delightful. Didn't both of you enjoy it? I happened to encounter an old friend of my father's, General Lewis, and I'm afraid that we spent the entire evening talking. He is engaged in such a worthwhile project right now. In fact, that's where I've been—to see what is being accomplished there—but how I do run on! Please tell me all about your evening."

Elizabeth thereupon plunged into a polite recital of all that had occurred, but Annis had slipped away into her own thoughts. She was preoccupied with a rather different problem than her sister had been.

Laurie had been importuning her steadily for drafts against his allowance. She had been adamant in refusing to allow him to purchase a curricle, which had put her quite in his black books, but she had been unable to curb his expenditures in any other way.

Even worse, she had wakened quite late the other night, and throwing on a wrapper, had found him stumbling around in the dark. He smelled strongly of drink, and it was only with difficulty that she managed to get him into his chamber. His sleepy manservant had come to her aid, and between the two of them they managed to haul Laurie's body into bed just before it went limp. She would have simply exited and left everything to Johnson, but her attention was attracted by a screw of paper that had fallen out of Laurie's pocket in the struggle. She reached down and pocketed it inconspicuously, then bade the servant a weary good night.

Back in her own chamber, she opened it and found it to be a voucher for over three hundred pounds, signed by some gentleman unfamiliar to her. It confirmed her suspicions. Laurie had been in some gambling den. The little piece of paper had an even more ominous significance for her. If Laurie had brought one home, wasn't it also possible that he could have signed some himself?

When she had confronted him the next day, it had only made a bad situation worse. Laurie was openly hostile, refused to discuss the matter, and said it was none of her concern. She could have cut off his allowance entirely, but she already had heard talk of the moneylenders and the danger young gentlemen faced at falling into their hands. It seemed that what little control she had over him was gone and that the situation was likely to continue to deteriorate. He had stayed for only a portion of the ball last night, and certainly had met his friends afterward, for she had heard him return in the small hours of the morning. His tutor had told her frankly that Laurie had no hope of joining his contemporaries at university unless he radically altered his mode of living. It was obvious that Laurie needed a firmer hand than hers at the reins, but where was it to be found?

As always, she thought of Richard and sighed. How odd it was that her thoughts of him, which should have been growing feebler every day, seemed to grow stronger instead.

Sir George Reeves, though not the first of the widow's suitors, was certainly among the most determined. He had followed his floral offering with a call the next morning, only to discover that Annis was out shopping. When he espied her driving in the park with Walter Ulverstone that afternoon, he realized that matters were desperate and he resolved to call on the widow daily in order to press his suit.

His persistence was rewarded, for he was to become a fixture at Burham House, a position denied more easily discouraged suitors. It perhaps could not be said that Annis enjoyed his company, but she tolerated it, mainly because he proved such an effective buffer against Don Alonzo.

The latter gentleman's attentions had become most pronounced. There was nothing to which Annis specifically could object, but he made her uncomfortable all the same. He insisted upon sharing the sofa, and sitting much too close to her. When she attempted to foil him by sitting in a chair, he merely pushed his until it was practically touching hers. The warm looks and lazy smiles he bestowed on her made her cheeks grow hot with embarrassment. When he kissed her hand, his lips lingered far longer than necessary, making her flesh crawl. Even worse, he always finished the act with a meaningful gaze, which made her want to snatch her hand back and slap him across the face with it.

She would have been happy simply to refuse him admittance, but he had an uncanny knack for rendering that impossible. On his very first visit, for example, he had happened to encounter Annis in the entrance hall, making it quite impossible for her to say that she was not at home. The next time, he had happened to encounter Laurie, who insisted upon bringing him home.

Sir George earned his welcome the first morning that he arrived and found Don Alonzo already comfortably ensconced beside Annis on the sofa. Unlike her other suitors at the ball, he proved impervious to Don Alonzo's withering gaze, for he merely acknowledged the introduction with a cold bow, then drew up a chair next to Annis while fixing the foreigner with a resentful pop-eyed stare. Elizabeth, who entered the drawing room a half-hour later, was hard to put to keep from laughing at the spectacle of these two contrasting suitors glaring angrily at each other across the top of her sister's head.

Don Alonzo, who at first glance saw that Sir George could not be considered any competition for a gentleman boasting his own personal charms, dismissed him as an annoyance. As the morning progressed, however, Sir George proved to be more of an irritation. Don Alonzo sought to drive his rival away by casual jests at Sir George's expense. The effort availed him nothing, for such references were lost on Sir George. The latter, unsure whether or not he'd been insulted, but still vaguely resentful, generally responded with some comment about his horses, always his main topic of conversation. Elizabeth was having a difficult time not giggling at these exchanges.

Don Alonzo would say, "My dear Lady Burham, I wonder that you do not find the present company too *boring,*" adding an expressive roll of his eyes in Sir George's direction.

Sir George angrily would respond, "My horse Cannonball won at Newmarket in less than nine minutes, which was close to a record for the course."

Annis herself found nothing amusing in the situation, but she had to be glad when Don Alonzo was finally too angry to persist in remaining. During the ensuing weeks, whenever the Spaniard arrived to find Sir George already installed in the drawing room, he kept his visit short and would depart in quiet fury.

It was thus that Sir George found himself rarely turned away from Burham House. Annis considered him by far the lesser of the two evils, for he was not one to take liberties, considering that his position there spoke strongly enough. If he was surprised that she consistently refused to go driving or riding with him, the only two activities which he thought held any allure, he never complained about it. He once or twice let slip that he considered Don Alonzo an interloper, for Sir George had been at school with Sir Richard and therefore, in his own mind at least, must be considered an old family friend. He was less resentful of Walter Ulverstone, another frequent visitor, for he knew that as a younger son, Walter's fortune could not compare with his own magnificent one. Annis might often go about with Walter, but Sir George knew that he could not be regarded as a serious rival.

10

THE play was delightful, Annis supposed, musing upon the faces all around her. Elizabeth and Walter both certainly seemed to be transfixed by it. Louisa looked as if it were holding her attention also. Annis glanced over in the corner of the box and surprised Laurie yawning. He grinned ashamedly at her and shrugged. "Sorry," he mouthed.

It had to be Walter's company that made everyone so agreeable. He was well-mannered, courteous, and the perfect host. He had the happy knack of paying the ladies compliments that always sounded as if they came from the heart. He had quite won Laurie over by treating him as an equal rather than as a callow youth, and Annis knew it was this circumstance that had persuaded Laurie to join them tonight. Laurie had not been able to resist Walter's frank appeal for an additional male escort for this evening's party. Annis was doubly glad of his company, for she knew it also meant that he would be kept out of trouble this one night at least.

She glanced around the theater and saw a pair of black eyes glinting at her through the darkness. Don Alonzo had been staring at her ever since their party had entered the box. It made her quite uncomfortable, and she wished that he had at least bowed or acknowledged her in some civil way. She quite dreaded the interval, and was particularly grateful for Walter's escort. He had managed to rout Don Alonzo on several occasions at the house and about town also. In fact, though he never said a word about the matter, it was clear that Walter held him in both suspicion and dislike.

To her dismay, Walter disappeared during the interval in order to procure some refreshments for the ladies. She could not object to such a thoughtful scheme, nor to his taking Laurie along to help fetch them. She tried to console herself with the notion that she had Elizabeth and Louisa to bear her company. She could have wished for Sir George Reeves also at this moment.

True to her fears, Don Alonzo materialized as soon as Walter had disappeared. He greeted them all perfunctorily, but took Annis' wrist in his hand in an urgent way.

"Lady Burham, if you would be so kind, I would like to speak with you for a moment."

"I cannot leave my companions just now," Annis offered.

The grip on her wrist became suddenly painful. "It will take only a few moments of your time," he said, coolly polite. "We will just be in the hall outside."

Annis was afraid that if she did not agree, he would haul her from the box by force. "Very well, then, I will see you, but only for a few moments."

Elizabeth and Louisa were too busy discussing their raptures over Kean's acting to pay much attention to Annis' departure.

Annis half-walked and was half-pulled by Don Alonzo. "What did you wish to say to me?" she asked with an assumption of indifference.

Sparks flashed from his dark eyes. "Do not toy with me, Lady Burham. I have been your suitor for over a year now—" He waved away her angry protest. "Oh, do not prose on to me about all your English proprieties—I do not care for them and neither should you." He released the pressure on her wrist, slipping her hand into his.

"What I mean to say is that I have no patience with these ridiculous observances—they should never stand in the way of a man and a woman in love."

Annis was both shocked and resentful, but before she could tell him so, he had seized her, dragged her into a nearby alcove, and proceeded to kiss her. The feel of his lips on hers nauseated her. She tried to push away from him, to no avail. "Let me go!" she demanded.

He smiled that same superbly confident smile that always irritated her so. "Protest if you wish, but I know deep down that you could not prefer that tame English squire, Ulverstone, to me. You need excitement in your life, and passion."

Annis could not believe that this was happening to her in a public theater. "If you don't let me go, I shall scream," she told him.

"It was kind of you to warn me," he said, and made clear his intentions by bending his head to hers again. She could not endure that disgusting sensation another time. "Let me go," she pleaded one last time, pushing him away with all her strength.

He chuckled, his lips reaching out for hers, when a dry voice sounded behind Annis. "I should let the lady go if I were you."

"Walter," Annis sobbed, spinning around. She had never been so glad to see anyone before. The Spaniard's arms dropped in shock.

Walter wrapped his arm about her shoulder in a protective manner. He nodded curtly to Don Alonzo. "Lady Burham, if you would return to the box, there are certain matters that Don Alonzo and I have to discuss." He lowered his arm and would have relinquished his hold on her, but she clung to him.

"No, please, I beg of you—there must be no trouble. I am certain that he has only had a little too much to drink this evening."

Walter, torn between what he saw his duty to be and what her wishes were, hesitated. She tightened her hold on him. "*Please,* Walter, we must go before Laurie sees us. You know how impetuous he is. He must not learn of this."

Walter felt himself to be in a dilemma. Clearly Don Alonzo should be made to pay the price for insulting a lady, but how was Walter to shake off that same lady in a gentlemanly fashion? He could understand her fears for her younger brother. He glowered at Don Alonzo. A compromise was obviously in order. He thrust out his jaw. "You will apologize to the lady immediately."

Don Alonzo, who had been staring at the two of them in stupefaction the entire time, seemed finally to have been awakened by these last words. He swept Annis a bow which lacked none of its usual grace. "I apologize, my lady. I *misunderstood* the situation."

There was an ominous irony in his tone, but his face had resumed its usual hooded expression, so Annis could not be sure what he felt or meant.

Walter would have been happy to tell him what he thought of his rather inadequate apology, but fortunately Laurie joined them at this moment, burdened down with glasses. He greeted

Don Alonzo with pleasure and would have attempted to draw him into conversation, but Annis said anxiously, "Come, we must return to the box. The play is about to resume."

Fortunately for Annis, the others were too much distracted by the arrival of refreshments and the excitement of the play itself to notice her high color. She saw with relief that Don Alonzo did not return to his seat. She would be able to enjoy the rest of the play in peace, but she could not help but vainly hope that it would be the last she would see of him.

The distance between her hopes and reality was to be made obvious the next morning when Greenlaw announced that Don Alonzo was without. A cowardly impulse prompted her to inform Greenlaw that she was not at home to this visitor, but she restrained herself. She did, after all, have every right to refuse to see him, but Annis could not doubt that Don Alonzo would return. She knew him well enough not to underestimate his tenacity. This interview would have to be faced, now or later. She was thankful at least that she had Louisa in the drawing room with her. "Show him in," she told the footman.

He entered with no appearance of self-consciousness and bowed gracefully to the two women. Louisa regarded him fondly. She was still rather smitten by the good-looking foreigner and would have been sadly disillusioned had she known what had occurred the previous night.

Don Alonzo was careful to pay both of the ladies compliments, but when he had done, he turned to Annis with a grave expression. "My dear Lady Burham, there is a most urgent matter which I wish to discuss with you—alone."

In spite of herself, Annis paled slightly. Louisa looked at her, uncertain whether to stay or go. His dark eyes rested on the companion for a moment. "It is a *private* matter," he said softly.

She folded her mending and rose, then looked at Annis again. Annis was forced to make a decision. "That is all right, Louisa," she said, adding for Don Alonzo's benefit, "The bell rope is within easy reach, after all."

Louisa sidled out the door. She had high hopes for this private conversation.

As soon as she had left, Annis turned to face Don Alonzo

with her heart racing though she prayed her appearance did not reveal it. "What did you wish to tell me?" she said coldly.

"May I be seated?" he asked, his face enigmatic. When she nodded, he selected a chair and lowered himself into it, carefully flipping back the tails of his dark coat so that they would not be crushed. He was silent for a moment, and Annis thought to herself that she was expected to admire the picture he presented in the biscuit-colored pantaloons that clung tightly to his powerful legs and the exquisitely cut coat that fitted him like a second skin. It was clear that Don Alonzo did spend a great deal of time on his cravat in the morning.

His voice startled her when he finally spoke. "First of all, I wish to apologize deeply for the incident last night. I regret that my passion got the better of my reason."

The memory sickened Annis. "You have already apologized once, Don Alonzo, so there is no need—"

"No, hear me out," he said, cutting her off peremptorily. "I cannot tell you how it has affected me to see that . . . that gentleman so constantly by your side."

Annis opened her mouth to speak, but he cut her off with an angry wave of his hand. "No, do not ask it. I am well aware that the idiot Reeves is only a decoy to keep the rest of the world at bay. You know that I am speaking of the other, of Ulverstone. It seemed that every other time I came to call, *he* was here. If I went shopping, there *he* was by your side. At assemblies, there *he* would be, dancing attendance upon you, and scarcely permitting me to exchange more than a word with you. It has driven me mad to see him insinuating himself with you in this fashion, and last night it was simply too much. I—"

"No, please . . ." These months in England had certainly worked a change in Don Alonzo, for he was speaking without a trace of an accent now, but Annis was too distraught to notice.

"It was when I was brought to my senses that I saw what my mistake had been. I had assumed that you were aware of my intentions, but I had never spoken of them to you."

"Please, no . . ." Her words were ineffectual, for he continued relentlessly, "In short, Lady Burham, I hope that you will do me the honor of becoming my wife."

The "I hope" was a mere concession to manners. His

declaration had no sort of question to it. She saw that supreme confidence in his eyes and realized that he had no idea that she would do anything but accept him. Her nausea was replaced by anger.

"No, sir, I will not," she told him curtly.

He leapt to his feet, his eyes burning, and she wished that she had phrased her refusal more politely. "*What* did you say?"

She stood her ground valiantly. "I said what I meant. We should not suit. And I have thought so from the moment of our first meeting and have done my best to discourage you in every way that I could."

"But this is monstrous!" He ran a hand through his hair distractedly and she thought that he must be angry indeed to disturb its careful arrangement. He paced about the room furiously while Annis observed him in silence, her hand itching to pull the bell rope.

Fortunately, this activity apparently helped him to regain mastery of himself. After a few moments he paused, turned to her, and said thinly, "Your decision is irrevocable?"

"Yes."

"Then there is little else for us to say." He paused for an instant, and Annis was struck by a sudden sympathy for the earthworm forced to face the scrutiny of the robin's black and beady eye.

"There is one other matter which I have not mentioned to you for some time. I cannot think that I will have much reason to remain in England now. Before I go, will you please do me the favor of selling me the parcel of land as your husband had previously promised?"

She had only to do this one thing and he had virtually promised not to trouble her again. It gave her a giddy sensation of relief and she would have agreed quickly, except for some deep-buried wariness. Her caution in most financial matters had stood her in good stead so far. "Why," the little voice inside her argued, "is that land so important to him?"

"If Sir Richard made you the promise, then I regret that he did not put it in writing," she told him coldly, "but at the moment, I do not intend to dispose of any of my land."

He took a step toward her and she could see the fury blazing out of his eyes. Reacting instinctively, she reached for the bell rope and rang it. Greenlaw, who must have been waiting just outside the door, appeared almost instantly.

"Show Don Alonzo out," she ordered woodenly.

She received a glance of searing hatred from those dark eyes; then he simply stalked out, without so much as a nod in her direction. She sank back in her chair. She could be glad she had escaped so lightly. She didn't think she would be seeing Don Alonzo again.

After undergoing such an ordeal, she felt in need of her family's and friend's support. She would have talked with Louisa first, but learned that someone had called for her and she had left without a word. Annis frowned to herself. These sudden disappearances were unlike Louisa and they had started becoming alarmingly frequent. She needed to speak with her about it. She must remind herself to do so when her companion returned. Failing Louisa, she went in search of Elizabeth.

She found her sister, happily curled up with a book, still in her wrapper, though the morning was quite advanced.

"Elizabeth," Annis said reproachfully, "what if someone should come to call?"

Her sister looked up with a startled glance as if she had forgotten about the existence of anything but the book in which she was engrossed. "I'm sorry, Annis, but no one will—except perhaps Lord Bainbridge or Lord Eversley, and you know that I am trying to avoid them."

"Well, you can't ever tell who may call," Annis said severely as she seated herself in a blue-silk-covered *fauteuil*.

"Oh, but Annis, this is such a good book! I know you do not generally like to read, but you would enjoy this one. The young lady in the book has already refused the gentleman, but she has changed her mind now, and it looks as if he means to propose to her once more."

The subject matter recalled the events of the morning unpleasantly to Annis' mind. "Elizabeth," she began hesitantly, "Don Alonzo called this morning."

"Oh, did he?" Elizabeth asked with some indifference. "Annis, would you mind terribly if I finished the book now? There are only five chapters left."

Preoccupied as she was by the book, Elizabeth could not be the sympathetic audience Annis was craving. "No, I suppose not," Annis said rather sadly, but Elizabeth had already pressed her nose into the book once more and didn't even glance at Annis as she left the room.

Annis went downstairs rather thoughtfully. Had all her efforts been for naught? Instead of becoming more and more fond of London life, Elizabeth seemed increasingly to shrink from it. The only times she seemed truly happy were when she was engrossed in some book or another. She did not complain, but she seemed to dread every rout, or musicale, or assembly that they attended. She enjoyed the theater and the opera, but only during the performances themselves. She had not attracted the notice of one worthwhile suitor who was her equal in station, wealth, or intelligence, though London was full of eligible gentlemen. Her sobriquet had persisted, and Annis thought unhappily that Elizabeth had done nothing to show that she was other than an "Ice Maiden." Why couldn't anyone else see the generous, loyal, and loving girl that her family knew? Even Aunt Berinthea was beginning to be discouraged and to make suggestions that perhaps Elizabeth might be willing to settle for a title, since she had such a comfortable fortune of her own.

There was no denying, also, that Laurie was the worse for their London stay. He was completely neglecting his studies. He spent most of his time in the company of young fellows who were both rude and vulgar to Annis' way of thinking. He was spending money profligately, and Annis feared that his dissipations might have a negative effect upon his health. Moreover, he had become increasingly resentful of what he considered to be meddling on his sister's part. Relations between them had deteriorated to the point where she almost feared to put a simple question to him, knowing the likelihood that it would meet with a sharp retort.

No, it looked as if all she had accomplished with her efforts was to waste a significant part of her fortune and to contribute to her sibling's unhappiness. A recent meeting with her man of business had done nothing to add to her cheer. Though he was quite sensible of the expense required to maintain an establishment in London, he considered that it would be wise for her to at least keep an eye on her expenditures. She was quite as shocked as he to see how much money had been pouring out of her coffers. It was little consolation to reflect that some of the new investments she had made were actually enhancing Richard's yet-intact fortune. She still, unreasonably, refused to touch it.

It was in this frame of mind that she encountered Laurie, still at the breakfast table. She wisely decided not to animadvert against this fact. He was used to keeping late hours by now, after all. He could not simply change his habits overnight.

The evening at the theater was the least combative time that she had spent with him in weeks. Perhaps she could build upon this harmony to create a new relationship with him. Besides, she had little choice about confidants. Therefore she greeted him kindly and asked how he felt this morning.

"I'm afraid it's almost afternoon," Laurie said carelessly as he buttered a muffin. "But a fellow has to get some sleep. 'Fraid we were racketing about town rather late last night." He cast a wary eye on her as he spoke, waiting for her reaction.

Remembering her resolution, Annis poured herself a cup of tea and with nothing more than mild curiosity in her voice asked if he had gone out after they had returned home last night.

"Oh, yes," Laurie said with the same studied indifference as before. "One of Luffy's particular friends was having a little party, don't you know."

"A party? How delightful. Was anyone else I know there?"

"Just the usual fellows," Laurie said, not entirely able to conceal his anxiety. "Of course, we didn't stay there the entire evening."

"You didn't?" Annis asked mildly. "Where did you happen to go then?"

"Oh, just to a coffeehouse," Laurie said. "It was capital fun, too. I had never been to one before, don't you know. But the real adventure came afterward."

By the utmost exertion of will, Annis was able to keep from revealing her dismay when her brother mentioned the coffeehouse. She might be from the country, but she had been in London long enough to know what sort of persons would frequent a coffeehouse. She would have been much relieved had she been able to read her younger brother's thoughts, for despite himself, he had been shocked by the low company there and not a little embarrassed by what his friends termed "capital sport." He had no intention of allowing Annis an opportunity for I-told-you-so's, though, and so he did not betray his true impression.

Since Annis was incapable of knowing what lay beneath this carefree exterior, it took her a few moments to master herself and ask, in a voice that betrayed no extraordinary interest, just what exactly had been the "real adventure."

Laurie had been quite agreeably surprised to find his sister this equable, but a little discretion seemed in order. He told her confidentially that it was "not the sort of thing one tells a female."

Managing to fix a smile upon her face again, she said, "Oh, I know many are easily shocked. But you know me better than that, Laurie. Now that you've roused my curiosity, pray tell me, what did you do?"

When she put things that way, it did seem rather nonsensical not to confide in her. After all, it had just been a humorous prank—the sort of thing that would probably have made her laugh too if she had been there. Luffy's female companion had certainly found it amusing.

"Well," he said, his eyes bright with amusement, "I suppose I really shouldn't . . . but I'll tell you if you promise not to be shocked."

Annis made the promise, managing to keep her worry hidden.

"It was Luffy's idea," Laurie disclaimed modestly. "There's one old charley—a watchman, that is—who has been persecuting him. We crept up to his box, saw the fellow was asleep, and we tipped the box forward on its entrance so that he was trapped there. You should have heard the old scout yelling!"

His laughter was cut short by the expression of outrage on his sister's face. "Laurie, how could you!" she exclaimed. "What if he had been hurt?"

Presented in that way, the anecdote did seem a trifle less entertaining, but he stuck to his guns. "Really, Annis, it's not as though we beat him, and he really has been most unjust to poor old Luffy. He's locked him up more than once just for being a trifle on the go."

Annis stared at him, fresh horror in her eyes. "Do you mean that your friend has actually been locked up in a watchhouse for the night?" she asked.

He looked sulky. "Well, it's not as if he were in Newgate, after all."

She caught a hand to her throat with a fresh fear. "Did no one else hear his cries? Were you not pursued?"

Laurie laughed scornfully. "Of course we were. Another charley came on the run, sounding his rattle, but we were long gone by then. What a set of gudgeons you must think us."

Annis let out a sigh of relief. "Oh, thank heaven. I can just imagine what Ambrose would say if he learned that you'd been locked up in a watchhouse at seventeen."

Laurie snorted. "No, of course I haven't been locked up in one yet."

These last words awakened Annis' anxiety afresh. She turned to him pleadingly. "Laurie, you must not be! Oh, can't you see how wasteful and destructive this way of life is?"

Laurie, having completed most of his breakfast, threw down his napkin angrily and rose. "That does it! I should have known how it would be. You can't resist the chance to read me a sermon at every opportunity, can you?" His irritation was heightened by a realization that there was some justice in what she said, and by a newly awakened sense of shame.

"Laurie, please do not—"

Ignoring her, he strode from the breakfast room into the hall. "If you ask me, you care too much for Ambrose's opinion, and for everyone else's," he told her brutally. "You always complained of Ambrose's running your life—well, it seems to me that that's just what you want to do to mine and Elizabeth's, and you do a poor job of it too, as far as I can tell."

She pursued him to the foot of the stairs. "Laurie, it needn't be like this. I only wish—"

He stared at her coldly. "I don't care a fig for what *your* wishes are. I am going upstairs to change my clothes and then I mean to go and pay a call on my *friends*. *They* at least care whether or not I am happy."

With a flourish of his silk-brocade dressing gown, he presented his back to her and began to march up the stairs. Annis leaned heavily on the balustrade. His words had wounded her deeply, whether or not they were undeserved. She turned and saw Walter standing in the entryway, an unwilling observer of the scene.

With anyone else she would have felt mortified, but then, she had always felt surprisingly comfortable around Walter. She took a step or two toward him. "I'm sorry."

He strode to her quickly and took her hands in his. "That young whelp needs to be taken in hand. I should like to have a talk with him myself."

"Oh, it's not important. Won't you come into the drawing room?" In marked contrast to her interview with Don Alonzo earlier, Annis now seemed to feel that there was no impropriety in closeting herself with a male acquaintance. As they entered the drawing room arm in arm, she added, "It's just that we've been at loggerheads ever since we came to London. It's so odd, too, for we used to get along so particularly well—and Elizabeth too."

"He's simply feeling the need to sow a few wild oats. Most young gentlemen do. It's nothing for you to worry over."

Although she was aware that she would be awakening Laurie's wrath by confiding in Walter, Annis could not help repeating the gist of Laurie's conversation with her, as well as mentioning the voucher she had found the other day. Walter looked grim. "It's as I say, he needs someone to keep a close eye on his doings. I would myself, but . . ." He broke off in the middle of what he was about to say. "There are far too many responsibilities that have been thrust on these slender shoulders," he said kindly. "Something else is troubling you. May I know what it is?"

Here was the sympathetic confidant for whom she had been searching all day. She poured the story of her interview with Don Alonzo into his ready ears. He was angered afresh by the man's insolence, and expressed a wish that he had been there to "teach the fellow a lesson," though he did not seem to attach the significance she did to the sale of the land. When she had finished her recital and told him of her final dismissal of Don Alonzo, he drew a breath of relief.

"I could not say anything to you, Annis, when I saw that he was a welcome guest in your household, but I never have trusted that gentleman. As you know, I work in the office of the foreign secretary, and because of that position I am able to find out a great deal of information not available to the general public. I made some inquiries about Don Alonzo and was able to discover nothing whatsoever about his background, a fact which in itself seems suspicious, although it is true that affairs in Spain are still a good deal jumbled as a result of the war.''

"Oh, how I wish you had seen fit to confide in me," Annis exclaimed.

He glanced in her eyes, then looked away uncomfortably. "I regret now that I did not, so that you might have been spared some of this unpleasantness. I hesitated to say anything because he had known you longer than I had and because . . ." He hesitated for a moment. "I hope you will not resent my making the observation, but it seemed to me that you had far too many people attempting to interfere with your affairs already."

What an estimable gentleman he was. The warm expression in her eyes revealed her gratitude. His brows drew together slightly.

"There is one other thing which raised my suspicions, and yet which I felt unable to tell you. Knowing you as I do now, I can have no fear that the word will travel any further, though I must ask you not to inform anyone, even your sister or brother, of it."

She nodded, a little surprised by his gravity.

"My bond with Richard was a unique one. I knew him to be completely trustworthy, as well as both observant and intelligent. A gentleman in his position, required to travel for business, could be of the utmost use to me in my position. Colonial territories are always particularly vulnerable, and especially when they border on the holdings of a country unfriendly—or at least traditionally unfriendly—to our own. It was also most unfortunate that the recent treaty of peace entirely failed to deal with developments which had been taking place within the Spanish colonies themselves."

He saw that his auditor's eyes were beginning to glaze over in boredom and he gave a little smile. "I am sorry to prose on so. What I meant to say was that I often sent Richard to discover what developments were, under the guise of managing his own business, of course. The fact that Don Alonzo claimed to have had dealings with Richard in the colonies was enough to make me suspicious of him.'' He gave Annis a sad smile. ''In fact, Annis, I have always held myself partly to blame for his death. I was the one who sent Richard off posthaste to Jamaica that fall. He had business to take care of, of course, but none so urgent as we made out. He even seemed a little reluctant to go at first, though naturally he was willing enough when I explained the situation to him. I can never quite escape the feeling, though, that he might still be alive if he had only delayed the trip.''

Annis' eyes were bright. So it hadn't been just business that had taken Richard away from her at the moment of their engagement. He had wanted to stay; he might even had been eager for their wedding. It made no difference now, but there was some cold corner of her heart that was warmed by the thought. She saw that her companion was regarding her with some anxiety, and she managed a trembling smile.

''Oh, no, you must not blame yourself. No one could have known—but thank you for telling me. It means a great deal to me to hear about that side of Richard.''

There was a period of silence between them, which strangely enough was not uncomfortable; then Walter frowned once more. ''My purpose in coming here today was twofold: first I wished to ascertain that you had suffered no lasting harm from that villain's attack upon you last night, and second, I wished to take my leave of you.''

''You are going somewhere?'' Annis' tone unwittingly revealed her desolation at the loss of her only ally of the moment.

''Yes. I just received word that my brother has met with a serious accident. I meant to set off for Oxfordshire immediately, but I felt that I must see you first.''

''Oh!'' Annis' distress was obvious. ''I would not have delayed you so long had I known. Your poor brother!''

He shrugged. ''I cannot be of any material help to him, except to comfort my new sister, but . . .'' He rose to his feet, and Annis followed suit, escorting him out of the drawing room and heading toward the front door.

"Of course it will mean so much to them to have you there," Annis said stoutly. "I hope that his recovery will be rapid."

They had reached the door and he took her hand and pressed it. "Thank you," he said meaningfully. He would have turned to go, but the entrance was abruptly blocked by the large figure of Ambrose, who was waving a piece of paper angrily in Annis' direction.

"I should like to know the meaning of this!" he articulated by way of greeting.

Walter glanced back at Annis with a frown. He had made Ambrose's acquaintance during one of that gentleman's visits to town, and had greatly resented his treatment of Annis and Elizabeth. A part of him would have liked to stay and shield Annis from his menace. She understood his unspoken message and shook her head. "You must go," she said in a low voice.

Accordingly, Walter placed his hat upon his head and departed, though not without casting a darkling look at Ambrose. The latter's face had drawn up in a sneer. "I should have known that every gentleman in town would have the free run of this house. It was only to be expected."

Not for the first time, Annis wished that Ambrose had a little less liking for making a public spectacle of himself. "Come into the drawing room, then," she said wearily, "and you may tell me what is the matter now."

11

As usual, it took quite some time to calm Ambrose down enough to learn what actually had excited his wrath this time. After listening to his sputtering rage for about a half-hour, Annis was having difficulty keeping her own temper. Fortunately Elizabeth, who had finished with the book and changed into a pretty dress of blue sprigged muslin, chose that moment to walk into the room. The combined efforts of the two sisters managed to reveal the truth.

Unluckily, as it happened, Ambrose's wife, Maria, was a bosom bow of Lady Penelope Fairfield, the daughter of an Irish peer and an aunt to Lord Bainbridge. Apparently all of Elizabeth's discouragement had not proved effective, for this lady regarded the match as quite a settled thing already. She had written with delight to inform her "Dearest Maria" that their families were soon to be connected by marriage. It was this missive that had sent Ambrose off to London, apoplectic with fury. That Elizabeth should ally herself with a fortune-hunter! And without even consulting her cousin and trustee!

Annis herself had to admit that she was troubled somewhat by the letter. "Really, Elizabeth! I thought you turned him down when he offered for your hand again last week. And now that I come to think of it, why is it that he continues to offer for you anyway? Has he been misled into believing that you will accept him eventually?"

Elizabeth's cheeks flushed with rare anger. "I think it is unkind of you even to suggest such a thing, Annis. I have tried to make it abundantly clear to him that his suit will never be acceptable to me. Can I help it if he is just too stubborn to credit it?"

Annis had pursed her mouth. "Well, it seems to me that you

must have offered him some encouragement, however unwittingly—''

''I did not! You simply do not know how blockheaded he is. The last time that he asked me and I told him that we should not suit, he asked if there were anyone else. Of course I had to tell him no, and he said that there was still hope for him then.''

''Oh, Elizabeth,'' Annis groaned, ''must you always be so honest? You could have made up another suitor and rid yourself of him for good.''

''And who was I to say, then? Any of these other dolts that I have attracted would probably take it as a declaration—''

''You could have told him that there was a long-standing attachment between you and a gentleman in Kent, and that you'd only come to London to oblige your family.''

The lively argument that had sprung up between the sisters served to convince Ambrose of the untruth of the report as all their protests would have failed to do. He held up a magnanimous hand. ''Peace! It is much too trifling a matter to be quarreling over.'' He did not add that it had occurred to him abruptly that such a rumor might go a long way toward discouraging other suitors.

The two sisters desisted from their argument, regarding their cousin with frank amazement. Annis was still perturbed by the letter. Of course, if Laurie had been there, he might have explained how a gentleman being dunned by his creditors might find it convenient to put about the news that he was on the verge of being engaged to an heiress. His creditors naturally would wish to do nothing to endanger such a match, since it was their only hope of recovering any of their money.

In any case, Ambrose's mysterious affability continued for the rest of his visit, which fortunately was not a protracted one. To Annis' relief, Laurie did not appear while their cousin was there. She had no doubt that she would have been read a homily on the evils attached to allowing her younger brother such license regarding dress, manners, and other matters. As it happened, however, Ambrose was able to finish his visit more in harmony with them than he had been for some time.

It was Elizabeth who found this circumstance suspicious. ''It seems so odd to me,'' she told her sister, ''the way he keeps appearing on our doorstep suddenly, without a trace of warning.''

"He never has advised us of any of his visits since we moved to our own establishment," Annis pointed out fair-mindedly.

"I know. But didn't it strike you as peculiar, Annis, the way he just abruptly decided not to chastise us further about Lord Bainbridge? I was expecting him to lecture us for an hour at least."

"I for one am glad that he didn't," Annis yawned.

"I know, and I do not wish to look a gift horse in the mouth. But it seemed rather sinister to me. He was so full of good spirits, after all."

Ambrose had been much cheered by the notion that although the Season was now becoming advanced, Elizabeth apparently had failed to collect one eligible suitor. Maria had said initially that she thought the girl was far too shy to "take," and her words were being proved right. Elizabeth as a spinster was no threat to his own well-being.

Although she could not guess the reason for her cousin's abrupt amiability, Annis dismissed her sister's suspicions. She was to recall them, forcibly, several days later.

Life in town had seemed rather flat to her lately. With his departure, Walter had left her without a confidant, or an agreeable gentleman to converse with at the assemblies and routs she still attended. Louisa's mysterious business seemed to be taking up more and more of her time. Annis had been unable to catch her companion and question her about it in detail, though Louisa had assured her that it was "a most worthwhile charitable venture." That, of course, could mean anything. It spoke well for Annis that she did not resent Louisa's absences, but rather feared for her safety, certain that her companion must be frequenting the poorer areas of the city.

Laurie had been avoiding Annis since their last set-to. Elizabeth had failed to attract any fresh suitors, and even Aunt Berinthea seemed to have lost all hope of her doing so. An intelligent girl like Elizabeth could scarcely be oblivious of the fact, and Annis supposed it was this that made her seem reluctant to spend time with her sister, even though Annis had no intention of giving her a scold.

The one quality of Walter's that Annis was best able to appreciate in his absence was his ability to remove her from her many unwelcome admirers. Without him, she was forced to endure a good deal of attention that she found unpleasant, though she supposed it was still better than being rescued by Don Alonzo. That gentleman's continued absence afforded her the greatest relief, even if it made life a little less exciting.

She supposed either that it was sheer boredom or that she simply was weary of saying no, but at Lady Edgemount's ball she found herself agreeing to go riding in the park the next morning with Sir George Reeves. Despite all his obvious failings, he was an accomplished horseman. It would do Annis no discredit to be seen in his company, and it would get her out of the house, at least.

She had dressed the next morning in the new riding habit which she had scarcely worn since arriving in town. In her usual black, it was quite plain except for a double row of braid down the front and braid applied about the neck and cuffs. An unornamented bonnet of black crepe finished the ensemble. The only thing to relieve the severity of her dress was the white frill she wore about her neck. The effect was eye-catching and the very austerity of it becoming to her. Sir George could not conceal his admiration when he arrived.

Annis had chosen to ride the little black mare Laurie had picked out for her so long ago now. Sir George had offered her the choice of any horse in his stables, but as Annis was no very dashing rider, she preferred a mount with which she was familiar. The mare was docile and sweet-tempered, not giving to shying, and Annis felt safe with her. It was a little frightening to ride in the city, but with Sir George beside her on his big chestnut gelding and the groom behind them, she supposed she had nothing to fear.

Perhaps it was that Sir George was more sensitive than she had ever imagined, for he seemed perfectly content to amble alongside her at a dull walk for most of their journey. She couldn't know, of course, that he was greatly enjoying basking in the attention she attracted. More than one acquaintance observed that Sir George was in a fair way to fixing his interest with the lovely widow, swearing that he was a "lucky devil." His good fortune was felt to be all the more outrageous, for until then Lady Burham had seemed to favor no gentleman, unless you counted Ulverstone or that deuced peculiar foreigner.

Fortunately, Annis was unaware of their scrutiny and speculation, her whole attention being centered on her mount. She had not expected much of the fashionable world to be abroad at this hour, and she would have been surprised at how quickly the word was spread.

They had only a little distance to go before reaching the park. Sir George then suggested they try a trot about the Ring. Annis was not averse to the idea, for though there were quite a few riders and people walking about, there did not appear to be anything here that might frighten the mare. She urged her horse into a gentle trot and was quickly joined by Sir George and the groom.

After a few minutes she was beginning to feel more relaxed and thought she might acquit herself on this outing with what Laurie would call prime style. She even felt happy enough to be able to respond to Sir George's compliments with tolerable composure.

She was attending to something he said, and not quite enough to her riding, when the incident occurred. Without warning, her usually gentle mare took off like a bolt from the blue, pulling the reins from Annis' unsuspecting hands. Frightened witless, she could only try to hold on to the pommel of the saddle and pray that she would not be thrown. It took just seconds for her to realize that she was in danger of being scraped from the saddle by the branches of the trees. She had a queer sense of being frozen in time, as if everything were happening extremely slowly.

The mare swerved close to one tree, catching the skirt of her gown and tearing it. Annis was aware that her bonnet had blown off. She could hear her own frightened gasps for breath and the unceasing thunder of the mare's hooves. As if in a nightmare, she saw a big tree straight ahead. A huge branch loomed at an angle from the trunk. She was certain to be dashed against it, she could remember thinking, and then abruptly there was another horse beside her and a hand on the reins. The mare was brought to a stop just a few feet from the tree.

Sir George might be found wanting in the conversational

department, he might have difficulty remembering the figures of a country dance, and the extremes he affected in dress might make him an object of ridicule, but everyone had to acknowledge his horsemanship. Seeing Annis in difficulty, he had responded quickly, overtaking her horse with his own, and in a daring show of skill, had snatched the trailing reins and brought the mare to a halt.

They were both out of breath, and it took them a few minutes to find their voices.

"Are you all right?" he finally gasped.

Annis just managed to nod, then exclaimed in a trembling voice, "Take me home . . . oh, please, take me home!"

After ascertaining that she felt able to ride home, Sir George turned their horses in the direction of Burham House, adjuring her groom sharply to keep a hand on his mistress's reins. The trip seemed interminable, but it was uneventful. Annis was glad that Sir George had instructed the groom as he had, for she was shaking so badly she didn't think that she could command the horse. She could feel the mare trembling beneath her also.

Sir George was wondering aloud what could have made the mare bolt the way she had. Although Annis did not feel up to making any reply, the same question started turning about in her mind. The horse had not reared or neighed before setting off at a dead run. Was it possible that this was not an accident? She certainly might have been killed, she thought, and shuddered. She abruptly remembered Elizabeth's suspicions, and a cold and clammy feeling began to take hold of her heart. Was Ambrose here even now, and was he trying to kill her? It would have been simple to aim a stone at the horse's rump. She would not have noticed him in all the confusion, and there was certainly cover enough for him to hide behind. Her shivering became more violent, causing even the usually unobservant Sir George to notice. He gave the groom a meaningful glance. Best to get her home without delay.

Her nervous exhaustion took its toll in sleep, and it wasn't until that afternoon that Annis ventured back downstairs. She found a worried Elizabeth in the drawing room, Louisa for once with her. After the question was broached, Annis could not but admit that she thought Ambrose might have been behind the accident. Elizabeth raised her objections in an orderly, logical fashion.

"Yes, but if he truly meant to do away with you, surely he might have found a more thorough way of doing so."

Annis sighed. "I know that all these incidents might still be coincidental, but think—he must make it appear as if it were an accident, after all."

"Well, why should they suddenly start beginning again—after he's left us in peace for so long?"

"I think that perhaps the report that you were to wed Lord Bainbridge frightened him more than we thought. Either he disbelieved us when we told him that you are not engaged, or it made him consider that you might easily become engaged to someone else."

"I still don't know why he would wish to do away with you, after all. Laurie and I would inherit, not Ambrose."

It was Louisa who had the answers to this objection. "I have been considering the matter for some time now," she said quietly, "and I think that if it is your cousin, he is hoping that perhaps without Annis around he may coax you to return to the Briars with him. Your fortune would be made even more considerable by your sister's death."

"You're right," Annis interjected, "and since Laurie would have no home if I died, Ambrose might be hoping to become his acting guardian once more."

"It is true that he always does seem to blame you for everything," Elizabeth said consideringly.

"Yes, and think, he has no notion that you also are aware of his double-dealings."

They were interrupted by a knock on the door. Greenlaw entered and announced, "Mr. Walter Ulverstone."

Though surprised, Annis told him to show the gentleman in. Elizabeth herself had the presence of mind, at least, to slip her spectacles off before he arrived.

Walter strode in, his face anxious. "Is it true?" he asked. "Are you all right?" he added, taking Annis by the hands.

After she assured him that she was, he greeted the other ladies in a perfunctory manner, though it was clear that his mind was elsewhere. He took the chair that was offered, exclaiming that he wished he had been there in order to prevent the accident.

"I thought you were not in town," Annis said curiously. "Have you just returned?"

"Yes, I arrived last night. I had some urgent business to dispatch at the office this morning. I was on my way back home when I saw Sir George Reeves, and he told me what had happened. Thank God he had the presence of mind to stop your horse as he did."

"How is your brother?" Annis asked.

His eyes met hers gravely. "That is a matter which I mean to discuss with you." He looked at Elizabeth and Louisa. "Ladies, may I have a few moments alone with Lady Burham?"

Annis nodded at Elizabeth and Louisa. Silently they rose and left her with Walter.

To Annis' surprise, he did not first address the question of his brother's health, but rather that of her accident. He asked her in some detail about how it had happened, and she felt comfortable enough with him to confess that she thought it to have been deliberate.

"That was what I was thinking," he admitted. "Have you any idea who is behind it?"

She had already admitted to him that they had difficulties with Ambrose as a trustee and that her cousin still controlled Elizabeth's fortune. Now she told him the rest, including mentioning the accidents that had occurred in the spring. Of course, she could not tell him about her false marriage. No one could ever know about that.

He raised the same sort of objections that Elizabeth had, but he listened respectfully to her replies, and agreed that she had cause to suspect her cousin. Then he fell silent, and she could see that he was turning something over in his mind. She waited in some suspense for him to begin.

"In many ways," he said, "my timing is damnable, but this incident convinces me that I must speak now. I think I know you well enough to be certain that you will not take offense at some imagined slight."

She was anxious for him to continue, but she could see that his thoughts were painful. When he spoke, it was with an effort. "My brother," he began, "suffered a serious accident, as I told you. When I arrived there, it was obvious that I did not know quite how serious it was.''

Annis could not help giving a little moan of sympathy.

''Although he will live, it is quite certain that he will never father a child. The countess is . . . is not expecting.'' He flushed darkly and refused to meet her eyes. ''I suppose you will think that I should not be discussing such intimate problems with you, but you see, my brother's accident has put me in a new position. Although I may never be the Earl of Worthington myself, it is certain that my son will be. In other words, it is incumbent upon me to marry.''

He looked up, still flushed. ''It is not a decision that I need to or would wish to make in a hurry. Nevertheless, your situation is such that I do not feel that delay is advisable.'' He swallowed, and began again. ''I realize that we have been acquainted with each other for only a matter of months, but I have come to know you and your family rather well. Even before you told me about your suspicions regarding your cousin, I could not help but mistrust him. Your younger brother has given you cause for worry, and he desperately needs a man's guidance. Of course, though we do not speak of it, I know of your anxiety for your sister.''

He gazed frankly at her, their eyes meeting without evasion. ''There have been moments when I wished that I could ease you of the burden of responsibility that has been thrust upon you. Although I am not a wealthy man, my fortune is not inconsiderable. I could be of assistance with Laurie, I know. If you will forgive my mentioning it, also, I imagine that Elizabeth might do better with a Season under our auspices than with the sponsor she now has, who seems to make no allowance for her shyness.''

How understanding he was. He was probably the only gentleman in London who guessed that Elizabeth's cool reserve was the result of timidity, though he could not know the cause. Annis let go an involuntary sigh, but he checked her before she could speak.

''Wait. There is something else I must say to you first. Then, if you wish, we need never talk about it again.'' He took a deep breath, then resumed. ''I am quite aware that your heart is given to another, to another who is no more. I cannot help but honor you for your constancy. Indeed, were matters less urgent, I would not think of approaching you now." Again those level gray eyes met hers. "I cannot pretend to you that I have tumbled headlong into love with you, as the world would have it. I hold little opinion of such a rapid and transitory emotion. Our marriage would be founded on sounder principles—those of friendship, trust, and mutual esteem. I would do my best to be a good and faithful husband to you, and I feel that in doing so I would be serving Richard's memory rather than dishonoring it in any way. Annis, will you do me the honor of becoming my wife?"

She could scarcely believe her ears. She had grown so comfortable with Walter, grown accustomed to thinking of him as a dear friend, but nothing more. And from what he said, he had regarded her in very much the same light. She had not considered the possibility of marriage with anyone at all lately. But what he said made such good sense. She did need help with Laurie and protection from Ambrose. And if she were wedded, or even engaged, then those unwanted suitors would finally have to leave her alone, giving Elizabeth a clear field. How could Elizabeth have any confidence in her own powers of attraction when her sister, even unwillingly, commanded such a court?

She did not love Walter, it was true, but she had begun to believe that she would never love anyone other than Richard anyway. Walter was so courteous and so charming, so thoughtful of a lady. Not only that, but he understood about Richard. It seemed there was no ingredient missing for a perfect marriage. What a shame it was that her heart rebelled.

"Yes, Walter, I will marry you," she heard herself saying as if a dream.

"You have made me very happy," he said, rising to kiss her hand.

Now that the formalities had been accomplished, neither knew for a moment what to say or do next. It was the first moment of awkwardness between them. Annis rallied soonest. She rose and strode to the door and threw it open. "Elizabeth, Louisa," she called. They appeared almost immediately. "You must give us your best wishes," she said, smiling. "Walter and I are to be married."

Even two ladies as aware of decorum as these were could

not forbear to emit gasps of pleasure and surprise, nor resist throwing their arms about Annis' neck. Walter was not forgotten. He found his hand shaken firmly by Elizabeth, who also bestowed on him a breathtakingly lovely smile which he had never before been privileged to witness. It quite made his senses reel, but fortunately he recovered and was able to accept her congratulations with composure.

The happy little party did not quite know what to do with itself. Louisa suggested that they ring for tea, but Annis insisted that tea would be much too tame. It was evident that the occasion called for champagne. None of the ladies were accustomed to spirits, but both Elizabeth and Louisa had noticed Annis' overbright eyes and neither cared to countermand her.

With the orders given, the talk naturally turned to questions regarding time and place for the ceremony. Annis' and Walter's eyes met in consternation. They clearly had a great deal more conferring to do.

"I should think," Annis suggested with some diffidence, "that with your brother ill, you should want a long engagement, pending his recovery."

Walter performed the first ungentlemanly act of their acquaintance by appearing relieved. "Yes, I should think we would want a long engagement," he agreed.

A happy thought struck Annis. "And of course the banns will take some time also."

"Yes, they will, won't they?"

The efficient Louisa had immersed herself in detail. "I suppose I had better draw up the announcement to send to the papers immediately," she said.

Annis was beginning to feel that she was being hurried. "Well, I thought we might announce it privately first," she said hesitantly.

There was no stopping Louisa. "Well, we shall have to plan the party, then."

"Our calendar is so full at the moment," Annis explained apologetically.

Louisa was thinking. "Let's see, there's the musicale on Wednesday, the Griffiths on Thursday, and you are engaged to dine with the Cheetwoods on Friday. Of course, Saturday . . ." Here her eyes brightened. "Saturday there is only Lady Pallinghurst's ball. We might easily have a dinner party for close relatives and intimate friends on Saturday before the ball." Suddenly abashed, she looked at Walter. "Although I suppose that the earl and countess will be unable to attend?"

He confirmed it with a nod, as he also did her question as to whether he planned to remain in town for a week. It occurred to Annis that this was the reason why the engagement should not yet be announced. It seemed in poor taste to do so while his brother was lying ill. She was not given the chance to raise this objection, for Louisa continued on, "I know you will want Lady Downage there. Do you think you would wish for your cousin and his wife to—"

"No!" Annis exclaimed, thereby losing her vote on whether or not she wanted the party at all. The champagne was making her head a little fuzzy and she was beginning to have some difficulty in expressing herself. There was something quite important that she needed to say, if only she could recall it. The thought was driven from her mind by the observation that her glass was empty, a problem which she speedily rectified.

It was left to Laurie to pronounce judgment. He found them about forty-five minutes later, all the ladies rather giddy and carefree. He paused on the threshold and assumed an expression of shock. "Good Lord, Annis! And to think that you're always reading me lectures about *my* drinking."

Walter, who happened to be standing by Elizabeth, managed to catch her as she went down. "Thurstan," he said pleadingly, "be a good fellow and give me a hand."

Laurie teasingly told Annis later that she was fortunate in her choice of fiancé, that a lesser man certainly would have cried off after seeing his wife-to-be castaway. "I was not castaway," she had retorted hotly, "only a little on the go." Her words made her realize that Laurie had been exerting an influence on her vocabulary that was far from desirable. Well, at least he seemed to be happy about the news of her engagement, for he both liked and respected Walter. Annis' relationship with her brother was now quite amiable and she could only pray that it would continue to be.

She had experienced a sensation of fluttering nervousness when she dressed for the ball that Saturday evening. Elizabeth had insisted that Annis could *not* wear black the evening her engagement was to be announced, and had gladly offered to lend her a gown of her own instead. Annis had refused all the brightly colored ones, and as a compromise had settled on one of pale lavender. It was trimmed with a most decorous use of lace, caught up under the high waist, around the bottom of the sleeves, and finished with one deep flounce of it about the hem. It was both suitable and becoming, but Annis could not help but feel odd at assuming a garment that was other than black.

Although her mind had accepted marriage with Walter as a wise decision, she had not yet been able to convince her heart. It pronounced her a traitor as she donned the lavender dress, but that was hardly a surprise, as she had lived with the feeling all week. Although she had always been haunted by dreams of Richard, they had never been so frequent and vivid as they had been the past week. This very morning she had awakened herself by calling his name out loud, in answer to his cry of "Taggy." She could not even remember what the dream had been about, save for a feeling of indescribable sweetness that remained when she woke. It was merely some part of her that could not yet accept that he was gone, she knew. Her decision to marry Walter had merely brought it out of hiding.

The dreamlike feeling remained with her all day. She could not escape a sense of unreality during the dinner party. Walter had been at his handsomest and most charming, winning over even Aunt Berinthea. Of course, Annis thought with a new cynicsm, Lady Downage would be happy to approve of Walter once she learned that his son was to be the heir to the title. Still, it was pleasant to accept her friends' and family's good wishes, even through the pall of sadness cast by the earl's and countess's absence. Annis hoped that they would approve of her when they met her, though naturally Walter had assured her that they would.

He had been so busy with his work this week that it was no wonder that the evening seemed unreal. She had hardly seen him since they had become engaged. She thought guiltily to herself that at least a part of her had dreaded meeting him. To see him face to face could only confirm that they in truth were engaged.

Not even the reassuring hand that Walter slipped into hers as he made the announcement could shake her from her trance-like state. She passed the party in a smiling fog. Walter was everything a gentleman should be. Why must her heart persist in telling her that she was making a dreadful mistake?

It was almost as if she were an outside observer, watching herself enter the carriage, forcing herself to make the usual talk on the way to the ball, and maintaining that falsely serene smile upon her face.

When they arrived, it was evident that no one had missed the signficance of Walter's escorting them to the ball. The fact that she had put off wearing black could not fail to excite comment; nor could his gently proprietary air toward her be ignored, even though she still refused to dance. Society observed and drew its own conclusions.

Annis, conscious of the scrutiny, felt a certain helplessness. Well, she had made her decision and must stick by it now. Didn't logic argue that it was a perfect choice?

Despite her efforts, she must have been somewhat less animated than usual, for Walter, who had remained by her side ever since their arrival, asked gently if something were wrong. She shook her head and replied that she was simply a trifle fatigued. "I certainly don't mean to keep you dancing attendance on me all evening," she said smilingly. "If you wish to join some of the other gentlemen for cards . . ."

He shook his head, but his eyes had been scanning the crowd rather anxiously. He apparently caught sight of whomever he was seeking, for he leaned down to her and said, "I would not desert you for such a trifle as that, but I have something of urgency to communicate to Lord Hartley. If you would excuse me for a few minutes, my dear . . ."

She acquiesced gracefully and turned her attention to the dancers on the floor. In some ways it was a relief not to be of their number, for the evening was seasonably warm, and she had already resorted to the use of her fan. The orchestra had struck up a waltz, and the ladies and gentlemen on the floor presented a picturesque spectacle to her eyes. Black tailcoats and silk gowns swirled gaily about the room in time to the music. It was an entrancing sight. She was experiencing an odd sense of having done this before, though she could not quite identify the memory. Perhaps it was a dream, or . . . Was it the ball a lifetime ago with Richard? Preoccupied with her thoughts, she didn't notice the sudden buzz of conversation. A few sharp exclamations failed to catch her attention; her eyes remained on the waltzers. It was only when she saw some of their number begin to falter in their steps and stop, their eyes fixed on the entryway, that she turned her gaze in that direction.

A man stood there, a tall thin man whose dark tailcoat and pantaloons hung unfashionably loose on him. He took a limping step forward, and as he did, Annis thought to herself that there was something familiar about that upright carriage, that proudly arched nose, that shock of blond hair. . . . Suddenly it was as if everything and everyone around her melted away. She could see only Richard, a painfully thin but unbowed Richard, who was making his limping way across the room purposefully toward her. She was not certain if she were breathing. The room began to wobble about her, and abruptly she knew what it was to feel faint. She fought off the nauseating sensation with a supreme effort of will. He was just a few feet away from her now. She held out her hands to him. "Taggy," he said. It was that deep masculine growl she remembered, with that faint trace of hoarseness to it.

"Richard." He put his hand in hers. "How . . . how thin you are," she added idiotically.

He grinned at that, and she could see that it was the same heartbreaking, unexpectedly boyish smile that she had known and loved all her life. It *was* Richard who had come back to her, not a shadow of himself, and not a stranger. She could feel the color mount to her face and she was aware that she was trembling. Her heart was pounding, her throat constricted with joy. There was so much that she needed to tell him, that she had been needing to tell him for so long.

Annis had absolutely no idea how long they stood like that, hand in hand, not speaking, all their communication silent. It might have been only seconds, or it might have been hours.

Her heart was full to overflowing. To be given a second chance to tell him how she loved him! "Richard, I . . ." she began.

He startled her by glancing quickly over his shoulder. The movement awakened her and she suddenly heard the lively hum of conversation that was all about them. She realized that they were the focus of attention by everyone in the ballroom, and blushed to be the recipient of so many curious gazes.

"We had better find somewhere else to talk," Richard said dryly, and he tucked her arm in his and began to proceed from the ballroom matter-of-factly, as if it were the most normal thing in the world to return from the dead. He acknowledged joyous shouts of greetings with nods of the head and accepted various embraces of welcome as they traversed the room. For a moment Annis feared that they would not be able to pass from it, but Richard made his way inexorably toward the far door, which led to a series of small salons. As they broke free of the crowd and entered the first salon, Annis abruptly realized the dilemma she was in. Richard certainly did not know that they were supposed to be married. How could she explain the deception to him?

It was only when they had removed themselves quite a distance from the ballroom that Richard halted and closed the doors of the salon they were in, taking the added precaution of locking them. He turned on his heel and crossed his arms. The stern expression on his face was belied by the twinkle in his eyes. "Now, Taggy," he said, "just what sort of mischief have you been up to since I died?"

12

DIFFICULT as it was, Annis knew she must make her confession straightaway. She could not quite meet his eyes. "Richard," she said, choking out the words with difficulty, "everyone thinks I'm married to you."

"Oh, I knew *that*," he said with great casualness, crossing the room. He plopped down on a striped silk sofa, muttering, "My deuced leg," and Annis sat down beside him.

"How did you know?" she breathed.

"Had a message from the foreign secretary's office. That's why I came to London. Would have wasted my time looking for you in Kent otherwise. Missed Walter at the office, and thought I'd run him to ground at his home. Manservant said he was at the Pallinghurst ball with *Lady* Burham. Lord, I must have looked a sight. Took me a minute or two to work it out."

His casual attitude was bothersome in the extreme. Tears sprang to her eyes. "Richard, where have you been? Why couldn't you let me know that you were alive all these months? They told us your ship went down with all hands lost. They *saw* it go down."

He lifted an eyebrow, but responded, "The ship *did* go down. Thing is, I wasn't aboard."

"Then why was there no word of you?"

He hesitated, and she could not quite read his expression. When he spoke, she felt that he was choosing his words carefully. "I was back in the jungle looking at additional forest for the logging camp's expansion. By the stupidest mischance, I wasn't wearing my boots one day and a snake bit me just above the ankle. Luckily one of the Indians with me was quick to act and sucked out the poison, but still . . . well, I suppose I was near death for about a week. Chap that saved me was too."

He shuddered slightly. "And the stuff they forced down me—indescribably foul."

"Oh, Richard." The tears had begun to slip down her cheeks, but Annis was unaware of them.

"Well, by the time I came to myself, so to speak, the ship had already sailed. It was clear I wasn't going to be able to travel with this leg anyway—the jungle's confounded hard going, you know, so there I was stuck in this Indian village. It was, let me see, about a week or so later that the fever hit."

"The fever." She had noticed that his complexion was yellowed and his cheeks sunken, but the obvious explanation had not occurred to her.

"Yes. I must have given the Indians the devil of a time too, for I was out of my wits for weeks, off and on. I'd seem to get better and then I'd relapse. I was too ill to be moved, and they were afraid that I would be—" He bit off the words that he was about to say.

"They were afraid that you would be discovered. You were in Spanish territory, weren't you?"

"What the deuce makes you say that?" Richard asked, considerably annoyed. She said nothing, and after regarding her fixedly for a moment or two, he simply ignored the question and continued. "In any case, I lay there in the jungle for the better part of a year. When the fever finally left me, I was too weak to travel. As soon as I had recovered enough strength, the Indians got me back to the lumber camp, but then it took several more weeks for the ship to arrive. As soon as we landed in Jamaica, I booked passage on the first ship back to England, and of course that crossing took a couple of months. Here, what's this?"

Annis' head had fallen against his shoulder and the tears that she had held in so long were cascading unashamedly down her face. She had his lapel crushed in her hands. She looked up at him at these words, the tears still flowing. "Oh, Richard," she managed to sob.

"Seems cursed mean-spirited of you to cry at me when I've returned from the dead," he said reprovingly, but he extracted a lawn handkerchief from his pocket and began to dry her face with it. "Tears just won't do, my girl!" he said gently, lifting her chin with one finger to look into her eyes.

She allowed him to perform his chosen office. "I . . . I'm just so glad you're alive," she stammered between sniffs.

"You have a deuced odd way of showing it," he commented wryly.

They were so close, their faces almost touching. The air suddenly seemed thicker to Annis, making it hard to breathe. A strange heat was coursing through her veins. Richard had the oddest expression on his face. She could feel his warm breath upon her cheeks. She could smell the familiar masculine scent of him. There was the little scar beside his right eye where he had fallen and split his brow. Without thinking what she was doing, she reached out a finger to touch it. He drew in a sharp breath, awakening them both from the spell.

"The devil, Taggy! I shouldn't even be here alone with you, since we're not married."

She had quite forgotten that they weren't. "Oh, Richard, what are we to do?"

He glanced about them uneasily. "We shouldn't be talking about all this where anyone might hear. We'd better go home and talk there."

"Home?"

He frowned at her. "Dash it, yes, Taggy. It's going to look peculiar to everyone if your long-lost husband stays in a hotel, isn't it?"

Accordingly, the carriage was called for, and Sir Richard and Lady Burham rode back to Burham House. It wasn't until they actually arrived that Annis gasped, "My goodness, I forgot about Elizabeth and Louisa!"

"Send the carriage back for them," Richard suggested. His face was full of pain and weariness, but Annis did not notice.

"Yes, but I did not even tell them where I was going, or . . . well, I suppose they will have heard of your return by now, so perhaps it will not seem so very odd."

"Mmph."

The carriage stopped, and Annis turned to look at Richard, but she could not see his features in the dark. She descended from the carriage in silence, but she could not miss Richard's stifled groan as he set his weight on his injured limb.

"We must have a doctor see to that," she said with concern.

"It's not much use. Saw one in Jamaica. Told me I was lucky I didn't lose the leg and that I'd always be crippled."

She gasped in dismay at his choice of words, but she could not say anything, for Greenlaw had spotted his master and was greeting him with an indecorous effusion of spirits. "Told me you were dead, they did, but I'd have none of it. Told them you'd be home. Lady Burham here has been in charge of things, but—"

"Please, Greenlaw. Sir Richard is not well, and he needs to go directly to his chamber to lie down."

"Yes, my lady." He called one of the younger footmen over. Despite Richard's growling that he was not an invalid, it was evident that he was glad of the support. With their arms about him, they helped him up the stairs and into his room.

Since Richard had not brought his man with hm, Annis gave orders that Laurie's valet was to be summoned, and set about making the bed ready herself. As soon as the footmen had departed, Richard limped over to her and caught her by the arm.

"We must talk."

She shook her head briskly. "You are too weary and feeling far too ill tonight. We will talk in the morning."

He would not let go of her arm. "I had already thought it all out, Taggy, and the thing is that we'll have to be married tomorrow, as discreetly as possible. I'll set off in the morning to get the special license and find a church."

Annis could feel her eyes beginning to fill again. How typical of him it was. Just when you least expected it, he would have to go and do something noble, without any sort of fuss. He had made no protest over the necessity of wedding to save her good name. "Richard . . ." she began brokenly.

He saw what was coming, "I say, Taggy, don't start the waterworks again." He gave her an awkward hug. "After all, we're a year and a half late for the ceremony as it is."

She looked up at him, smiling gratefully through her tears. She meant to give him an appreciative sisterly peck on the cheek, but somehow her lips found his and the kiss turned into something quite different. It sent the blood racing through her veins and her arms twining up about his neck. She was molded to him inseparably, and she thought that she would die of happiness. A knock on the door ended the moment, and the two sprang apart guiltily. "Come in," Richard called.

It was Laurie's valet, Johnson, who entered. Annis saw that it was time to excuse herself. "We will talk tomorrow," she told Richard softly.

"I think we'll do rather more than that," he murmured softly, but he merely kissed her hand decorously before she left the room.

Bemused, she went to prepare for bed herself. With the maid's help she removed her dress, stockings, and petticoats, untied her corset, and donned a filmy nightgown of lawn, abundantly trimmed with lace. The maid loosed her hair and began to brush it, and Annis, staring at her reflection in the glass, thought that she looked like a bride. It was possible that by tomorrow she would be. The thought sent an unanticipated warmth spreading through her. She blushed for her own thoughts.

The maid finished and Annis dismissed her. She clambered into bed, extinguishing the candles, but she knew she could not sleep. She lay unmoving in her bed, her eyes refusing to close, her mind on Richard. The temptation proved too great, at last.

She rose and opened the draperies, letting the light of the full moon flood the room, obviating the necessity for candles. She opened the door that separated her room from Richard's. She could hear his heavy, even breathing. Since the night was so warm, he had left the window thrown open and the room was as light as it were day.

In sleep, his face had reverted to that of a boy. Even though thinner, it was the face of the boy she had loved, had adored for her entire childhood and beyond. She drew closer, fascinated. As she came nearer, it was more obvious how drawn the face was. There were new lines about the mouth and eyes.

He muttered something in that hoarse, deep voice and turned his head restlessly on the pillow. The sensible thing would have been to leave the room, but Annis could not bear to go yet. She knelt gently beside the bed. One hand reached out tentatively to rest for just an instant on the dark blond hair. "Richard," she whispered. He did not stir. "Richard, I love you." He lay unmoving as before. It was a foolish fancy of hers. Such confession might easily be left until tomorrow. They had the rest of their lives, after all. Though the night was warm, she could not repress a shiver, and she drew her arms about her. Fortune could not desert them now. They had been through too much already.

She took one last lingering look at that face, kissed a fingertip, and touched it lightly to his lips. His mouth twitched, but there was no other reaction. She rose silently, then made her way from the room, closing the door softly behind her.

The brief visit had given her the peace of mind she had been seeking. Nonsensical as it might seem, she had at last told Richard that she loved him. Surely it could not be so much harder to tell him when he was conscious. She had a second chance, an undeserved second chance. Underneath that coolly self-possessed exterior that was habitual with him, she had sensed a depth of feeling. Even given her inexperience, she was certain that he felt more for her than just a physical passion. Their kiss had touched her down to her very soul. She was positive that it had been the same for Richard, that it must be. She had been given her second chance. She would marry him and win his love. It was as simple as that. With these happy thoughts, she drifted off to more pleasant dreams than she had known in ages.

Though Annis was to enjoy peaceful, undisturbed slumber that night, the same could not be said for Richard. It may have been that he unconsciously missed the pitching and rolling of the ship, for his sleep became increasingly restless as the night went on. It was somewhere around three in the morning that the caterwauling awakened him.

He opened his eyes, not certain for a moment where he was. As his tired brain began to digest the information that he was in his own room at Burham House, it took on the additional task of trying to analyze the noise that poured in through the open windows. He sat up in bed, shaking his head, and covered his ears.

Sir George Reeves, still unaware of events at the ball, had been enjoying the congratulations of his friends at the club. It was clear that by actually rescuing the lovely widow from peril he had all but secured the position of prospective husband.

Betting had commenced as to the date, and Sir George, who had been imbibing more deeply than he ought, had confidently advised his friends to wager on an early one. As must always happen with any proposed endeavor, the doomsayers appeared almost instantly, and increased in number as the night progressed. An ugly suggestion was made that the widow might intend to preserve her single status. Sir George scoffed at the notion, though it planted the first seed of doubt in his mind. An observant gentleman remarked that the widow might well prefer a foreigner, since one had only to recall how much time she had spent with that questionable Spaniard. Sir George pretended to laugh at the idea, but it made him rather uneasy. The Spaniard was a handsome dog, after all, and there was no denying that females were apt to be taken in by such. He defended the honor of his intended by declaring that she had far too much sense to prefer a slimy foreigner to an honest Englishman. The devil's advocate noted that foreigners were well known for the insidious ways that they used to capture a female's affections. A long and tragic history followed of one such female, taken in and later deserted by a penniless Italian. Through the increasing thickness of the alcoholic haze, Sir George perceived that his self-confidence might have been seriously misplaced, and beads of perspiration caused by more than the heat stood out on his forehead. If he had considered the matter, he might have realized that despite all his outward devotion, he was hardly in love with the widow, and moreover, that he had no need of her fortune, but logic had little to say to a man who had already downed the better part of three bottles of port.

His honor was clearly at stake, and he must devise an immediate way to secure the widow's affections. He begged his companions to leave him alone so that he could think, which quite startled them, for it was not an activity in which he often indulged. Several more glasses were needed to aid him in this process, which apparently culminated successfully, for an unwontedly devious and cunning look came into his eyes.

If the foreigner knew how to insinuate himself with the widow, Sir George was more than willing to play the same game. There was no law that said that honest English gentlemen were obliged to desist from using identical sorts of tricks. He called over the well-informed gentleman who previously had been plaguing him so and pleaded with him to reveal the ways in which the Italian gentleman of the story had managed to enslave the poor female's heart. This gentleman was both pleased and bewildered to be so addressed, for though he enjoyed being a font of knowledge, none that he possessed was very specific in nature. For want of a better reply, he scowled deeply and replied that the Italian had used typical foreigner's tricks. This was not enough for Sir George, who desperately grasped the fellow by the sleeve and in a most touching manner entreated the gentleman to cite an example, at least one. Realizing that at last he had found the one person that understood the depth of his perspicacity, the gentleman searched his memory for information regarding the customs peculiar to foreigners and managed to come up with one idea. The Italian had serenaded the lady, of that there could be no doubt. Women were so susceptible to music and love songs and such, particularly when delivered in a foreign language. Beside himself with gratitude, Sir George thanked the gentleman, told him that he would always be his servant, and departed the club in haste.

To hire a group of musicians sometime after midnight for a performance the same evening was a difficulty, but not an insurmountable one for a gentleman so handy with the ready as Sir George. The idea of singing in a foreign lauguage troubled him for some minutes, particularly since he was not familiar with any tongue but his own. Happily he recollected that he had once been complimented for his performance of a group of Scotch airs, and he could not doubt that that particular language must be considered a foreign one. The disclosure that none of his little band of musicians were familiar with these songs did not trouble him in the least. They might easily follow him.

The time required for his operation had not served to sober him overmuch. He arrived at Burham House with his troupe, and was delighted to see a set of upstairs windows open. Luck was smiling on him tonight indeed. He arranged the group of musicians to his satisfaction and bravely launched into "The Birks of Abergeldie."

Sir George had long been renowned as the possessor of a

pleasant voice, and he had every confidence that this manner of wooing could not fail. He had forgotten to take into account a few minor circumstances. For one, although he did possess a good singing voice, it had been some years since he had employed it regularly, and his instrument had not benefited from this disuse. Also, he had failed to calculate what sort of volume would be necessary to rouse a sleeper in a second-floor bedroom. Though he continued to sing louder and louder, it appeared for several moments that his fair audience was not going to awaken, and the strain of singing at the top of his abilities was beginning to tell on him. Finally he had totally forgotten, if he ever knew, that large quantities of alcohol are apt to play havoc with one's sense of pitch. The musicians beside him winced and, lacking a particular key to employ, played rather tentative random notes, adding to the general discord.

Bemused Sir Richard, sitting in his room above, could hear a drunken tenor voice screeching, "Ye shall get a gown o' silk and a coat of callimankie" to the apparent accompaniment of several cats in heat. There was no humanly possible way to make sense of the cacophony, so he resignedly rose, and in his night-gown made his way to the balcony.

The sight of a drunken dandy singing a Scotch air at the top of his lungs, surrounded by a shabby-looking and embarrassed group of musicians, did not offer any obvious explanation to Sir Richard's mind. He was oppressed by the need to end this noise somehow, anyhow.

"What the devil are you doing?" he growled, striving to make himself heard over the din.

The star performer paused in the midst of singing "my minny will be angry" and gazed up at the white form that shimmered and swayed in the moonlight above. A servant, he reckoned. "I'm here to serenade Lady Burham. One of her suitors. Sir George Reeves."

A feeling of disgust and anger smote Richard. Was this the sort of fellow she had meant to replace him with? A well-known idiot? Well, it was too late now. "I'll thank you not to annoy my wife any further."

The deep voice rolled sepulchrally out into the sudden silence and echoed off the buildings in the empty street. A cold feeling began to edge its way down Sir George's spine. Surely he was at the right house. He squinted upward to try to bring that pale figure into focus. He could see a loose white garment of some sort billowing about the fellow. There was a bloodless face, and with an effort he could make out stern features, with a familiarly arrogant nose, deep-set eyes, a firm chin, and . . . He blanched. "My God! It's Sir Richard's ghost in his winding sheet!"

His companions, already dubious about this late-night engagement, needed no more encouragement to scatter like the winds. Sir George was left staring only a moment longer before he abruptly realized that he was alone. Without further ado he took to his heels with an agility that belied the amount of wine he had consumed.

It was some twelve hours later that Richard and Annis stood hand in hand in a small church on the outskirts of London and exchanged their vows. Annis had borrowed one of Elizabeth's dresses, of white muslin decorated with French work. It was quite modish, with a little ruff around the neck and sleeves composed of a series of puffs extending all the day down the arms. Richard looked as well as he could in a blue coat and fawn-colored pantaloons, though his clothes hung sadly loose on him. The reverend gentleman performing the service thought that both of the participants looked a trifle pale, and hoped that he was not officiating at a runaway match, although the extreme youthfulness of the bride made him fear otherwise.

Richard's hand was surprisingly cold in hers as they spoke, though Annis thrilled to the sound of that deep and husky voice as he made his responses. Richard had seemed rather remote this morning. The intimacy of the previous night was gone. Of course, he had a great deal on his mind. Many details had to be taken care of, and he doubtless was fatigued. She was not entirely aware of just how fatigued he was, since she had slept through the entire visit of her would-be suitor, and Richard had not informed her of it.

Richard had accepted the welcome and good wishes of her family most gracefully. They had seemed to think their abandonment at the ball the most natural thing in the world, fortunately. Laurie had appeared genuinely delighted to see Richard also. She couldn't help but be proud of him as he stood beside them. He had forsaken the horrid spotted kerchief about his neck for a plain one, and his clothes were quite as sober as Richard's, though they certainly fitted him better at the moment.

It would have been nice to have Elizabeth here also, but her sister, against her own wishes, had wisely insisted upon remaining home. If they were to keep this delayed marriage a secret, Elizabeth would be needed there to fob off those curious about Sir Richard's return.

"You know that Aunt Berinthea, for one, will come over here immediately. It would seem most peculiar for the entire family to be gone today, and I am the logical one to remain." She had given her sister a warm hug and added, "I will be there with you in spirit anyway." The bespectacled blue eyes had gazed directly into Annis' dark ones. "This . . . this *is* what you want, isn't it, sister?"

Annis had smiled at her. "Yes. You were right all along. It is Richard for me, and it always has been."

"Then I am so glad for you." Tears had sprung to Elizabeth's eyes, but she had given her sister a playful little push. "You had better be off, then—you wouldn't wish to be late to your own wedding."

Her words had given Annis pause for thought. If even Elizabeth had believed that Annis might be in love with Walter Ulverstone, it was evident what the rest of London would think. Of course, they had not announced their engagement yet, or had they? She tried desperately to remember what the overefficient Louisa had said about sending in a notice to the papers. Perhaps she should have glanced at the *Chronicle* this morning. No, someone surely would have mentioned it. She must remember to tell Richard about it, though. He probably would think it a great joke. Her thoughts were jerked back into the present as she heard "You may kiss the bride."

She would have been quite happy with a repetition of their performance on the previous night, but as it was, Richard managed only a brief chaste salute on the lips. He doubtless was concerned for decorum, she thought, forgetting that Richard had always been renowned for his scorn of the proprieties. His lips seemed cold to hers, though, which was odd on such a warm day. He was still so ill, of course. She must begin the task of nursing him back to health.

Although Elizabeth thought she was prepared for every contingency, she was caught off-guard when their first visitor was announced. It was quite a dilemma. She did not feel that she could simply refuse to see him. "Send Mr. Ulverstone in," she told Greenlaw with a feeling of trepidation.

He entered the drawing room, his face downcast. When he looked up and saw her, he could not disguise his surprise.

"Annis and Sir Richard have gone out," Elizabeth told him quickly, "but I thought it best to tell you in person. I'm sorry," she added inadequately.

"What? Oh, thank you," he replied absentmindedly. "Do you know, I never knew you wore spectacles."

Drat! She had been so rattled that she had forgotten to remove them before he entered. She slipped them off quickly now. "I wear them only at home," she replied truthfully.

"Don't remove them on my account," Walter told her. "Truth is, they give your face a different sort of expression, cleverer somehow." He realized what he had said and sounded embarrassed. "Please forgive me. I am often too forthright. But do leave them on."

Elizabeth was reluctant to assume the disfiguring objects, but Walter urged her. "No, I meant what I said. Do you know, I never really had the impression you were actually looking at me before? I always felt as if you were looking a little beyond me."

Honesty was Elizabeth's chief vice. In a tight, constricted voice she replied, "I cannot see very well without them."

"Well, then, put them on." He added with an expression she could not see, "After all, we were almost family."

Was he in pain? Was he jesting? It did seem ridiculous to stand on ceremony with him at this awkward moment. She put the spectacles back on. He looked at her with approval. "That's better."

His face was grave. She could not tell how troubled it might be. They were remarkably intelligent gray eyes, she thought, admiring her first clear view of them. If not outlandishly handsome like Don Alonzo, he was nevertheless a very attractive man. It was a strong face, a kind face, and an open one. It well matched what she already knew of his personality. She suddenly remembered her manners. "Won't you sit down?"

He hesitated. "I'm sorry. I have already been unforgivably rude, and prying, and dictatorial. Perhaps I should leave instead."

He stood before her, abashed, and Elizabeth felt a sudden rush of pity for him. Although he was gentleman enough to conceal it, it must be terribly painful to lose a fiancée in such an abrupt and unexpected way. She smiled warmly at him. "After all the trouble you have taken to make me replace my spectacles in your presence, it would be a shame to render the effort naught by leaving. I was rather bored by myself anyway. Would you care to join me in a cup of tea?"

How odd it was that this girl whom he had always thought of as being rather stiff and stupid could set him at ease with so little apparent effort. He found, suddenly, that he wanted to stay. "Thank you, I would," he said, settling gracefully into a chair.

As she rang the bell and asked the servant to bring tea, Walter reached over to take hold of the folio she had laid aside. "Do you mind?" he asked genially. When she shook her head, he opened it.

"I can't believe that you were bored with this. A Caxton, too. Wherever did you get it?"

She shrugged slightly as she resumed her chair. "I brought it from our library at Thurstan, where it was lying, covered with dust. I doubted anyone had looked at it in years, and I thought it would do no harm to bring it with me to London."

He looked up from the page to regard her keenly. "Do you actually enjoy reading Chaucer?"

Elizabeth dropped her eyes, embarrassed. "I suppose it would not be considered suitable fare for a young lady"—she looked up and met his eyes defiantly—"but yes, I do enjoy it."

He stared at her for a few moments, his expression enigmatic. She could not stand it. "What is it?" she demanded.

Recalled to himself, he gave his head a little shake. "Nothing," he replied. "It was merely . . . that is, it *is* unusual reading matter for a young lady. Most of my acquaintance are uninterested in reading, except for novels, or perhaps poetry."

Elizabeth's chin raised another fraction of an inch. "I enjoy novels *and* poetry also," she said. "Should one type of reading preclude another?" She was beginning to be impassioned about her subject. "It is so easy for you gentlemen to despise our mental capacities. After all, did I ever have an opportunity to learn Greek? Will I ever read the *Aeneid* in the original Latin? It is hardly likely." She snorted contemptuously, realized she had just poured out her heart to a stranger, and flushed with embarrassment.

"You would *like* to learn Greek?" Walter asked, just short of disbelieving.

She shook her head. "I have said too much. Please forgive me. I know this sort of topic must bore a gentleman."

"Not this gentleman, it doesn't." He leaned foward. "I'm interested, truly."

She did not look up. "Annis told me it was worse to be considered a bluestocking than merely shy. As if I knew enough to be a bluestocking! Please forget what I have said. It is just . . ." Her hands curled into fists; she was having trouble keeping a tight rein on herself.

"What? Go on," Walter urged.

All her pent-up resentment began to boil over, all the humiliation she had endured since she had been in London, all the slights, all the catty remarks. "It is just not fair! Look at Laurie, bored out of existence by his lessons, yet he is forced to endure them anyway. It would have been considered a waste of time to spend one of those lessons on either Annis or me. Why did the good Lord give females minds, if all they are expected to be is attractive breeding stock?"

Her emotions had quite run away with her, and she uttered these last words in a heartfelt tone which carried well. It nearly made old Hickeringill drop the tea tray he was carrying in.

She had said the unthinkable. "Oh, no," she moaned, blushing quite bright scarlet and covered in confusion. With a whisper, she managed to assure the butler that they required nothing else as he set down the tray. To his credit, Walter handled the situation with aplomb, acting as if she had said nothing out of the ordinary. He expressed his preference for sweet tea, thus giving her a chance to regain her own composure as she poured. By the time they were settled with cups and cakes, she was able to regard him more or less calmly and say, "I am most sorry for my outburst. I have always been far too outspoken."

There was a speculative look in his eye. "I see no need for an apology. I find your opinions most fresh and interesting. Pray, tell me, how far have you progressed with the Chaucer, or did you just begin it?"

She was able to reply to his commonplace question with some equanimity, and from this topic they proceeded on in an unforced way to discuss Kean's performance in *Othello*, the mysterious author of the Waverley novels, and finally a new poet Mr. Ulverstone had discovered and was certain that Miss Thurstan would enjoy.

They might have continued chatting happily on in an unexceptional way had not another caller been announced. Walter took this as his cue to depart, and so Elizabeth was left to cope with the first of a series of curious visitors. It was not until much later in the day that it occurred to her that she and Walter had never discussed Richard's return or the end of the engagement. When she considered the matter, one fact struck her as being even more peculiar. Admittedly, she did not know him well, but nothing in his speech or looks had made him seem like a man whose heart had just been broken.

13

THE thought of leaving immediately for the country after the wedding had been contemplated and then discarded with regret by Annis. Although it would be understandable that she and Richard would wish for some time alone, he was rather weak to set off instantly on another journey, even a short one. Besides, Annis had not entirely despaired of finding Elizabeth a suitor, though the Season was nearing its close. One could never tell, after all.

With an unexpected display of tact, Lady Downage had invited Elizabeth and Louisa to be her guests for dinner and the theater. Laurie had an engagement with some friends, so the newly wedded pair were left with the house to themselves for the evening.

Annis had borrowed from her sister a most becoming gown in a brilliant shade of crimson silk, heavily embroidered about the neck and hem. She had completed her toilette with particular care, and her maid had arranged her hair in a most attractive new fashion upon the top of her head. It was wonderful not to have to wear a toque or a veil or a cap for once. She knew that she looked well, and the reflection in her mirror confirmed it, though it was owing more to the glow of happiness in her face than to any external adornment. She adjusted one long kid glove and sallied forth to meet her bridegroom.

If Richard were impressed by the charming picture she presented, he certainly did not say so. Nor could she read any admiration in his eyes. In fact, it was hard to read anything whatsoever in his eyes, for they simply refused to meet hers.

Of course, the topic of the wedding was one that could not be discussed in front of the servants. Still, there were many other things they might have talked about. Richard hardly spoke a word, and his countenance was wooden. She was beginning to be a little irritated, on the surface, but deeper down there was hurt. Certainly she had expected better things for the evening of their wedding, and hadn't last night seemed to promise as much? She tried to stifle her resentment. After all, there were servants here, and perhaps Richard did not want to cause talk. Drat it! Why couldn't she have thought to dismiss the servants tonight? She and Richard might easily have eaten a cold collation instead. Then again, she thought, looking at the drawn face across the table from her, it had been a fatiguing day too. Perhaps Richard was just too exhausted to make trivial conversation. He might even be concealing pain with this impassivity. No one was quite as good as Richard at being remote.

A thought abruptly sprang to mind. She had never yet told Richard about Ambrose and their suspicions regarding him. They had simply been too busy today. Of course, they could hardly discuss that in front of the servants either. She must let him know that she had something to talk over with him in private. Another nagging thought occurred to her. There was something else she had meant to remember to tell Richard. Now, what on earth was it?

Dinner seemed interminable to her, but the clock was striking just half-past nine when they finished. She rose gracefully and, trying not to blush, informed Richard that she was feeling quite weary and would be retiring early tonight. She kept her face lowered, afraid that she would encounter a knowing look in the eyes of one of the servants' expressionless faces. When she did raise her eyes, she could not read anything in Richard's impassive countenance. She went upstairs with a heart that was beating somewhat faster than normal.

The maid had quite entered into the spirit of things, laying out the beautifully embroidered lawn nightgown for Annis to wear, and brushing her hair until Annis finally had to order her to stop. She dismissed the girl, and feeling both excited and nervous, took a turn about the room.

She had looked handsome earlier this evening, but tonight in the flickering candlelight she was almost beautiful. She listened eagerly for Richard's footsteps upon the stairs. Had she been Elizabeth, she might have whiled away some of the time with a good book, but Annis had no such resources at her command, for reading always bored her. She did, however, have a fashion magazine, and after quite a while she was forced to resort to perusing it. She could not have any true interest in leghorn hats or limeric gloves at the moment, though, so the pastime left something to be desired.

It was well after eleven when she finally heard Richard's tread. Although she listened hopefully, he did not pause at her door, but went on to his own instead. At first she was both disappointed and angry, but then she realized that he would wish to make himself ready for bed first. She could hear the voice of Laurie's valet, and Richard's responses from the next chamber. There, they had his coat off, and now the manservant was tugging at his boots. Richard had yanked his own cravat off, apparently, and was unbuttoning . . . She realized suddenly what she was doing, turned bright red, and scurried to the other side of the bedroom. It took her only a moment to decide. She slipped under the covers, arranged her hair wantonly over her shoulders, and picked up the magazine with an assumption of carelessness. Even from this distance she could hear Johnson's voice bidding Richard a good night, and the sound of the door closing was unmistakable. She waited, her heart pounding, hardly remembering to breathe.

The door that led to his chamber opened slowly and Richard entered in his dressing gown. She hoped that the smile on her face was more inviting than nervous. My word, he was thin. It was even more obvious in his nightwear. He was pale too, paler than she remembered his being at dinner.

"Annis," he said. She didn't even notice that he was not calling her by her usual nickname. "I thought I'd better tell you . . . that is . . . well, to be frank, my physical condition is such that I cannot perform the duties expected of a husband."

She gazed at him in shock. "Oh." It was not quite a question and not quite an exclamation.

"Yes, well, I thought I should tell you so. Good night."

She watched speechlessly as he walked away, closing the door behind him. Disappointment, hurt, and anger warred within her for several minutes. How dared he? Without so much as a hint! *Duties* indeed! He certainly hadn't seemed incapacitated the previous night. After several more minutes, sympathy asserted itself. He was very tired, after all. Hadn't he looked pale? His illness was one that was likely to come and go. It had probably humiliated him to have to come and confide in her. He had probably been dreading it all night—that was why he had taken so long to come upstairs to bed. She should have gone to him and kissed him on the cheek, smoothed that tired brow, and told him that it didn't matter, that they had the rest of their lives before them. What sort of an inhuman monster was she, anyway?

She leapt up from bed and crossed over to the door. She opened it and peeked into his chamber, but it was dark. She listened for a moment, but she could hear nothing but quiet breathing. Her poor darling! He had probably fallen asleep before he landed in the bed. She shook her head and closed the door. She was certainly starting off on the wrong foot if she were hoping to win his love.

As the door closed, Sir Richard sighed and opened his eyes again. Annis' worry might have taken quite a different direction had she known that in his wastebasket lay a crumpled copy of that day's *Morning Chronicle,* with a page torn out of the section where engagements were announced.

When Annis arose late the next morning, she discovered that Richard was already gone. The servants could not enlighten her as to his destination. He had told them only that there were matters he had to take care of and that he would be gone for quite some time. Annis had forgotten all about his packet for the foreign secretary's office. Doubtless he needed to dispose of that as well as to check on business matters. She hoped that he would be pleased with what she had accomplished in that department. Given that Richard was likely to be away the better part of the day, Annis did the only thing a sensible young lady could do when her husband suddenly returns from the grave. She went shopping.

It was evident that an entire new wardrobe would be required immediately. She would need shoes, gloves, bonnets, reticules, dresses, all sorts of things to proclaim her new status. What a joy it was to examine the red, yellow, blue, and amber silks instead of being forced to choose between black crepe and black bombazine, or perhaps net. Annis did not care that black was fashionable, or how well it became her; she never intended to wear it again.

She had placed a handsome order with the dressmaker and another with the milliner, which of course left all the sundries to be purchased. It was heaven not to have to worry about the cost of everything, as she had begun to do lately. That reminded her about Ambrose. She must write him a letter, informing him of Richard's return, and she must remember to share her suspicions about him with Richard. She had complete faith in her husband's ability to take care of that situation with the minimum amount of fuss.

A shop window had caught her eye, in particular a lovely scarf of blue net woven with a floral pattern in yellow silk. It would look charming with the new yellow ball gown she had ordered. She turned to her sister to ask if she did not think so, but Elizabeth's eyes were cast hungrily upon a bookstore across the street. It seemed Louisa had espied a particular much-desired volume sitting right in its window. Elizabeth had been looking for it for the longest time, and would Annis mind too much if they stopped there? Annis had a pessimism born of experience concerning Elizabeth and bookstores. She knew that once her sister went in, no one would see her again for hours. Elizabeth assured Annis that she was wrong, that once she purchased this volume she would be happy to return and help Annis with her decision. Fortunately, with Louisa's help, a compromise was struck. Annis might take the maid with her and go in to examine the lovely scarf more closely. Elizabeth and Louisa would go across the street. They would return as soon as Elizabeth had bought the book. Annis could not help but be suspicious, and she had no intention of being caught for hours in a musty old bookstore, but she had little choice but to agree to such a reasonable request.

A closer view confirmed that the scarf was every bit as handsome as she had thought it. It was evident that she must buy it. There was also a charming reticule in amber netted silk which would, if she were not mistaken, perfectly complement her new pelisse. She was tempted by some ribbons and some truly beautiful lace handkerchiefs, but she decided that she must curb her expenditures somewhat. It would not do to be too extravagant the very first day of her married life.

Elizabeth and Louisa had failed to appear by the time she had paid for her purchases, so Annis decided to await them outside the shop. Perhaps if they saw her standing vulnerable to the gazes of the Bond Street loungers, it would incline them to make their selections more rapidly and leave.

The maid was already quite burdened with parcels, since they had left the carriage some distance back. Annis had decided to carry this latest one herself, for it would be ruinous for it to be dropped in a puddle. She was growing impatient, however, and unfortunately she began to fidget. She was twisting the strings of the parcel in her hands when it suddenly came untied. With a cry of dismay she stepped forward and tried in vain to keep her latest prize from fluttering to the ground. She was unsuccessful in the attempt, but as she was leaning forward, she felt a sudden rush of air behind her, followed by a crash. Fragments of something shattering caught at the back of her skirts, scratching her legs. She picked up the scarf and reticule and turned around. Her maid's face was white. A matter of inches behind her lay a broken flowerpot. Dirt, pottery, and geraniums were scattered for several feet.

"Oh, my lady, you might have been killed." Tears were starting to flow down the girl's cheeks.

Almost unthinkingly Annis glanced up at the building above her. There were no anxious faces to be seen, no apologetic cries issuing from above, no loud reprimands being given to a careless servant. Louisa and Elizabeth came rushing from across the street. The commotion had begun to attract a crowd. Annis suddenly felt very exposed. "Let us go to the carriage quickly," she ordered.

Annis spent the rest of the day in some anxiety, awaiting Richard's return. She alternated between irritation with him for leaving for the day on such little notice and fear for his safety. Laurie was no help to her, for he had returned quite late last night, and upon arising sometime after noon, had taken himself off to Luffy's lodgings. The latter gentleman was considering the purchase of a "prad," and Laurie's opinion apparently was requisite for a "look-in" at Tatt's.

A book had arrived for Elizabeth during their absence. At another time Annis might have found it strange that her sister did not mention whom it was from. As it was, she only noticed that Elizabeth soon had her nose buried in it, entirely oblivious of the possibility of her sister's imminent murder.

Louisa likewise provided little support. After an hour or so of watching Annis pace about the room, she had ventured to ask hesitantly whether her presence were required. She would not wish to abandon Annis in such a time of crisis, but then again, she had promised Mr. Williams that she would make a great effort to come today. Oh, hadn't she mentioned Mr. Williams? Yes, it was the same—well, the same one who had been so helpful in the matter of the you-know-what. Yes, he was aiding her with the project the general was helping to sponsor. Why, hadn't she told Annis about it? She must do so, in great detail, but the problem was that the hour was becoming rather late and she was afraid she might miss him entirely if . . .

Annis sighed and told her she might go. Louisa spurned the suggestion that she take the carriage, but she did accept the company of the maid when offered.

It wasn't until after she left that Annis recalled the matter of the engagement announcement. She must remember to ask Louisa if it had been sent to the papers. She supposed that yesterday's paper had been disposed of long ago.

Her questions on that head were soon to be answered. A clamor in the entryway heralded the arrival of her aunt. Lady Downage entered, waving a copy of the *Morning Chronicle* and asking Annis what she intended to do about it. Annis took the paper from her and grimaced. The announcement of her engagement to Walter was featured prominently. What a mercy it was that Richard hadn't seen it. She turned around to see what Elizabeth had to say, but somehow that damsel had managed to sneak out of the room before her aunt's arrival, in order to ensure that her enjoyment of her new book would be uninterrupted. Meanwhile, there was still her aunt's question to be answered. She wrinkled her nose.

"Well, really, Aunt, I don't see that there is anything to be done. Almost everyone in town knows the truth by now, or will shortly, I'm sure."

Lady Downage refused to take the situation so lightly. "But had you considered the scandal? You and Sir Richard will be the subject of discussion wherever you go. I think you should leave London immediately."

As usual, Annis was beginning to be a little irritated by Lady Downage's dictatorial manner. There was some sense in what her aunt said, but there were other things to be considered. For one, there was Elizabeth, who might yet find a husband. For another, there was the matter of Richard's business. She didn't even know what it was that he was doing today, let alone how long it would take. He might need to remain in town for weeks. She drew herself up to her full five-foot-two-inch height. "That is surely a matter between Sir Richard and me."

Her aunt, having made herself comfortable in a chair, merely shook her head. "You needn't get on your high horse with me. If it's Elizabeth, you may leave her with me, although I am not sanguine about her expectations. Had you considered, Annis, that it is you who will suffer the most? At the very best, you will be seen as inconstant in your affections, while at the worst . . ." She fanned herself with the paper absentmindedly, shaking her head all the while.

Annis was doubly offended. At first she had been touched by her aunt's offer to take Elizabeth, but that feeling of gratitude was quickly squelched by the criticism of her sister that followed. She could not think of leaving Elizabeth with someone who understood her so little. The idea that anyone would venture to animadvert upon her own conduct enraged her. Hadn't she worn mourning well beyond the prescribed period? Hadn't she taken her place with the dowagers, refusing to dance? Hadn't she repulsed all her suitors, or almost all, anyway? No other person could know what was in her heart—the pain she had lived with for well over a year, a pain that had invaded when she awoke every morning and that had been there when she went to bed every night. Neither could anyone know of the danger she had been facing, a danger that had made Walter's offer of protection most attractive. If it had not been for that, and family considerations, she would not have accepted him. She was so furious that it was hard for her to speak, but finally she managed to say chokingly, "I do not care what anyone in London may think of me. I consider that my conduct has been beyond reproach. I could not have known that Richard was still alive when I became engaged to Walter, and you yourself were urging me to marry."

"You are not attending to me," Lady Downage said with

some severity. "I did not say that you had done anything wrong. I am merely talking about how it might *appear* to others."

"You think we should run, then?" Annis asked her angrily.

"I think it would be easier on you to remove yourself from any unpleasantness. Some other scandal will oust you as a topic for discussion, but you may be very uncomfortable until then."

"We will just have to live with that." Annis' chin was up and she regarded Lady Downage with defiance. "Would you care for tea?"

Clearly there was no point in Lady Downage's arguing further with her thickheaded niece. Well, the next few days would prove the truth of what she was saying. She herself might brush through the thing easily enough. She accepted Annis' offer, and by the time tea was finished, some measure of peace had been restored.

It wasn't until well after Lady Downage's departure that Richard finally came home. Annis, who thus had been given a great deal of time to reflect upon her grievances, was simmering with anger by the time he arrived. When he entered the drawing room and plopped down casually in a chair, without a word of either explanation or apology for his absence, she could scarcely contain her wrath.

"That's a devilish peculiar table over there," he observed, waving a hand in the direction of one of the acquisitions in which Annis took great pride. In the latest, Gothic, mode, it consisted of a thick hexagonal wood surface supported by three grotesquely leering gargoyles. He shuddered with distaste as he encountered the glare of the nearest one. "That's an evil expression the fellow has in his eye."

Goaded, Annis could not control a sarcastic bent. "It may interest you to know," she remarked, "that someone tried to kill me today."

He did not endear himself to her by his response, which was to break into laughter. He saw that she was serious, and controlled himself, though a smile remained on his face. "Come now, Taggy, what is it? Have you been reading some of those rubbishy novels?"

"You know I don't read," she retorted angrily. "This was only the latest attempt. There have been others."

She could see by his face that he still did not believe her, though in her anger she did not notice how tired that face was. "Very well, then, you'd better have a seat and tell me about it."

Notwithstanding the reluctance of the offer, Annis proceeded to tell him what had happened that morning, followed by a description of the incident in the park. She did not notice the little spasm that crossed his features when Sir George Reeves's name was mentioned, nor did he see fit to enlighten her about the serenade. From this beginning she proceeded to delve into the entire history of Ambrose's double dealings, from her first suspicions to the confrontation before she left for Jamaica.

"No wonder you were so eager to marry me," he said softly, but caught up in her recital, she did not hear his words.

She continued on, describing Ambrose's suspicious behavior upon their return, his attempts to block the dissolution of the trust, and the two suspicious carriage accidents. Didn't it seem odd that he had made these trips to London to try to persuade Elizabeth to leave, and that he had been visibly upset when he thought Elizabeth was to be married? And wasn't it an odd coincidence that the accidents had begun happening just after his last visit? It occurred to Annis that Richard wasn't expressing the surprise he ought. She remarked on it.

He shifted uncomfortably in his chair, but Annis had forgotten about the pain his leg might be causing him. He replied carelessly, "Surprised? Good Lord, no. I was fairly certain about Ambrose before I left. That was why my will read the way it did. I wish I'd had time to take care of him before I left, but other matters were more pressing." He shrugged. "I can't imagine Ambrose going to the lengths you describe. He's just not the sort. I suspect it was just an unlucky series of accidents. Why, a rein might break or a horse might bolt any day. Happens all the time. You're becoming fanciful in your old age, Taggy," he added unsympathetically.

Any gratification she was feeling at the mention of the will was obliterated by these last few sentences. "I am certainly not fanciful," she said, firing up again, "and it is no very pleasant thing to have these narrow brushes with death. I *insist* that you do something about Ambrose *immediately.*"

He shifted again, not meeting her eyes. "Well, you needn't worry about *him* in any event. I've spiked his guns fairly effectively."

"What do you mean?"

"Went to talk to Fishwick today. Had papers drawn up making me Elizabeth's new trustee. Mean to go down to the Briars tomorrow to have him sign them."

Hope flared in Annis' face. "Oh, Richard, do you think he will?"

"He won't have much choice. He wouldn't like to be dragged into court for mishandling the trust, not that I should like it either, but I think the threat is enough. Besides, he can't afford to pay back what he's taken." He looked up at her. "Sorry about the money that's gone, Annis, but I look upon it as the price we pay for ridding ourselves of him. I thought I might even offer to buy him and his wife passage to Jamaica. He could make a fresh start there."

The ominous threat that had been hanging over her all these months abruptly dissipated. With a few sentences Richard had merely blown it away. He made it all look so easy. It was as she had always known, that despite his careless manner she could depend on him absolutely. Her eyes began to moisten. "Oh, Richard," she said softly.

He sighed, unobserving. "Meant to tell you also. Spent some time with Robbins, the man of business in the City. You never told me you had a shrewd head for figures, Taggy. Seems that investment you made in the shipping company is paying off a hundredfold. Have to thank you for making me, or us, richer." He was having trouble paying her the compliment, but it made her eyes even fuller. His last words struck her. Surely he had seen that she hadn't touched a penny of his money, that it was all his? "Richard—" she began.

He pushed himself awkwardly to his feet. "Sorry, Taggy. I think I'd better go upstairs and rest. The leg's giving me the devil of a time. Too much walking today. Would you send dinner upstairs for me?"

Again she was struck by her own monstrous selfishness. "I'm sorry. Shall I call a footman to help you?"

"No, think I'll manage."

She watched him limp from the room, holding back her tears only with difficulty, and it wasn't until he had gone that she realized she had not yet told him about her engagement. She must tell him soon. Tomorrow, without fail.

14

ANNIS had quite forgotten that Richard would be in Kent all the next day. He had decided to spent the night there, which hurt her feelings somewhat, though she told herself that there was no sense in his posting back to arrive in the wee hours of the morning. He was also gone the better part of the second day, but he had already warned her that he meant to meet with the manager of his estate to see how matters stood. She was at first disappointed, then angry when night fell and he again failed to materialize. With the threat of Ambrose removed, she no longer felt the need for remaining confined to the house, so she decided to enact her own sort of revenge by going on another shopping spree the next day.

Although Elizabeth was unaccountably missing, Louisa professed herself happy to accompany Annis when she was ready to set off the next morning. Unfortunately Annis simply could not take the interest in clothes that she had a few days before. She told herself sternly that Richard was taking care of important business and that some of it was her own, but she could not help feeling abandoned, and reflected that she had imagined that at least the *first* few days of her marriage would be happy.

She was torn between two conflicting feelings. On the one hand she wanted to be sympathetic to Richard, to realize that he was still very ill and that he needed her care. On the other hand, a quiet little voice inside her had begun to whisper that because of her love for Richard, she might have imposed her own desires on him. She might have dreamt so fervently that he was in love with her that it seemed to her that he was upon his return. After all, Richard had never spoken a word of love to her, not before going to Jamaica, and not after coming back. He felt an obligation to her and her family, particularly since he was Laurie's guardian. Was that all there was to it? She tried to tell herself that a friendship was all that was needed for a good marriage, but it was cold comfort to her. "I am tired, let us go home," she exclaimed abruptly, startling her companion.

Elizabeth, in a different part of town, was also worrying about her sister. After receiving an urgent note from Mr. Ulverstone, she had taken her maid and gone to meet him at the British Museum. There were pleasures associated with this outing, for she had not previously had an opportunity to examine the treasures there. When Walter came up to her with an apology for asking her to meet him in such a place, she therefore was able to respond honestly that it was quite a treat for her.

"I am sorry," he said ruefully, "but I needed to speak with you privately and I thought it might cause talk if I took you driving in my carriage."

Elizabeth smiled. "I am perfectly sincere. I have just been looking at the Rosetta stone. It was a thrill to me to finally see it. But what did you wish to discuss with me?"

He indicated a bench and they seated themselves, the maid maintaining a decorous distance. "Would you mind putting on your spectacles?" he asked. "I can talk with you much more easily if we can see each other." There were few people about at the moment, so she complied.

Walter smiled at her, then began, "I am afraid that Sir Richard is taking the news of the engagement in rather the wrong way."

"What do you mean?"

"I saw him the day before yesterday—he had a packet to give to me—and I thought it best to bring up the subject, in order to do away with any unpleasantness."

"What did he say?"

"That was it. He said nothing, nor would he listen to any of my explanations. He treated me much the same as ever—you know that lighthearted way of his—but he simply wouldn't let me say anything about the matter. All he said was that he already knew about it and that there was no sense in discussing it at this point."

"Perhaps he did not regard it as a serious matter," Elizabeth suggested, watching Walter's face closely.

"I would swear that is not true, for he pokered up whenever I came close to talking about it. I think he may be laboring under some misapprehension. He needs to know that there was nothing between Lady Burham and myself but mutual respect and friendship. Certain circumstances simply pressed us into engaging ourselves to each other."

A burden that she did not know that she bore began to lift from Elizabeth's heart. She dropped her eyes and toyed with her reticule. "Perhaps he would not quite believe you, even if you told him."

"That is why I called upon you." Despite herself, she had to look up into those frank gray eyes. "You know your sister better than anyone else, I should think, and I am happy for you to speak on my behalf as well. It was always clear to me that she was still in love with Sir Richard. I should not have offered for her had I not believed that she was in some danger and that I could help her. You must go to Sir Richard and convince him of that."

Her protective shell had fallen away completely. She knew herself now to be open and entirely vulnerable, in direct opposition to the advice of her intelligence. "How?" she asked simply.

"I do not know, but you must do your best. I think if your sister had been able to convince him, he would have been willing to hear me out. They need our help and I do not know anyone else in a position to talk with him."

Elizabeth frowned. "He has been gone for the past two days."

"That confirms what I have been thinking."

She looked at those expressive eyes again and saw the appeal in them. "Will you speak to him?" he asked.

Elizabeth, though she had never experienced any animosity toward Richard, never could understand her sister's attraction to him or Annis' joy in their madcap exploits. He was rather an alien being to her. Though undoubtedly shrewd, he was not at all bookish, and like Annis, he rather scorned the things Elizabeth adored. She couldn't imagine that he would listen to anything she had to say. "I will try," she said finally.

There seemed to be nothing else to say, but he surprised her by asking abruptly, "Have you had a chance to look at the book I sent you?"

She smiled with genuine warmth. "I couldn't put it down. I'm afraid Annis was quite disgusted with me. I shall certainly have to look for other works by him."

"Alas, I am afraid that there are no other books available. This was not received as it ought to have been, but he is a young man yet and I trust that we will see some more from him fairly soon."

From this beginning, it was quite natural for the conversation to turn to a discussion of the specific poems and the merits of each—a thought that captured the fancy, a particular line of sublime beauty—and it was well over an hour later that Elizabeth realized she must be going.

"I can't think what possessed me to remain here so long," she told Walter apologetically. What a bore it must have been for him to have engaged the Ice Maiden in conversation for an hour!

He smiled at her and she could swear that his words were sincere. "I enjoyed every instant of our talk," he said. "One may easily find persons of intellect in a city of this size, but it is rare to encounter someone whose heart beats in such harmony with one's own."

His words made her blush, though they were not intended to produce that effect. Frowning in confusion, she rose and held out her hand. "Thank you, I . . . I shall remember to speak with Sir Richard about the matter we discussed."

To her surprise, he caught her hand in his and did not release it. "Miss Thurstan," he said, "I should . . . I should like to talk with you again sometime."

Heavens, what was she to say? "I would like that too," she replied with innate honesty, though she turned an even darker shade of crimson.

He dropped her hand as if he were startled himself to find it in his, but his smile was warm. "Your servant, then, Miss Thurstan."

She was almost out of the museum before she realized that in her preoccupation she had forgotten to take off her spectacles.

For the rest of the day Elizabeth battled her own confusion and did her best to avoid Annis. It was just so difficult to interpret the situation. She could not rid herself of the notion that she was stealing her sister's suitor, though that of course was nonsense, since Annis was married now. And Annis had said that she had always been in love with Richard. Walter had said the same, and added that he himself had not been in love with Annis. Could she trust his words? His explanation for their engagement certainly seemed believable. It was hard to doubt someone with such an open countenance as his. Perhaps he had that same effect on everyone. Perhaps everyone felt immediately that they could trust him and confide in him. She shook her head. Whatever *he* was, it was certain that *her* heart beat more quickly when she was near him, that a warmth passed through her whenever she met his eyes, that time ceased to exist when she was in his company. All of her intellectual powers could make no sense of this sad puzzle. To be courted by her sister's former fiancé! She could not make a coherent decision yet. She must wait and see what might happen.

Richard was to return late that afternoon. Elizabeth did not have an opportunity to speak with him, for by the time he arrived, both she and Annis were already dressing for Mrs. Weedon's musicale.

When she heard her husband's voice, Annis hurried from her chamber to the top of the landing. Richard looked up at her in some bemusement. She was most becomingly attired in a dark blue gown of net over a matching satin slip. The gown was heavily embroidered about the neck and hem, and caught up under the high waist with a dark blue ribbon. Her maid had not quite finished with her coiffure and her dark curls ran riot about her face in a charming effect that added even more to her appearance of youth. On her cheeks there were spots of color produced by the excitement of her husband's return, and all in all she presented a lovely picture. She gave him a dazzling smile. "Oh, you are home."

"You are going out."

"Yes, to Mrs. Weedon's musicale, thought I must finish dressing and we intend to eat dinner first." He was looking tired, so she added hastily, "But you needn't accompany us. We intend to call for Aunt Berinthea, so we will be adequately chaperoned."

His face, which had relaxed into a smile at the sight of her, now changed at these words, though Annis could not appreciate the cause for this metamorphosis. "So, you've not missed me, I see. Your calendar must be very full." He began up the stairs to her. When he reached her side he said in a low voice, "I will escort you tonight, madam. I, at least, intend to do *my* best to squelch any talk about our marriage."

As if she hadn't been sitting at home waiting for his return! Annis thought angrily. She had meant to tell him how tasteless life had become with him gone, but she certainly would not gratify him now with such a recital. "Very well," she said coldly. "I will put dinner back another half-hour."

He gave her a half-blow in that mocking sort of way that always made her want to slap him, and passed into his chamber, closing the door behind him.

So much for the tender reunion. Annis spun on her heel furiously and returned to her own room.

Although she was still angry with Richard when they sat down to the table, Annis could no longer deny her curiosity. Despite herself, a note of trepidation crept into her voice as she asked what had transpired with Ambrose.

"He signed the papers," Richard said curtly. He glanced at his sister-in-law and his tone softened slightly. "I am your new trustee, Elizabeth—that is, if you have no objection."

She murmured an assent.

"Mr. Fishwick is to bring the documents by tomorrow for you to sign."

Annis could not contain herself. "But what happened? Is he going to Jamaica?"

Richard studied his wineglass for a moment and she knew that he was deciding what he might tell her. Drat the servants anyway, she thought.

"He and Maria booked passage to America next month. She has some sort of cousin there who apparently has some sizable holdings, and the gentleman has offered to employ Ambrose as a manager." Richard returned to his plate with the carelessness that was so typical of him.

Annis and Elizabeth exchanged looks expressive of their relief. With the papers signed and Ambrose soon to leave the country, there was no longer any need to fear for their own safety or to worry that Elizabeth's fortune might gradually be disappearing. The nightmare they had been living with all these months finally was done.

The new harmonious mood was shattered abruptly when Richard asked in a testy voice where Laurie was this evening.

Annis replied that he had a previous engagement, to which Richard responded that he had hoped that Laurie had enough of a sense of responsibility to escort his sisters. Annis, usually the last one to defend Laurie, fired up on his behalf.

"Really, it is unfair to expect a young gentleman to be at his sisters' beck and call all day long. We do not at all depend on his accompanying us and we never have."

Richard replied gravely that he cared little what Laurie did during the day. At night he would like to see Laurie escort his sisters.

Annis gave a brittle laugh. "I am not at all sure that Laurie would welcome your interfering in his affairs."

"It matters little what he thinks about it," Richard said calmly. "I am his guardian."

Annis lapsed into angry silence, but the incident did not bode well for the evening.

Elizabeth, seated nervously between the two, thought that perhaps she should talk with Richard soon. There clearly was something wrong.

They arrived at Lady Downage's house a half-hour late, which irritated their aunt and added more unpleasantness to an already difficult situation. More clearly than any of them, Lady Downage could foresee what effect the unusual history of their marriage would have on the gossips of London, and sadly, she was not to be proved wrong.

The moment they entered Mrs. Weedon's saloon, all voices died and many of the persons there indulged in frankly curious stares. Talk resumed with an intensity and a volume that suggested that this delicious new topic had done much to aid flagging conversation.

Annis could feel the color rising to her cheeks, but she lifted her chin and greeted her hostess with a fair assumption of obliviousness. It was the sort of situation in which Richard's aplomb could be considered an asset. He had no difficulty appearing coolly self-possessed. Elizabeth for once was glad that she could not see the sly glances, and she was able to preserve her reputation as the Ice Maiden without making any great exertion of will.

Richard's friends began to greet him joyfully, and since he tucked her arm firmly into his, Annis was naturally swept up into the welcome. The snubs that Lady Downage had been fearing failed to materialize. It was true that there were still some surreptitious looks and comments, but Lady Downage began to hope that the full-blown scandal she had been fearing would not result. Perhaps the gossip would die down more quickly than she had expected.

She allowed a cautious optimism to infuse her thoughts. Richard and Annis were conducting themselves with propriety and presenting to the world a picture of a close, if not outwardly doting couple. Surely no one would wish to cause them any unpleasantness, particularly considering the tragic nature of Sir Richard's disappearance. Lady Downage's hopes were to be abruptly crushed by the arrival of Walter Ulverstone.

Annis, on Richard's arm, was the first to see him. She felt sick to her stomach and her knees began to buckle. Richard, whose attention had been captured by this unexpected pressure on his arm, looked at her in concern. She was deathly pale.

His eyes followed the direction of her gaze, and his jaw tightened imperceptibly. She was yanked rather harshly upward, until she was standing straight once again. Richard's voice boomed loudly into the sudden silence that had fallen. "If it isn't my oldest friend, Walter Ulverstone," he commented to the room. "We must go and greet him immediately."

He took a step forward, but met some resistance from Annis. He tugged on her arm angrily and hissed in her ear, "Come on, you little fool. Don't you see that this is the only way we can possibly carry the thing off?"

In despair, her eyes met his and read the knowledge there. How had he found out about her engagement, and why hadn't he mentioned it to her? He pulled her forward again, and she went along with him, unresisting.

Walter's impeccable manners did him credit on this occasion.

He appeared glad to see Sir Richard, complimented his wife and her lovely sister, and appeared oblivious of the awkwardness of the situation.

Richard himself played his part well, even going so far as to invite Walter to join their group in finding seats, since the music was to begin shortly. Walter, only too aware of the public scrutiny, quickly agreed with the suggestion.

Annis, who had forced herself to utter the usual commonplaces, could not quite bear to look at Walter. She had never seen him to tell him their engagement was over, after all, even though he must have known it soon enough. She remained pale and slightly nauseous, but she hoped that she was projecting an attitude of great calm and indifference.

She had to be grateful to Elizabeth, who undoubtedly guessed the difficulties she was in and who promptly took upon herself the task of entertaining Walter. Indeed, Elizabeth seemed well able to occupy his attention until the chamber group began, which fortunately relieved them all of the necessity of making polite conversation. Elizabeth proved herself even more selfless, however, for once the quartet had finished, she engaged Walter in a spirited discussion of the merits of various composers. Her countenance was more animated than polite London had ever seen it, and for the first time society was treated to examples of her trilling laugh.

Annis' head was aching dreadfully and she could only just manage to hold it up. Had she thought about it at all, she would have been thankful to her sister for showing that there was no awkwardness between their family and Mr. Ulverstone. All Annis' thoughts, however, were on her husband.

She could not read his expression at all, but then, Richard was better at concealing his thoughts than any other person she knew. That he was angry she suspected from the suppressed violence with which he had handled her and from a certain iciness of manner that would have been apparent to no one but herself. She still could not solve the enigma. Why hadn't he mentioned the engagement to her, if he had already learned of it? It was evident that she had been sadly mistaken believing that he would regard it as a laughing matter. Of course, she thought shamefacedly, she had not brought up the topic either.

She heaved a sigh. She had embarked upon this marriage with such hopes and dreams. All she had met with so far were disappointment, hurt, and anger. She glanced from under her lashes at the impassive countenance beside her. Why did it have to be like this?

From somewhere deep inside her, an old determination asserted itself. She would not allow things to remain in this state. Richard and she had been better companions as mere friends than they were now as husband and wife. There must be a way to reclaim at least that part of their relationship. She would have to talk with him and try to pull from him exactly what was troubling him.

The carriage ride home was filled with tension. Even Lady Downage did not feel secure enough to comment upon the evening. When they had deposited her at home, the silence in the carriage became even grimmer. Elizabeth studied the two brooding faces opposite her in some worry. Walter was right. She must speak with Richard without delay. Of course, there would be no opportunity to talk with Richard tonight. She would have to try to see him before he left in the morning.

When they arrived home, Elizabeth bade the other two a swift good night and fled to her chamber to reflect pleasantly on some of Mr. Ulverstone's more personal observations. Richard and Annis, some little distance behind her, ascended the stairs without speaking. When they reached the second floor, Richard simply would have gone to his chamber without another word, but Annis caught his sleeve. "I must talk with you."

His face expressionless, he followed her into her chamber. She glanced at the waiting maid and dismissed her, then turned to her husband.

"Richard, we must talk about what happened tonight."

He shrugged and threw himself down into a delicate little chair with red cushions. The action might have reminded Annis that his leg was undoubtedly paining him and that he was probably exhausted after his long journey today, but she had only one matter on her mind.

"Why didn't you tell me that you knew of the engagement?"

He looked at her with a gaze of calculated indifference. "There didn't seem to be any point to our discussing it. After all, since you had put it about that you were my widow, we had no choice but to be married. I am sorry to have overset your plans," he added in his most sardonic manner.

Annis did not hear the almost imperceptible note of hurt in his voice. "Of course, I should have known. Everything is always all my fault, isn't it? I should have known that you weren't really dead. I should have gone back to Ambrose like a good little girl and waited for you to return and rescue me instead of trying to give my sister a Season—"

He cut her off. "And just whom was that Season for, Annis—you or Elizabeth? I haven't noticed any of *her* suitors dangling about the house, and *she* certainly isn't engaged. In fact, until tonight I had the distinct impression that she was a very unhappy young lady."

How dared he! When all her sacrifices had been for Elizabeth, the charade had been for Elizabeth, even the engagement had been undertaken partly with the notion of clearing the field for Elizabeth. And of course there was the danger, too, the danger that Richard had scoffed at so cavalierly. That was one of the primary reasons Walter had offered for her, to lend her his protection. Naturally Richard wouldn't listen to this explanation, since he didn't believe in the danger himself. Well, she was not going to give him the satisfaction of trying to justify her action to him. He could believe whatever he wanted, for it was evident that he would not believe what she said anyway.

"Well, I am sorry now that I ever took on this masquerade, though I will say that being your widow was certainly more pleasant than being your wife." The hateful words were out, and it was too late to stop. Annis, horror-stricken, threw out a hand as if she might pull them back from the ether, but the damage was already done.

Richard's lips were curled into a cold and bitter smile. "It certainly seems as if there were no limit to your pleasures," he remarked insinuatingly. He rose. "Good night, madam," he said in a voice that sent a chill wind through her heart. He turned and walked from the room, into his own chamber, closing the door firmly behind him.

Annis had been strong for so very long. Now she realized what she had done, that she had been given a second chance for happiness and had thrown it away forever. She threw herself onto her bed and dissolved into bitter tears.

Rising early the next morning, Elizabeth managed to intercept Richard as he was preparing to leave the house. His face was drawn and wore one of the blackest expressions she had ever seen upon it. Her heart plummeted, but she had promised Walter and would keep her word now. She would have given much to have conferred with the older and more pragmatic Louisa, but that lady already had departed that morning. Really, it was odd how much of the time Louisa seemed to be gone nowadays. She must talk to her about it.

Richard scowled at her fiercely, recalling her to the matter at hand. "Well?" he said uninvitingly.

"I must speak with you."

He looked as if he were ready to turn her down, but there was something compelling in her forthright gaze. With a sigh of repressed impatience he threw his gloves down. "Very well, then. Where shall we talk? The drawing room?"

She agreed and they made their way there. They took their seats and he frowned at her. "What is it?"

It was difficult to know where to begin, but Elizabeth did not lack courage. "I have had a conversation with Mr. Ulverstone." He said nothing, so she swallowed and went on. "He feels that he has been the cause of a misunderstanding between Annis and you. He thought that if he could explain—"

"There's nothing to explain," Richard said shortly. "Your sister placed herself in a position in which she had no choice but to marry me, so we did the thing. It's as simple as that."

"No, you do not comprehend the matter. Walter told me particularly to assure you that . . . that the arrangement they entered into was based merely on mutual respect and liking, nothing more."

"A good deal more than we have now," Richard muttered under his breath, but Elizabeth did not catch the words. She looked at him anxiously.

"He said that certain circumstances pressed him into offering for Annis. He feared for her safety for one thing, and wished to offer her his protection."

Richard merely shook his head, and to Elizabeth his countenance seemed unbelieving.

"Walter also told me last night, confidentially, that he had felt a certain obligation to protect and help your widow because of your long-standing friendship. He said—"

Richard raised a hand to stop her. "You needn't go on," he said with surprising gentleness. "If the point is to convince me that *Walter* was not in love with Annis, I had already guessed it, and everyone at the musicale last night probably guessed it too."

Elizabeth was caught off-guard. She blushed in a most becoming way. "I . . . I think that you misinterpret our—"

"I have eyes, my dear." He rose, his face set in grim lines. "If that is all you have to say—"

"Oh, no, it is not." Elizabeth, having stumbled, attempted to recover quickly. "I have not yet told you how it was all those months when we thought you were lost—how Annis was and . . ."

His expression became glacial. "I have plenty of evidence as to how Annis *was* then, rather too much evidence in fact."

Desperate, Elizabeth rose also. "But you *cannot* know what pain she suffered—waiting all those days and weeks for word of you, never giving up hope, and then . . ." She could not prevent a shiver. "I shall never forget the look on her face when they told us you were lost—"

He snorted in a contemptuous way, effectively cutting her off. Observing the uncomprehending expression in those clear, wide, bespectacled blue eyes, he twisted his face into a rueful grimace. "Thank you for your efforts. I am sorry that you have wasted so much of your time."

"Oh, please don't go. Please hear me out!" She was beside herself, but she did not have the temerity to catch at his sleeve. He sighed and she could see how weary he was.

"I am sorry, Elizabeth. I know that you are a loyal sister and that you wish to do your best for Annis, but she and I understand each other tolerably well, I think. I know that you mean well, but"—he hesitated for a moment before finding the word—"your concern is misplaced. Good day to you."

He bowed and exited the room, leaving Elizabeth to stare hopelessly after him.

Her meeting with her sister was hardly more auspicious. She was nearly through with her breakfast by the time Annis joined her. The latter was simply but charmingly dressed in a gown of white lawn. The lack of color served only to exaggerate her paleness and the dark smudges beneath her eyes. Given an entire night to reflect, Annis had realized that in addition to having destroyed her own marriage, she was also a good deal to blame for other troubles. She refused all offers of food and requested a cup of tea instead. Her sadness hung about her in an almost physical way, thereby depressing attempts at conversation. Elizabeth studied her with some pity. Whatever Richard and Annis' "understanding" was, it was not a pleasant one.

Elizabeth was startled when Annis addressed her abruptly. "Elizabeth, are you unhappy here?"

It seemed an odd question. Annis took one look at her face and gave a sad smile. "I am sorry. I never have been in the habit of consulting your feelings, have I? Not even upon the matters which most nearly concern you. Have you been so very unhappy in London all these months, then?"

Elizabeth hastened to reassure her. "Why, Annis, I don't know what would make you think that. Only think of the libraries and the bookstores and the plays and the opera! Country life will be bound to seem very flat when we return."

Annis almost had to smile. Laurie's vocabulary was creeping into even Elizabeth's speech. Stirring her cup of tea, she gazed into it as if to read her future in its depths. She suddenly spoke. "Would you like to go home again? Now, I mean?"

A week or so before, Elizabeth would have jumped at the opportunity. Not to spend her days and evenings either ridiculed or forced to listen to the flattery of idiotic young men! To have the time to read some of those books she had acquired, to return to all those peaceful country pursuits. She realized on the instant that they seemed rather dull at the moment. She would much rather spend an evening discussing Restoration comedy with . . . Her thoughts were taking a dangerous direction. Aloud she exclaimed, "But you are only bamming me! There is the Vanbrughs' ball on Saturday and Lady Otway's breakfast on Tuesday, to say nothing of a dozen other invitations we've already accepted. Besides, you know that I have not had time to visit the museums or galleries as I would like. That reminds me, Annis, I have not yet been to see the summer exhibition at the Royal Academy and I would like to do so. Would you care to go to Somerset House with me? I have heard that they have six to seven hundred paintings, and the admission is only a shilling.''

Annis was prepared to make sacrifices for her sister's happiness, but this was asking rather too much of her. ''You'd better take Louisa,'' she advised, grimacing as she sipped her tea.

''She's gone today again,'' Elizabeth said. They were interrupted by the arrival of a footman. ''You have a caller, miss.''

''I wonder who it can be,'' she said in a careless fashion. She left to greet the visitor, only returning to inform Annis that Mr. Ulverstone had called and that he meant to take her to the exhibition himself. She would bring her maid along, of course.

Annis bade her farewell absentmindedly. She was smitten afresh by remorse. Did anyone deserve to have such a thoughtful sister as hers? Both she and Walter were going to heroic lengths to stop the gossip. She might as well admit it to herself. Aunt Berinthea was right, for once. Annis had found the remarks last night intolerable, and her feelings were exacerbated by the knowledge that her marriage truly was on shaky ground.

The dismal train of thought was interrupted by the arrival of Laurie, who looked as if he felt every bit as dreadful as Annis did this morning. Without saying anything, she poured him a strong cup of tea and handed him a plate of muffins. He accepted them gratefully as he sat. He sipped at his tea, then took a bite of muffin. The two sat together in harmonious silence for almost twenty minutes while they companionably traded sections of the morning paper. The tranquillity might have continued for hours had not an idea suddenly occurred to Laurie.

''I say, Annis, I shall need another advance against my allowance, for I mean to go out of town for a few days.''

''Where are you going?''

''Oh, Luffy thought it might be a bit of a lark to pop down to Ascot for a bit.''

Her blood ran cold at the thought of Laurie alone in such company for several days. She sipped her tea with outward serenity. ''It's no use to apply to me anymore, for Richard is your rightful guardian, you know.''

Laurie's brows drew together, perplexed. "That's right." Thinking deeply, he polished off another muffin. "I shall have to speak with him, then. Daresay he'll understand. Does he happen to be around at the moment?" he asked with an assumption of carelessness.

Annis could not help wincing for an instant, but she immediately resumed her expression of placidity. "No, I think he is out."

"Oh, well, if that is the case," Laurie said cheerfully, "perhaps you would be good enough to lend me a—"

"No," Annis said flatly.

Laurie was indignant. "Dash it, you don't even know what I was going to ask for."

"It makes no difference. I won't lend you the money. Richard would have my head, and rightfully so." Annis thought that she could not sink further in Richard's estimation, but she was hardly about to tell Laurie that.

He grimaced. "Thoughtless of him to go loping off like that when I particularly need to speak with him. Just came back to town, too, didn't he?"

"Last night."

It occurred to Laurie that his sister was not looking well, and he commented on the fact rather tactlessly. She dismissed his worries with a wave, though she thanked him dryly for his concern. He was not to be fobbed off so lightly.

"I say, Annis, are you certain that everything's all right? You look positively hag-ridden." He thought for a moment. "Seems the last time I saw you—I suppose it was the day of the you-know-what—you were in blooming good looks, I thought."

"I have a touch of the headache, that's all."

He eyed her with a not entirely selfless concern. "I say, everything's all right between you and Richard, isn't it?"

She did not reply.

"You can tell me, after all," Laurie said encouragingly. "I'm your old partner in mayhem, you know."

"It's nothing—nothing that can be fixed, anyway." She gave a heartrending sigh.

Although he made another, admirable attempt to get her to confide in him, his efforts were unsuccessful. He decided that the best course would be to withdraw to prevent his succumbing to a fit of the blue devils, since they were often contagious. The encounter had given him food for thought, though. If Annis was this mopish, it was unlikely that Sir Richard was dancing happy little jigs. It made the timing for his advance most unfortunate. He liked Sir Richard, but could not be sanguine about his request's being met even under the most auspicious of circumstances. He had enough of the ready to get him to Ascot and back, and enough to pay for a room. One didn't like to be a charge on one's friends, but there it was. He couldn't pass up such an opportunity and he might make a lucky wager, after all. He hadn't been on a spree for quite some time now. His mind made up, he called for his valet and began issuing orders about which clothes to pack.

15

DURING the ensuing days, Sir Richard and Lady Burham were constantly to be seen in each other's company. One might find them at a play, a ball, a dinner, or a card party almost every night of the week. They presented a charming picture of a devoted couple. There were still detractors, of course, but society had begun to look upon their story as the stuff of romance, and was inclined to smile kindly upon them as a result. This should have alleviated the strain on Annis, but with each day she found it growing progressively worse. It was murderous to have to go out and play the happy couple when she in truth rarely saw Richard at home, and then they hardly spoke to each other. It was the latter circumstance that prevented her asking him about Laurie. She supposed that he had given his consent to the expedition, and although she could not like it, she trusted in Richard's judgement in that type of matter.

She was greatly relieved when at the end of a few days Laurie returned without having suffered any visible harm. Doubtless he was just going through some sort of phase that all young men went through. She could trust Richard to know where to draw the line. In other circumstances she might have been hurt that Richard had not consulted her about his decision, but the cold silent stranger she was married to rarely exchanged more than a word with her, except in public. He hadn't even commented to her on Laurie's going or on his return, though she supposed he might not have been aware of the exact dates.

She herself had seen Laurie on the day of his return. Had she been less preoccupied with problems of her own, she might have noticed that his high spirits seemed rather forced, but as it was, she congratulated herself on having held her peace. He had seemed a little taken aback at the number of tradesmen's accounts that had arrived for him in his absence, but he quickly assured her that he would take care of them. It showed a new sense of responsibility on his part, she thought.

Annis was blind to things other than Laurie's situation now. It did not strike her as odd, for example, that Elizabeth disappeared with regularity every morning. On the few occasions that Annis bestirred herself enough to ask where her sister was bound, she did not find it singular that Mr. Ulverstone was to escort her sister to the particular museum or gallery she wanted to see. She merely thought her loyal sister and Richard's friend were doing their best to quell gossip, and after all, they did have many interests in common. It did not occur to her that Elizabeth and Walter were becoming the subject of talk themselves.

Although Annis was oblivious to the talk, the same could not be said for the two new principals involved. Walter had escorted Elizabeth to the Dulwich Gallery today, partly for the remarkable collection it housed. It also had occurred to both Walter and Elizabeth that they would be less likely to encounter many of their acquaintances in such a removed spot. The use of such a stratagem pained Elizabeth's honest heart and kept her from full enjoyment of what otherwise might have been a pleasant outing. It was not to be presumed that her attentive escort should fail to notice such lackluster spirits.

They had paused in front of a magnificent Rembrandt, but it was obvious to Walter that his companion hardly noticed it. "Elizabeth, what is wrong?" he asked gently.

She gave a little shake of the head, which prompted a gentle smile from Walter. "My dear Elizabeth, I am afraid that deception is not your strong suit. Let us be seated and you may tell me what is troubling you."

It was hard to speak with those clear gray eyes upon her. Conscious of the maid, who was standing discreetly at the opposite end of the room, Elizabeth said huskily, "I am not certain that we should be here."

"Come, now," he said, teasing her gently, "we did purchase our tickets, after all."

She could not even summon up a smile. The matter had been bothering her for days. She fought to keep the tears from rising to her eyes. "You cannot be unaware of the stares and the remarks when we are seen together. Why, even my aunt, when we met her yesterday . . ." She could not continue.

"Hmm. Well, yes, I admit that it was a bit indiscreet of us to go driving in the park, but after all, my dear, London will have to get used to seeing us together sometime."

She ignored the implications of that remark and continued miserably, "I am ashamed of myself, for as much as I do not wish to cause talk, I cannot feel proud about our meeting in places where we might avoid the public eye. It seems . . . duplicitous to me, somehow."

He was frowning now. "Elizabeth, I will take you anywhere you choose. I would happily take you driving in the park every day at five o'clock. You seemed uncomfortable there, and that is why I brought you here today instead. All I wish is to make you happy."

She shook her head. "You have been most kind and most thoughtful, but you do not understand. There can be no happiness for me, knowing that it was purchased at my sister's expense."

"At your sister's expense?" Walter's frown had deepened. "What on earth do you mean by that? And by the way, I should inform you that I haven't been 'kind' in the least—I operate strictly according to self-interest."

There was a moistness in her eyes now, but she had turned her face to hide it. "You are too much of a gentleman to say anything else. But as innocent as our meetings have been, can you imagine the pain it would cause Annis if she heard of the gossip that was the result?"

Walter was scowling now. He took her by the shoulders and turned her so that she was forced to gaze into those angry gray eyes. " 'Kind' and 'innocent'? My dear girl, if you imagine that I have some sort of fraternal interest in you, you are dead wrong. The gossips are entirely right. I mean to marry you, and I don't care a fig for whatever anyone says."

To her utter surprise, Elizabeth found herself being crushed in a powerful set of arms and ruthlessly kissed in a way that dislodged her spectacles and made her head spin. More astonishing was her own regret when he abruptly released her, particularly since she had been aware the entire time that they were in a public place. She straightened her spectacles, her cheeks flaming, but she did not attempt to avoid his gaze.

He chuckled, eyeing her appreciatively. "By gad, you are beautiful. My dearest heart, I love you and you might as well not attempt to deny that you love me."

Hardly trusting her voice, she replied huskily, "I think you are mad!"

He laughed out loud. "Not mad, my own dear love, only blind. I was blind for such a long time, wasn't I? I engaged myself to your sister, never dreaming that a woman like you could exist. How could I have known you so long and so little?"

She did not attempt to excuse herself. "It is a shell I have built up. I have always felt awkward about not being able to see and recognize people, and I found that if I said very little, I avoided many awkward situations." She realized what she was saying and added hastily, "But you cannot love me. We hardly know each other."

"Perdition catch my soul, but I do love thee!" Walter exclaimed, caught off-guard.

She frowned at him with the first gleam of her old humor. "I cannot say that I like your source, sir."

There was an answering sparkle in his own eyes. "True, but then, Othello had interfering Iago to contend with."

Her flush had died and she was becoming pale. "Oh, what a dreadful fix we are in."

"Let me not to the marriage of true minds admit impediments—is that better?" he asked her innocently.

"But I am serious, Walter. Can you think of the scandal this will cause? And poor Annis is so unhappy already," she added wistfully.

He smiled at her. "My dear naive little love. Do you truly imagine that our affairs can interest anyone half so much as the hastily contracted marriages that most of the royal dukes are on the verge of? I don't deny that our marriage will cause talk, but it is likely to be supplanted within days by something far worse. As for myself, I would happily marry you tomorrow and simply disregard the gossip that results, but I know that it would pain you. Difficult as it may be, we shall delay announcing our engagement for a while yet. That will give the talk time to die down first."

Her heart was racing. Could this joy be real? He was moving much too fast for her. She looked at him evenly. "But you haven't asked me to marry you," she pointed out.

He assumed an equally grave expression, though a light shone far back in his eyes. "A serious omission. My own dear, true, and only love, will you marry me?"

"I . . . I don't know." Her eyes were troubled. "I can't help wondering what Annis will think—"

"Ah, I see that I will have to convince you again," he said with his best attempt at a suggestive leer.

Since a couple had recently entered and were standing just a few feet from them, Elizabeth shrank from him, though a part of her would have been happy to comply with his suggestion. "No, that is—"

He had her hand in his. "I love you, Elizabeth. Will you do me the honor of becoming my wife?" he said simply.

Aware of two pairs of curious eyes on her, Elizabeth blushed fiercely. "Yes, I will, but please let us leave now!"

"What a beautiful sentiment." He rose, assisting her up also, bowed politely at the strangers staring openmouthed at them, and escorted her decorously from the room. Her maid, a quick-witted lass, had long ago taken an interest in a picture in the next chamber.

Elizabeth was thoughtful on the ride home. Walter could not help but notice her abstraction, but wisely refused to comment on it. It was clear to her that she needed to talk with someone, particularly someone older and wiser, and that the last place she might search for a confidant was at Burham House. She knew that her chance of encountering Louisa there was slim and her desire to avoid Annis was great. A surprising idea occurred to her. She abruptly spoke aloud.

"Walter, would you mind taking me to my aunt's, that is, Lady Downage's house?"

In a far different part of London, Louisa removed a blood-stained apron and began to wash her hands. "I am sorry," she commented to the gentleman standing beside her, "but I cannot remain any longer. My young ladies will be wondering what has become of me."

"Haven't you told them of your work here?" he inquired in some surprise.

She shook her head. "No." She hesitated for a moment, then continued, "They still need me, you see, and they were so kind to me when I had no prospects at all. If they knew how I enjoyed my work here, they might feel that they were depriving me."

"So you haven't informed them of Mrs. Woolcott's offer?"

"No, though it was most kind of her to say that she needed a companion, and though I shall always be grateful to her and the doctor, I am afraid that I shall have to decline it. My first duty lies with Lady Burham and Miss Thurstan."

"Your loyalty does you credit, though"—he gave a sigh—"we certainly could use you here. Even though you were born into another station in life, you have a god-given talent for caring for the ill, and it seems a shame to waste it."

"I myself could not think of a *higher* calling," Louisa quietly. She had finished drying her hands and had rolled her sleeves down once again. "I thank you for saying so. I will be back when I can."

"I know, and thank you."

Annis was seated in the small drawing room at Burham House, perusing a fashion periodical with no real interest, when the butler entered with a perturbed look on his face.

"What is it, Hickeringill?" she asked.

He frowned uncertainly. "My lady, I am afraid that young Mr. Thurstan has a caller, a rather insistent caller, a Mr. White."

She crinkled her forehead. "My brother is not in?"

"No, my lady."

She gave a sigh. "Well, show him in, then."

Hickeringill returned in a few moments with a most curious-looking individual. Annis had never seen such a well-padded jacket before, nor such a magnificent waistcoat, nor such high shirt-points. When the visitor spoke, he confirmed her surmises. He was Laurie's tailor.

Sheer desperation had driven the little man to make this visit. Suspicious at first, Annis soon found her sympathies awakened by the tailor's pitiful story. He had come from the provinces hoping to make a success in London. Knowing that it was customary, he had extended credit freely. Even after months of polite reminders, his patrons still neglected to pay their accounts. His creditors were on the verge of seizing his shop and all its assets. His family would be left homeless and destitute.

Annis' pity turned to wrath when she learned that Laurie was among those who had never paid the poor fellow so much as a penny. Her brother seemed to have plenty of money for cockfights and coffeehouses and horse races and such. Well, she would settle accounts with Laurie later.

Quite alarming the tailor by her scowl, she rose and announced that she would go write him a draft on her bank immediately. True to her word, she returned in a few minutes' time with the draft, which she thrust into his hands.

"I hope that this will content at least a part of your creditors," she said sincerely. Her jaw tightened once again with anger. "I regret that my brother took so long to settle his—" Her words were cut off abruptly. The tailor turned to see that a tall, thin gentleman with an autocratic expression had entered the room.

"Paying Laurie's debts for him, Taggy?" the new arrival asked softly. Though he spoke in a low voice, there was something in his tone that sent a shudder up the tailor's spine. He looked at the intruder and back at Annis in some confusion.

She did not reply to her husband, but addressed the tailor instead. "Go on. It was owed to you and my draft is good."

He bowed obsequiously, took a look at Sir Richard and decided hastily that one bow would suffice, then left the room as quickly as possible.

"Well, wife?" Richard asked coldly.

She waited until the door had closed behind her visitor. "Yes, it was Laurie's tailor. He had owed him money since last September, and the poor man was about to be dispossessed by his creditors, so—"

"Is this a habit with you, taking care of your brother's bills?"

She flushed angrily. "No, it is not, though I do not see why you—"

He interrupted her. "Had you forgotten that I am your brother's guardian? I suppose you will think my views narrow, but I consider that his allowance might be better spent on settling the bills he has run up than spending it gambling or carousing or entertaining low company.''

How quick he was to put *her* in the wrong. ''Well, I haven't seen *you* trying to discourage him.''

He drew a hand across his forehead painfully, than sank into a chair. ''I have hardly seen your brother since . . . since my first day in London. I would certainly like to speak to him, given the opportunity.''

Stung, she responded, ''Well, you saw him long enough to give him an advance on his allowance so that he could go to Ascot with those companions of whom you say you disapprove.''

He stared up at her blankly. ''What on earth are you talking about?''

He was not to get off the hook as easily as that. ''You needn't pretend you don't know. He asked me for an advance before he left, and I said he'd have to apply to you, since you are his guardian.''

He leaned forward, frowning. ''Am I understanding you correctly? Do you say that Laurie has gone off to Ascot?''

She suddenly felt her position weakening. ''Do you mean that you didn't know?'' she asked falteringly.

''Of course I didn't know,'' he snapped. ''Do you think I'd have allowed a seventeen-year-old boy to go jaunting off with such a set of . . .'' He stopped, arrested by a new idea. ''But why didn't you tell me, when you learned of his plan?''

''I thought he had asked you,'' she said blankly.

He rose slowly and she had never seen him so angry. She had to tremble before that icy gaze. ''My word, Annis. I begin to think that Ambrose was right when he said you weren't fit to be Laurie's guardian. Just what else have you been allowing him to do? What other sorts of expeditions have you been funding for him? I thought he was looking a trifle worn-down, but I can see that I haven't guessed the half of it.''

How awful he was being. He could not know how many anxious hours she had spent worrying about her brother, how useless speaking to Laurie had proved to be, how she had feared that denying him money would drive him into even worse predicaments. She had spent all those months wishing that Richard were around to help, and yet he, who had done nothing for Laurie since his return, could only blame her for all her brother's excesses, as if she approved of them! Her lower lip trembled, but she fought back the tears. She would not give him the satisfaction of seeing her cry. She would have resented his words less if she had not had a deep suspicion that at least some of them were true.

He stared at her for another moment without speaking, and she could feel herself turning into ice beneath that gaze. "How odd it is that you can know someone for so long and yet not know her at all," he said reflectively. "How did you expect that he would learn to manage an estate, Annis, if he couldn't even manage his own allowance? Were you too busy to care?"

There was no reply to be made. She could feel the tears begin to sting her eyes. Richard was not the only one who had been deceived. Why had he ever asked for her hand, if all he wished were to make her life miserable?

Richard, too, seemed to feel that there was little left to say. "I will be in my chamber," he said wearily. "As I recall, this evening was free of social obligations." Not looking at her, he continued, "You will please give orders that your brother is to be shown to my chamber as soon as he arrives, no matter what the hour is."

Before Annis could respond, another voice cut in, "That won't be necessary." She looked up through swimming eyes to see that Laurie had entered the room, a grave expression on his young countenance. "I'm here now, and whatever you have to say would best be said to me. I've been all kinds of a fool, I know, but Annis is not to blame for that." He pressed his lips together and nodded at his sister. "She tried to stop me, but I wouldn't listen."

Richard wheeled on him angrily. "Are you aware that a *tradesman* called upon your sister here in this house today for an account of yours?"

"I am sorry." His young eyes were bleak. "Did you pay him, Annis? You must tell me what I owe you and I will repay you."

"Doubtless you were too taken up with your own pleasures

to cast your mind to such a trifling matter as an overdue account. You and your sister have that in common, at least."

Laurie paled, though the latter part of the reference was lost on him. "No," he said quietly, "I deliberately did not pay it, for that is what my . . . my *friends* told me to do." The word seemed to have a bitter taste for him. "I see now how wrong it was."

Richard was at his most sardonic now, and Annis hated him for it. Just because he was angry at her, he needn't take out his foul temper on Laurie. "I suppose you have spent all afternoon at prayers in the chapel, then?"

Laurie flushed. "No, I was at Tattersall's."

"Making a wager on a promising prospect?"

"No, selling my horse." Laurie looked at Annis for some kind of approval. "It was my money that bought him, after all, wasn't it?"

Annis knew what a source of pride the elegant bay gelding had been for Laurie. "Why did you sell him?"

"In order to settle my accounts. I know the money won't pay for everything, but I mean to sell my gig when I get home, too, so there will be some more money also."

"What happened?" she asked softly, no longer trying to hide her tears.

"You were right all along. I went to Ascot, made a wager on a 'sure thing' that ended up running a close second, which left me without a penny. Luffy and his friends seemed to regard it as a good joke. They didn't even see why I shouldn't make other wagers, and then they actually abandoned me there, for sport, I guess. I was fortunate enough to find a good-natured farmer who was bringing some chickens to London, and he was willing to give me a ride on his cart. I . . . I didn't even have a shilling to give him. I asked for his address so that I might repay him later, but he wouldn't give it to me, just insisted that it wasn't necessary."

"He would have done better to have put you to work on his farm for a few days," Richard growled.

Laurie turned to him earnestly. "I have no doubt that you are right—but you don't know how I've been feeling, to be under an obligation that I can't repay. Why, he even shared his dinner with me, for he could see that I was hungry." His gaze drifted downward. "In any case, it made me think about all the things Luffy considered capital jokes, and suddenly they didn't seem funny to me at all. I spent several days trying to think of how I might meet my obligations without drawing against my allowance further, and then it occurred to me to sell my horse."

There were a few moments of silence, and then Richard spoke. "Will you please leave us, Annis? There are matters which Lawrence and I have to discuss alone."

Laurie looked as if he did not relish the prospect, but he nodded in agreement. Annis gave her brother a tremulous smile. No matter what Richard might say, selling his horse had meant a great sacrifice to Laurie and she was proud of him. She hoped that Richard would not be too hard on him. She left the room, closing the door behind her, and began up the stairs, thinking her own troubled thoughts.

She had to face the fact that she had failed utterly at everything she had tried. When she had begun the masquerade, she had thought to ensure a better education for her brother. He had been given a sort of education, she supposed, but it was of a type to horrify most right-thinking people and it certainly was not what she had intended. For her sister, she had hoped to find a husband. Instead, as Richard had pointed out, Elizabeth had endured months of misery as one of London's most prominent wallflowers.

Still worse was the muddle she had made of her own life. The one dream she had clung to for most of her life was that Richard would someday fall in love with her and marry her. He had married her; owing to her foolish lies about her situation, he had been given little choice. Instead of being wedded to a Richard who loved her, she found herself trapped into a marriage with a man who despised her. It was a far worse torment than anything she could have imagined. If she had been able to hate him in return, at least she might have salvaged her pride, but although he was a master at irritating her, she still could not help loving him. Every detail of that countenance was as dear to her as it had ever been, and whatever he might think of *her* character, *his* had not sunk in her estimation.

Loving him, what could she do? A divorce was unthinkable. An annulment, though technically possible, would be just as scandalous by now. Perhaps he would simply wish to maintain separate establishments, so that they saw each other as little as possible. It was a common enough arrangement, after all. The thought caused her agony, but if that was what he wanted, she would agree to it without any sort of argument. After all, she had destroyed his life as surely as she had destroyed her own.

With these thoughts in mind, she was not too surprised when Richard's valet knocked on her door some hours later and informed her that the master wished to see her in his chamber. Her heart was heavy, but she nodded and resolutely opened the connecting door.

Richard was lying in bed, swathed in a dressing gown of plain brown flannel. When she looked into his face, she noticed for the first time how tired it was, with the lines of pain seeming more deeply etched than usual. He waved her to a chair. "Please be seated, my dear."

The sobriquet and the gentleness of his voice alarmed her more than open hostility would have. She seated herself and waited for him to begin.

"First of all, I would like you to know that I have apologized to your brother for losing my temper earlier." He hesitated, then continued, "We had quite a long conversation, wherein he disabused me of several of my misapprehensions. I would like to offer you my apologies also, my dear. I am afraid that my illness has made me quite snappish, but that is no excuse for my jumping to conclusions in the way that I did."

Annis could not stand it any longer. "Please, Richard," she said, "say what you have to say to me, but do not continue to call me 'my dear' and to address me in that saintly manner, as if you were on your deathbed, because I cannot bear it."

Did the ghost of a smile flicker in those blue eyes for an instant, or did she imagine it? "Very well, Taggy, I'll have done with pretty manners. What I have to ask you, and what I hope that you will agree to, is that we leave London as soon as we may."

His request was so far from what she had been expecting that she could only stare at him in astonishment. "Do you mean that *all* of us will go?"

He looked troubled. "Yes, I know that it will mean giving up all your amusements, but—"

"Oh, Richard." Tears of relief started to her eyes. "I would be happy to go, indeed I do not know of any reason why we should stay."

He seemed a little taken aback by her enthusiasm, but he said, "Yes, the Season is almost over, so I don't see much point in remaining for Elizabeth's sake. And although your brother is considerably chastened at the moment, I do not doubt that word of some mill or cockfight or horse race or such would be enough to make him recover enough to entirely neglect his studies once more. I think our only hope of getting him into university is to return him to Kent once more." Something else moved in his face, but she could not read it. "My doctor also has advised a period of rest in the country for me."

He was looking ill; she was certain of it now. She leaned over to him and took him by the hand. It was hot. "Why didn't you tell me you were ill, Richard? Perhaps you should take a few days to recover before we leave."

He grimaced. "The physician seemed to think that it would be better for me to leave for the country immediately." He saw her anxious expression and gave a wintry smile. "He thinks that London is not very beneficial to me and that perhaps I have been jaunting about a bit too much lately and will do better away from these distractions."

Her conscience smote her. There had been hardly an invitation declined, hardly an evening when they might have been found at home. Even Elizabeth had mentioned that Richard seemed weary, but Annis had scoffed at the notion. Could she have been more thoughtless? Unthinkingly she reached out to smooth a stray lock of blond hair that had fallen across his forehead. He jumped back as if he had been bitten. It served to remind her of the state of affairs between them.

"Did you tell Laurie?" she asked quietly.

"Yes, and surprisingly, he agreed. I have never seen him in such a subdued mood before. You will need to tell Elizabeth, though."

"Yes, well, I suppose I had better go do that immediately." She rose, took a last painful look at his face, then left the room. He still wanted her with him. That was something, at least.

16

ANNIS first went to Elizabeth's chamber in search of her sister, but was surprised to meet with no answer to her knock. She vaguely recalled that Elizabeth had gone out on some sort of pleasure trip this morning, but surely she should be back by now. It was almost seven, after all, which reminded her that she must go change for dinner as soon as she spoke with her sister. She went downstairs and looked for Elizabeth in every room. She was nowhere to be found. Perhaps she should return upstairs and see if Louisa knew where Elizabeth was, although she herself hadn't seen Louisa today. Her eyes lit upon Greenlaw, and it occurred to her that he would certainly be able to tell her if Elizabeth were out. She approached him, but before she could ask, the door swung open. To her amazement, there stood Elizabeth, Walter, and Lady Downage, all apparently in the most congenial of moods. She stopped dead, staring at them in surprise.

Never at a loss, Lady Downage bustled in and addressed her elder niece. "Annis, we must talk with you immediately." She then turned and addressed Walter with a smile. "We will see you on the morrow, I think?"

He bowed politely. "Certainly." He took Elizabeth's hand and kissed it, and Annis thought that there was a warm look she had never seen before in his eyes. Elizabeth, too—why, Elizabeth was actually blushing as she bade him farewell in a soft, shy voice. Annis regarded the scene in stupefaction, but her aunt caught her by the elbow and pulled her into the drawing room with her. "Elizabeth, close the door," she commanded.

She dropped Annis none too gently onto a chair and sat down herself. "You must hear the exciting news," she said. "Your sister and Mr. Ulverstone have become engaged."

"Engaged?" There must be something wrong with Annis'

ears. She shook her head as if to clear it, then happened to glance up at her sister's face. She saw the mixture of happiness and uncertainty shining from those eyes and she realized that she was not dreaming. "Oh, Elizabeth, is this true?"

Annis' tone confirmed her sister's worst fears. Elizabeth crossed the room quickly to kneel beside her, taking her sister's hands in her own. "Oh, I am so sorry, Annis. The last thing in the world that I wished was to make you unhappy. Walter and I simply had no choice, you see. We fought against our attraction, but—"

Recalled to herself, Annis managed to interrupt the flow of words. "*Sorry!* You goose, why should you be sorry? I'm very happy for you—it just took me by surprise, that is all."

Elizabeth searched her sister's countenance. "Annis, are you sure? I know you said that you were always in love with Richard, and Walter said the same, but . . ."

Annis stroked her sister's hair gently. "Of course I'm certain. Haven't I been wanting you to make a creditable marriage? I think that Walter is a fine person and I always thought that you had a great deal in common. In fact, I . . ." Her eyes opened wide as she realized what this marriage meant. "Oh, no, and here I thought that the talk was beginning to die down!"

Lady Downage, who had restrained herself for several minutes, could not help making her contribution now. "You may safely leave all of that to me. I know exactly how the thing should be managed. To begin with, Elizabeth and Mr. Ulverstone have agreed to delay the announcement of their engagement until after the Season is over. There will be less talk with fewer people about to discuss it."

Her words reminded Annis of a more pressing problem. "Elizabeth! Richard means for us to leave London tomorrow!" To her surprise, her aunt began to chuckle in a self-satisfied way. "Excellent. That makes my plan even easier. You see, in order to avoid another opportunity for gossip, I had intended that Elizabeth should come to stay with me. And what could be more natural than that she should, with her sister returning to the country?"

Bemused, Annis looked at her sister. "Elizabeth?"

Her sister smiled. "Yes, Aunt Berinthea and I talked it over this afternoon and we decided that it would be best. Walter agrees with us too.''

Annis looked from Elizabeth to their aunt, who was regarding her sister with a look of fond approval. Love certainly was capable of working miracles if it improved their relationship so much in one day. Her aunt's next sentence gave her part of the solution to the mystery.

"Yes, Elizabeth could not have done better than to come to me as she has. And Mr. Ulverstone and I are in agreement that she should keep her spectacles on at all times. It is far better to admit having weak eyes than to be thought haughty. You know, I shouldn't be surprised if that young gentleman has a great future as a politician or a diplomat.''

"I'm sure he has," Elizabeth stated with simple faith.

As the dinner hour was approaching, Annis invited her aunt to join them, but Lady Downage declined, saying that she had to return to have a chamber readied for her guest. She did venture to whisper in Annis' ear that she had begun to doubt her matchmaking abilities, but this obviously showed that she had not lost her old touch. How she could venture to take credit for this engagement was beyond Annis, but she certainly would not argue with any idea that put her aunt in such harmony with Elizabeth.

They had scarcely bidden farewell to Lady Downage when they were met by Louisa, who had come downstairs, properly dressed for dinner, at the correct hour. A glance at the two sisters served to inform Louisa that something had happened, and the three women closeted themselves in order to discuss the interesting news.

When she was informed, Louisa threw her arms about Elizabeth and hugged her, saying that though she had hopes, she had been fearful of expressing them. Her words brought home to Annis precisely how blind she'd been. Details were discussed, including Elizabeth's move and the proposed trip to Kent. Louisa clasped her hands and regarded them both with some anxiety. "Does this mean that you won't be requiring my services any longer?''

Annis laughed. "Oh, Louisa. You know you shall always have a home with Richard and me.''

Her sister, more perceptive, commented, "I don't think that is what Louisa is asking us, Annis."

Louisa blinked and twisted her hands nervously. "Yes, well, that is . . . I am much obliged to you, of course, and I can never truly express my gratitude for all you have done for me, but if you have no objections, I am going to take up a new position."

"A new position? What is it?" the sisters exclaimed.

"Well, I had been reluctant to speak about it until now, feeling that my first duty was to you, but I have been working in my spare time at a new hospital . . ." Seeing the blank looks on their faces, she hurried on, "The West London Infirmary and Dispensary on Suffolk Street. It is the first hospital to open in London in eighty years, so as you may imagine, the need is great. The people that live in the area are generally impoverished Irish laborers who are unable to pay for any sort of medical care. I cannot describe to you the misery and the want . . ." She hesitated.

"I should like to visit there sometime with you," Elizabeth said quietly.

"But, Louisa, where will you live?" the more practical-minded Annis asked.

"Doctor Woolcott and his wife, old friends of my father's, have concerned themselves greatly with this project. They have offered me a home with them so that I may continue my work there. Mrs. Woolcott suffers from ill-health, so I will be of some help to them also, and not feel quite a charity case." She saw the consternation in Annis' face and smiled. "My dear Annis, I know that it sounds the grimmest sort of occupation in the world, and it is, but I can tell you that I have never felt as useful or as needed in my life. I also feel that in some way I am carrying on my father's work." She blushed slightly here. "You will not credit it, I am sure, but some of my connections have enabled me to render a unique service. For example, the other day there was a hodman killed, which left his wife and child without any means of support. Well, I need not tell you what is usual in such cases, but . . ."

She continued on with what Annis thought was a rather boring story of having been able to find this widow employment in the household of some general. Annis could not quite believe that this was the sort of life that Louisa would prefer, but seeing the glow in those gray eyes as she talked and the animation in that angular countenance, she could not doubt that Louisa was happy.

When Louisa had finished, Elizabeth was the first to speak. She took her companion by the hand and squeezed it warmly. "I think it is a wonderful project that you are engaged in. Mr. Ulverstone and I will be glad to help, however we may."

Annis addressed her with some lingering reluctance. "Richard and I will be glad to help too, Louisa, but are you certain that this is what you want?"

Louisa saw her disbelief and smiled at it. "I have never been more certain of anything."

It was a sentimental group who gathered around the dinner table that evening. Richard had remained in his chamber. Laurie was still in his subdued mood, taking in even the news of the engagement with gravity. Louisa and Elizabeth, though excited about their futures, could not help but feel regret at the imminent parting from Annis and Laurie. Annis' conspiracy had drawn them all together. They had passed through two long sea voyages, several threats of danger, and a wedding together, and it had made them closer than many families or friends could ever be.

Annis had no bright prospects to sustain her. All she could think of was the support these two had lavished upon her and how it would soon be gone. From now on there would be no Louisa to furnish an impossible solution to her dilemma, no Elizabeth to confide in when she was utterly miserable. There would be no bright moments to relieve her wretchedness.

Annis had many faults, but cowardice was not among them. The same determination that had kept her from shedding tears when she learned of Richard's death kept her eyes dry now. Her sister and her friend must be able to enjoy their futures without any sort of remorse. She talked brightly about how they should be gathering before too long for Elizabeth's engagement party and wedding and how they should all spend the holidays together and so forth, until the other two began to be cheered and think that perhaps there was no real need to feel that they were deserting Annis.

The following day dawned wet and surprisingly cool for summer. Laurie, quite heedless of the weather, set off for home in the early part of the afternoon in Richard's curricle. Annis had looked at Richard questioningly when he had volunteered to let Laurie drive it, but he had whispered that he was tired of seeing such a hangdog expression on her brother's face. His solution certainly proved effective, for Laurie was beaming as he wheeled the horses out into the street. Annis was understandably concerned, but her fears were assuaged somewhat by the sight of Richard's groom seated beside him. Richard caught her gaze and remarked that Brown could be trusted to take care of him.

Within a half-hour the few trunks they had chosen to bring were loaded into the post chaise and they said their farewells to Elizabeth and Louisa. The latter two ladies had assured them that the rest of the packing and the closing up of Burham House might safely be left to them, it being agreed by everyone that Richard's health took precedence over all else. Louisa had even, touchingly, offered to accompany them back to Kent to help nurse Richard. Annis had turned Louisa down, remarking that it was now her own job.

Bidding farewell to her sister was even harder. Elizabeth had stared her in the eyes and said, "I hope . . . oh, I pray that you will be happy, Annis. I do not know what is wrong between you and Sir Richard, but I do know that he loves you and that you love him and that you can overcome any difficulties with that." Annis was amazed that her usually perceptive sister could be so wrong about something. She merely gave her a tight smile and told Elizabeth that if she wasn't happy, Mr. Ulverstone would have a great deal to answer for. "Oh, but I am happy," Elizabeth had replied with shining eyes. "I never knew it was possible to be so happy!" She gave her sister one last fierce hug, and Annis stepped into the carriage and they were soon on their way.

Richard was busy with his own thoughts, and he kept silent

as they left London. It wasn't until they were well away from the confines of the city that he spoke.

"Annis," he said with obvious difficulty, "I hope that . . . I hope that it was not too hard on you, learning of Elizabeth's engagement so abruptly."

Still gazing outside, she replied indifferently, "No, why should it be? I'll admit that I was a good deal surprised, but she seems happy enough. I always thought that they had a great deal in common." She turned to see that he was studying her closely, which unnerved her a little. "Why? Did you suspect it was going to happen?"

"Yes, I did." He offered nothing else, so after enduring another moment's scrutiny, she turned her face to gaze at the wet countryside rolling by.

Perhaps fifteen minutes passed before she thought to make another comment. "It's fortunate that Laurie took the curricle. I should hate to have you driving when it is so cold and damp and you are fighting a fever." She turned to glance back at him as she spoke, but his illness had proved too much for him and he had fallen asleep. In repose, he looked like a boy again, and it made her heart ache dreadfully. If only they could return to that happier time, to that time when he was her idol and she the willful tomboy who accepted his every dare. Tears began to rise to her eyes and she dashed them away angrily with the back of her glove. This sort of thinking did her no good. She had been up all night, fighting loneliness and sadness and self-recrimination. The rocking of the carriage was soothing. In a few minutes she had joined her husband in sleep, her head unconsciously dropping to rest on his shoulder.

She awoke in the midst of falling, landing on top of something large as a shriek sounded in her ears. She opened her eyes to find herself lying on top of Richard, the chaise at a standstill, resting at an awkward angle. She realized that the scream had been her own.

Richard's face was nearly touching hers. "Are you all right?"

"Yes. I should think you're the one who was hurt, since you padded my fall." She struggled to free herself from the tangle of limbs, but found it nearly impossible to do so.

"Wait, I fancy they're about to help us." There was indeed

the sound of voices outside the chaise, and presently there came a tugging on the door, which abruptly opened, spilling them both the short distance to the ground. One of the postboys, a squat dark fellow with a badly broken nose, helped Annis up. She did her best to restore her appearance by disentangling her rumpled skirts and replacing her bonnet, though with the rain streaming down, she knew she would soon look like a drowned rat. Richard had risen slowly, with a grimace, and she was very afraid that his leg had been injured in the accident. They turned to see that the other postboy, a man with hard eyes and a pockmarked face, was studying the left-rear wheel, which was lying in pieces beside the carriage. Richard let out a low whistle. "It looks as if we won't be going anywhere anytime soon," he said.

"You're right, sir." He straightened up and gazed down the road. "I believe there is a village not too far distant. I suppose the only course will be for us to ride and see if there isn't some sort of vehicle to be hired there."

Wet and already beginning to be chilled, Annis would have preferred to borrow the horses and ride on ahead herself, but she was long used to deferring to Richard's judgment. She looked at him and saw the pain in his face and knew that the journey might well be beyond him in the rain and in his weakened condition. She would have demanded of the postboy whether he meant them to stand in the rain until their return, but he had another suggestion. "There's an old windmill on the hill. I can't say whether or not there's still a miller, but you should find some shelter there in any case."

Annis, who had begun to take the man in some unaccountable dislike, thanked him briefly and called Richard, who was busy examining the pieces of the wheel. He looked up, listened to the advice, and took Annis' proffered arm without comment. He leaned on it heavily, confirming her fears about an injury, and they began to make their way slowly to the distant windmill.

The track that led to it was overgrown, making the going even harder as they walked through the tangle of weeds and slipped on the soft ground. Annis' hopes began to evaporate. It was evident that there would be no miller and his wife snug in front of the fire in the nearby cottage. She only hoped that the roof would still be sound enough to keep out the damp. She could not help but growl aloud to Richard that it was no wonder the man had gone out of business with a mill in such an out-of-the-way spot.

"Well, it is a high point," he observed wearily, "and they have to do their best to catch the breeze."

She hardly thought it the time to be making observations on the operation of windmills when his weight was sinking her inches deep into the mud, but she would not have thought of complaining. Neither would it have occurred to her to ask if he were in pain, since he so obviously was. She well knew Richard's dislike of anyone's calling attention to what he perceived as a weakness.

They struggled on through the rain and the dirt for the rest of the way in silence, and it took no more than a look at the miller's cottage to see that it would afford them no shelter whatsoever. "We'll go on to the windmill," Richard said. "They generally are built to last."

It was a stout-looking octagonal structure built of wood, and it looked to be in fairly good repair, with the sail frames still intact. They had little choice, after all.

A little more limping progress led them to the mill. With some difficulty Richard slid back the heavy wooden bar that held the door shut, and opened it. They entered, finding that the structure was dry inside. It was musty and dirty and the dust made Annis sneeze, but it was better than being outside in the rain. It took a moment for her eyes to adjust to the gloom, the mill's few narrow windows affording little light on this dark day. It was a complicated structure, with all sorts of irregular platforms and ladders leading up from one level to another. She could see all sorts of belts and gears and other machinery, as well as the huge spouts through which the flour must pour downward. "Well," she said briskly, "if you'll find somewhere to sit, I'll see if I can get a fire going."

His chuckle surprised her. "You wish to put a period to our existences?" She frowned up at him in the dusky light and saw that he was serious.

"My dear Taggy, *no one* lights a fire in a windmill—it is a miller's greatest fear." He saw her look of consternation and smiled. "They don't burn—they explode. The flour dust has explosive properties, you see. Then there's the grease and all the oily rags also. Almost everything in here is conducive to burning, including all this dry wood. It takes only a spark from the grinding of the stones or a lightning strike to destroy a mill and everyone in it."

"Well, how are we to get warm, then?" she demanded.

"There should be some of the rags still lying about . . . ah, here are some grain sacks." He arranged a few of them to make a pallet, then sat down. She hesitated. "Come down here," he ordered. "We'll need each other if we've a hope of keeping warm."

She obeyed, and he drew her roughly to him, covering them both with another couple of the flour sacks. It was the most miserable set of circumstances she could imagine and yet she was delighted to be so near him and to be treated as his "Taggy" once more. She could not very well say that to him, so instead she asked gruffly how he had become such an expert on windmills.

He pretended hurt. "And here I thought you used to hang on my every word," he complained. "I know I must have told you about my exploits at school—that we used to take dares about who would ride the sails."

His words brought the memory back to Annis' mind. She remembered now how he had told her about clinging to the sails as they traveled some eighty feet into the air, before returning to deposit him gently on the ground. "It's a wonder you weren't killed." She shuddered.

"Yes, well, we took care to do it only when the wind was dying or the miller was shutting down operations."

"I wonder that he let you do it."

"*Let* us! Taggy, it was an operation that required the utmost skill, management, and subterfuge. He would have had our hides if he had caught any of us, and rightly so."

He was making rather bright and quick conversation for a man who was weakened, chilled, and in pain, but she did not think to wonder at it. Instead her attention was attracted by a rustling and squeaking above them. "What is that?" she exclaimed nervously.

"Probably just mice and bats," he said with what seemed to her an inadequate amount of concern. "I daresay it's been their home for some time."

"Mice and *bats*!" she exclaimed, shrinking involuntarily closer to him.

"Taggy, don't tell me you're afraid of mice," he said teasingly.

"No, it's the *bats*," she replied frankly, pushing her bonnet down even more firmly on her head. "Ugh!"

He would have responded, but the slow creaking of the door caused them both to swivel their heads around to look at it. "I hope they've found a closed carriage—" she was saying, but her words were cut off abruptly as she saw the figure who stood in the half-light before them. "Don Alonzo!"

He was certainly the last person she had expected to rescue them, but she was not about to turn down any help. "How odd to meet *you* here! My husband, Sir Richard, and I have been stranded by an accident to our carriage and would greatly appreciate your help in . . ." She did not finish the sentence, for Don Alonzo had not said a word, but was merely gazing at Richard in a way that sent a shiver down her spine. She could feel the tension in her husband's body. There was a prolonged silence; then at last Richard broke in wearily.

"So it was you, Davies. I should have guessed from the description, though apparently you made a most convincing Spaniard."

Don Alonzo made no reply, but took a step into the room. He had withdrawn a cocked pistol from his greatcoat, and now he leveled it at Richard. Annis gasped.

"Whatever your business is with me, let Annis go. She can have nothing to do with it."

Davies shook his head and said in an accentless voice, "I wish I could oblige you, Sir Richard. I did my best, but unfortunately the lady did not succumb to my charms. I suppose it worked out for the best, since you surprised us all by returning."

Richard was grim-faced now. "You have us where you want us. That was a neat job that you did to the wheel, by the way. It must have taken some time to file through five wheel spokes. Still, it accomplished what you intended."

"How very observant you are, but then, that's always been your problem—you're a little too observant."

"I would have known before we left London if I'd bothered to take a look at those 'postboys' of yours. I suppose I've gotten careless, being sick." He stared into the barrel of the pistol resolutely. "Well, what is it that you want? Or are you merely taking care of a little job for a certain government with which we are both familiar?"

"You attach too much importance to your abilities," Davies replied sardonically.

"Richard, who is he?" Annis could not help whispering.

"The manager of one of my lumber camps in Honduras, my dear. Or should I say that he formerly held that position, until evidence of wrongdoing forced me to discharge him. He has engaged in many professions, including that of actor, which may explain why he was able to pass himself off so well. I hired him as a *favor*"—Richard spat the word—"to a friend of mine, whose unacknowledged son he is."

The dark eyes regarding them held a scornful expression.

"Have I failed to do you justice?" Richard asked mockingly.

"But . . . but I know you to be wealthy," Annis said to Davies unbelievingly. "Your clothing, your horse, your curricle—why, you would not have been accepted into society without having some means."

He inclined his head. "You are right, Lady Burham. I have some wealth—and I intend to have a great deal more."

Annis' brain, stunned at first, was slowly beginning to operate once more. "That parcel of land—has this something to do with that?"

He gave her a cold smile. "Very astute of you, Lady Burham. Yes, as it happens, among Sir Richard's holdings there is a piece of land on which, by an odd coincidence, gold was discovered. I had been mining it in a discreet way with the use of Indian labor, but after my discharge, that naturally became more difficult. I would have preferred to own the land outright, but I doubted that Sir Richard would sell it to me, considering the terms on which we parted. The news of his death came as quite a godsend to me. I hoped that you, as his widow, would be willing to sell the land with a minimum of difficulty, but I didn't count on your obstinacy. After meeting you, it occurred to me that it might be easier to acquire the land by marriage, although I can't deny that the rest of Sir Richard's fortune, as well as your own obvious attractions, made it a particularly alluring prospect."

Richard gave a contemptuous snort, but Annis, who was still trying to piece things together, looked up at Davies, her eyes large in a white face. "Then the accidents—the carriages, the horse in the park, the flowerpot—it was you trying to kill me, and not Ambrose!"

He had nothing to lose by his admission. "Regrettably so, once I found that you wished to marry someone else. As far as I could determine, the first two mishaps were only accidents, but I thought them convenient if they gave you a distrust of your cousin. He was certainly not one of my admirers. Those accidents helped to spark my own plan for doing away with you. It should look as if your villainous cousin were responsible, and I should have your signature forged on a bill of sale so I might say that you had sold the land to me before you perished."

Annis could not help asking the question: "Then why did you attempt to hit me with the flowerpot after Richard had already returned? Your forgery would have done you little good, since he was the rightful owner all along."

Davies looked vexed. "The, ah, person I employed proved to be not altogether reliable. He was supposed to be observing your home during that period, but either he relaxed his vigilance or did not quite appreciate who Sir Richard was. That attempt was made quite against my wishes."

Sickened, Annis could no longer look at those cruel and perfect features. This was a man with whom she had spent hours of conversation, with whom she had eaten dinner, a man who had actually kissed her! She buried her face in Richard's shoulder as if to shut out the awful reality before her. A hand slipped reassuringly into hers and squeezed it.

Davies, who had lowered himself to a squatting position during their conversation, now raised himself again, with the pistol still trained on Richard. "I do regret the necessity for this," he said politely, "but I was forced to spend all my newfound wealth just to keep up appearances. When I ran out,

I went to the moneylenders, who are not terribly polite about waiting for reimbursement, so you see, I have little choice.''

Richard spat an epithet at Davies which was indicative of his origins, but Annis looked up at their captor bravely. ''How will it help you if we die? That won't get you the parcel of land.''

He smiled without humor. ''Oh, but you see, I've already had a bill of sale drawn up and Sir Richard's signature forged on it.''

''Pity you didn't think to do that in the first place,'' Richard said scornfully.

Davies' brows drew together angrily, but after a moment he replied, in a heated voice, ''If the reason for my dismissal had been less public, I might have. I knew no one would believe then that you had been willing to grant me such a favor, and I thought it would be easy to persuade the widow, particularly with the pathetic tale I concocted.'' He looked at Annis with a hint of admiration. ''I underestimated your wife.''

''You caused the talk yourself,'' Richard said coldly, ''and what makes you think anyone will believe that I sold it to you now?''

''Time has passed, and you have been known to be gravely ill, almost out of your head with illness in fact. Your only heirs will be your wife's family, who already know and trust me as Don Alonzo.''

He seemed to be finished with what he had to say, but Richard unexpectedly prolonged the conversation. ''It was most fortunate for you that the carriage broke down where it did, since you obviously could not control that circumstance.''

''Yes, wasn't it?'' Davies remarked. ''Though it was the postboy who spied the mill here and sent you to it. Rather a good touch, I thought, since it's unlikely that we'll be interrupted here. I meant to have dispatched you in the carriage and have it put about that highwaymen did it, but the fellow had a certain squeamishness about the job being done there in his sight.''

''It's rather an unusual highwayman who leads his victims to a mill before shooting them,'' Richard pointed out coolly, his voice revealing none of the desperation he felt.

Davies gave his cold smile again. ''Oh, the highwayman theory is quite out now. This is a dry old wood structure and it should burn nicely. You sought shelter here and lit a fire, which obviously got out of hand. There won't be enough remaining to show that you were shot first. And now, if I have satisfied your curiosity on every point, I must be going. I have to go procure a tinderbox somewhere to start my little blaze. Good-bye, Sir Richard.'' Annis clutched Richard to her, instinctively trying to shield him, but with an oath he cast her aside. With an expressionless face, Davies leveled the pistol at Richard's heart and pulled the trigger.

17

ANNIS had closed her eyes reflexively, but as there was no report, she opened them again. Davies was staring at his pistol with a foolish expression upon his face and Richard was grinning up at him. "Need to be careful to keep your powder dry on a day like this."

"But I did—it must have misfired somehow. I . . ." Davies suddenly realized that he didn't need to explain anything to his would-be victim, and he assumed control again. "I have another, anyway, and I doubt that it will misfire too."

He made the mistake of glancing down inside his coat to locate the pistol, which gave Richard the opportunity for which he had been waiting. He leapt up, taking Davies off guard and knocking the second pistol from his hands. It went clattering across the floor, and as the two men grappled, a suddenly inspired Annis ran to fetch it. She cocked it and pointed it at the writhing ball of flesh in the middle of the floor, praying that she wouldn't shoot Richard. Despite his infirmities, he was giving a good account of himself, but he had forgotten that Davies still held the first pistol in his hand. With an adroit twist, Davies managed to get one half of his body free and bring the heavy butt down on Richard's head. The shock made Richard loose his hold, enabling Davies to land a more powerful blow to the top of his head. Richard was half-stunned, and another few thumps served to complete the job. Davies rose, giving the prostrate form a kick as Annis took aim and pulled the trigger. Nothing happened. "Damnation!" she exclaimed.

Davies seemed to notice her once more, and he gave a lazy smile. "My luck is not out yet, you see." He strode toward her purposefully, and Annis' blood ran cold. Glancing about her, she noticed a ladder. She ran up it quickly, and stared down at him from the comparitive security of the platform above.

"Lady Burham, I have no time for these ridiculous games," he said as he placed one foot on the first rung of the ladder.

Her heart pounding, she climbed up another ladder to the next platform. It was a shorter climb than the first, and with a great effort she managed to pull the ladder up after her.

Davies squinted up at her in the darkness. "It is useless to try to get away, you know." He stood, one foot on the ladder, considering for a moment. "Well, if you prefer it, you may have it this way. It will look as if you climbed up there in an attempt to escape the fire."

He put his foot back down on the floor, walked over to Richard, and gave him another kick, which produced no response. Satisfied, he walked out the door. Annis could hear the heavy bar being drawn back into place. She held her breath for another minute, but it was evident that he truly had gone to find a tinderbox. Breathing a little more easily, she managed with some difficulty to replace the ladder, and climbed back down to the floor.

She ran over to Richard, crying with fear and shock. "Oh, Richard, he's gone. We must find a way to escape!" She shook him, but to no avail. She tried to pull him over on his back, but he was deadweight. She did manage to turn his head, and saw that he was still breathing. A rivulet of blood streamed down his forehead and over one eye. "Oh, Richard," she gasped.

She realized instantly that it was all up to her. She must save them—save Richard and herself. She took out a handkerchief and wiped the blood away tenderly, then covered him with a few of the sacks in an attempt to keep him warm.

What could she do first? She walked hurriedly over to the door and tried it. It was useless. The bar held it secure. They were trapped. Think! she told herself. She looked all around her. There was no other door on the ground floor. She looked up. The windows! Perhaps she could make her escape out a window.

She climbed rapidly up the ladder to the first platform and rushed over to the window there. Even at this height, it was a dizzying prospect—a straight fall of more than twenty feet, with the hill falling steeply away on this side. She would do neither of them any good if she escaped from the mill only to break her leg or her neck, even given that the ground was soft.

She gave a slight shudder and climbed up the ladder to the next floor. Here she had to crawl around a huge spout to reach the window. She tried not to notice how far the floor was beneath her, but as she reached the window she could see that it was an even less attractive prospect than the last. She was busy thinking to herself. Perhaps she could make some sort of rope from the grain sacks. Of course, that would take time, and she didn't know how much she had. She wasn't even sure that there were enough to do her any good. She looked about the platform in despair. It was useless. She would have to try to continue upward and see if there were anything else she might discover.

The next platform, where the huge stones lay, was at an even more frightening height, and she was suddenly aware of nearby squeaking and the scurrying of little feet. She was obviously disturbing the inhabitants. Their droppings were everywhere in the dust, making her task even more unpleasant. She noticed for the first time a heavy chain hanging down to the floor, which she guessed was used to haul the heavy sacks up to the top of the mill. She tried to see whether it might sustain her weight, but her chilled hands would hardly grip the cold iron, even after she removed her gloves. She tried to lift it and realized that it was far too heavy for her to drag even the bottom of it over to a window. She must discard this possibility.

There were no windows on this floor, but as she climbed up to the next, the light filtering in above made her uncomfortably aware of the dark shapes hanging from the rafters about her. Bats! She climbed onto the platform, and turning about, accidentally bumped one with her shoulder, causing it to give an angry squeak of protest. She jumped, only narrowly avoiding brushing against another, and gave a shudder. They slept during the daytime, she knew, but she could hear the rustling of wings about her as they adjusted themselves.

She made her way cautiously around the great machinery to the window, with no real hope in her heart. Looking out, she once again saw no footholds of any kind, just a sheer drop, but something in the view made her pause. From this window she could see the great sail frames. This mill had the more common arrangement involving four sails, and they had been left or had come to rest in a position almost perfectly vertical and horizontal, like a cross. The lower vertical sail stretched nearly to the ground. It almost appeared to be a ladder, the frame over which the canvas was usually stretched looking like a series of rungs leading down. Some dim memory surfaced in her mind, a memory from her childhood. Hadn't she seen the miller in their neighborhood climbing up the frame to make repairs? With about five minutes' effort she managed to force open the window. She reached out an arm, then leaned dangerously far out the window. It was no use. The sail was out of reach.

She thought to herself for a moment. The windows were staggered, winding in a spiral up the side of the mill. That should mean that the next one was almost directly over the sail.

She glanced up above her at the gloom spilling from the topmost floor. She could not doubt that it was home to the majority of these creatures that she abhorred. The noise of rustling and squeaking was very pronounced from above. For a moment her heart failed her. She had no choice. She tried to think of what Laurie had often told her. They are beneficial creatures. They eat insects. They do not harm people, she told herself. She took a deep breath, put her foot on the ladder, and climbed resolutely upward.

Using every bit of determination she possessed, she forced herself to move slowly toward the windows, trying to disturb the bats as little as possible. When her high-crowned carriage bonnet bumped a couple of them, she dropped to her knees and untied it, laying it on the ground gently. It was even worse to walk with her head uncovered, but she tried not to think about it.

Her spirits plummeted as she approached the window. One beam had fallen, resting at an angle as it projected from the window frame. In a small patch of shade, one lonely bat hung. She would have to move him if she intended to reach the window.

She might simply have tried to pick up the beam and move it, but she guessed if she didn't wish to have them all flying about her ears she would be better off disturbing him as little as possible. She stretched out one nerveless gloved hand. Even with the protection of a layer of thin kid, she couldn't help shuddering as she touched the membrane of the wings and gently exerted pressure. The furry little creature blinked at her sleepily and shifted sideways obligingly, without even a squeak. She let out an abrupt sigh, not even aware that she had been holding her breath. She reached the window, which fortunately opened with little exertion.

The sail rested immediately below her, stretching, as she had pictured it, like an enormous ladder to the ground. Well, it was now or never. She prayed that it was not rotten. She took a deep breath, stuck a leg out of the window, and found the first support. Turning, and trying to keep her skirts from catching, she thrust out her other leg and found herself standing on the sail.

The wind at this height was much fiercer than it had been on the ground. The sail rocked and shook, but held steady, and it seemed able to bear her weight. Saying her prayers, she started the climb down.

She worked her way downward slowly and methodically, one foot, then one hand, then the other foot, then the other hand. She gazed steadily at the mill itself, refusing to glance at the ground below. A single downward look, she knew, would prove her undoing. Besides, she needed all her concentration, for the frame was slippery from the rain. The climbing seemed to take an eternity. She began a new series of prayers, that Davies would not return and catch her halfway down the sail. He would need only to yell at her to make her start and fall. A gust of wind shook the frame, and she clung to it, unmoving, for a second. Her heart pounding in her ears, she gathered her courage and began her way down again.

The descent seemed to take hours, although she knew in reality that it involved only a few minutes. It was with a sense of relief and fear that she felt the last support. She placed her other foot down with the first, braced herself, and dropped. It was not a very great fall. She was lucky that the sails had been facing this direction and not the steep drop on the other side of the hill. She would be a little bruised tomorrow, but that was all. The thought brought Richard vividly to mind. She gathered herself up and raced over to the door.

"Richard, I'm here. I'm outside now." She could hear no reply to her shouts, so she began to try to draw back the bar. It was a simple business, surely. She had seen Richard do it.

She pulled and tugged, but she could not shift it. The weight was too great and it was wedged too firmly. She tugged at it again. Tears sprang to her eyes.

"Richard, I'm here, but I can't undo the bar!" There was only silence. She drew in a deep breath, gathered all of her strength, and gave a mighty heave. Nothing happened. "Richard," she called hopelessly. Was all her effort to be for naught? She leaned against the door and sobbed despairingly.

After she had vented the worst of her anguish, the will that had sustained her so far came strongly to her rescue. She considered her choices rapidly. She might wait here for Davies' return and steal his horse, but that would undoubtedly be too late to help Richard. She could try to find some place to conceal herself and lie in wait for him, she thought dubiously, but she had only the most pessimistic view of her chances of overcoming a muscular man who was a foot taller than she, even given the element of surprise. No, it was clear that the best course was to obey her first impulse and go for help. Davies was nowhere in sight anyway. She must take heart from that and remember that he would not wish to appear hurried or have people think his buying of a tinderbox remarkable in any way.

She set off back toward the road at a trot. There must be some cottagers about for the mill to have existed at all. The postboys, if they could be believed, had said that the village had lain beyond them. If so, that was probably the direction Davies would take. In hopes of avoiding him, she would try the other. Perhaps she would be lucky and meet some sort of carriage or cart along the way.

She fought her way through the weeds and mud back to the road, but found it deserted. She tried to remember that this was good news, for it meant that Davies was still not here yet. She turned in the direction from which they had come, hurrying along as fast as she was able, though now she was beginning to be short of breath. She half-ran, half-walked for what seemed an interminable length of time. Gasping with her efforts, she could not quite fight back the despairing tears, though they blurred her vision. Was there no rescue to be had? She sent up another prayer, and as she stumbled around a tree-lined curve, she saw a cottage. It was not in any way elegant, nor was it even in good repair, but it was clearly inhabited, for a trail of smoke curled out the chimney. She raced toward it with all that remained of her strength and fell against the door, breathless, pounding it.

"Help me! Help me!" she cried.

The door was opened and she found herself being regarded with some astonishment by a plump round-faced woman who was busy wiping her hands on her apron. "Eh? What's the matter then?"

"There's a man trying to kill someone . . . up at the old windmill . . . you must help me," Annis managed to say between gasps.

"Here, you'd better have a seat and catch your breath," the woman said, not unkindly, for it was obvious that the wet, mud-spattered, wild-eyed young woman in front of her was quality, even if she had managed to escape her keeper.

Annis shook her head with impatience, but it was a few minutes before her breathing eased enough to give a more or less coherent account of what had been happening. The woman had called in her husband, and it was evident from their carefully interested expressions that they didn't quite believe her. She sighed with exasperation. Precious minutes were fleeting. How could she stir them to action? An idea occurred. She didn't have her reticule, but it was back at the mill and she knew that Richard had money too.

"I'll pay you," she said desperately, "but my money is back at the mill. You must have some sort of cart and a horse, don't you? Hitch them up and drive me over as fast as you can and I'll see that you are well-rewarded. If you have a gun, it would be wise to bring it too."

The couple looked at each other in a consulting way. Their thoughts ran in perfect unspoken harmony. If the young lady was mad, wasn't it better to humor her? And wasn't it likely that there would be some sort of reward at the end? The husband made the decision. "I'll have my boy hitch up the horse." He cast a speaking glance at his wife. "Might want him with me when we get there," he said with a little toss of the head in Annis' direction.

"Oh, please hurry," Annis said impatiently.

Luckily the operation was accomplished in less time than she might have expected, though she did shake off the farmwife's offer of food and drink while accepting the loan of a warm cloak. When she saw the horse the cart was hitched to, her spirits sank, for it was clearly not an animal meant for speed. She had found an unexpected ally in the person of the son, Tom, who was at an age to be deeply affected by such a picture of beauty and distress. Although their household did not boast a firearm, Tom had included a stout shovel and a hoe from the barn. As soon as Annis was seated, he whipped up the horse in a way that brought an exclamation from his father, though an appealing look from Annis made the latter hold his peace. Dusk was beginning to fall and she despaired of reaching the mill before dark.

Thankfully, their journey passed at far greater speed than her flight to them had. They soon reached the track that led to the windmill, and Annis, peering through the misting rain, thought she saw a horse standing next to it.

"Oh, hurry," she cried.

Tom responded as best he could, clucking to the horse and giving the reins a shake to ask for more speed, but the animal was performing at the height of its abilities now. He was forced to slow to turn onto the track, and had some trouble coaxing the animal back into a trot. Annis had to bite her lip in order to keep silent. She could see as they drew closer that there indeed was a horse beside the mill. A feeling of dread all but overwhelmed her. "He is there! Oh, hurry!" she cried.

The words had scarcely left her lips when there was the loud sound of an explosion and the mill seemed to tremble for an instant before bursting into flame. The horse standing near it had been knocked over by the force of the blast, and now was running away with shrill neighs of fear. Annis could not believe her eyes.

Reacting instinctively, Tom pulled up the cart, and now Annis prepared to jump down from it. The farmer saw her intention and caught her by the arm. "Don't, miss. It's too dangerous. There's no telling where that fire could travel."

"Let me go!" Annis yanked her arm free of his grasp success-fully and ran as hard as she could toward the burning mill. She ran to where the force of the heat would permit her to go no nearer. She stared with eyes wide open, trying to focus through the shimmering waves of hot air, but she could see nothing. She could see no one. Her eyes were blurred with tears. If Richard were in that windmill, he was dead. There could be no doubt.

Shattered, emotionally and physically drained, she collapsed to her knees and began sobbing, not caring who saw her, not caring that she was still alive.

She remained on her knees like that, all hope lost, crying in the rain and the heat and the soot. After several minutes she felt a light touch on her shoulder and realized that the farmer must have come to lead her away.

"Oh, leave me alone," she said despairingly.

"Taggy?" It was a deep voice, croaking rather than husky now with all the smoke swirling about them. She opened her eyes and looked up. Could it be? There stood Richard, a disheveled, blackened Richard, but Richard nonetheless. She launched herself upward and threw her arms about his neck. "Richard! You are alive! You are alive! I love you! You are alive!"

Then and there, despite the heat and the soot and the smoke and the rain, they kissed, and it was as Annis remembered their first kiss to be, but with a passionate intensity that the other had lacked. Two people who had nearly lost their lives and each other in such a short space of time could not be expected to adhere to the rules of decorum, after all. Annis could have wished that it would never end, but Richard, more practical-minded at the moment, broke his hold upon her. Leading her, he began limping away from the fire.

Their arms about each other, they marched back in the direction of the cart, Annis tightly supporting her miraculously returned husband. When they had withdrawn a safe distance, she turned to him. "But how can you be alive? We saw the explosion. We didn't see anyone running away."

He shrugged. "I fell out the door—it's around back, the other side from here, you know—just a bare minute before the mill exploded. It was a near thing."

"And . . . Davies?"

He shook his head. "I tried to save him, the fool, but he wouldn't listen. I must have awakened ten minutes or so before his return. Anyway, I thought it best if I pretended I was still unconscious. I kept my eyes barely cracked open and watched him walking about, talking to you. He supposed you were still in the rafters. Well, I did too. Anyway, he heaped a pile of rags in the corner and had out his tinderbox before I knew what he was doing. I yelled that he was a fool and started to my feet, but of course he didn't give me a chance to explain. He just hit out at me—as a reflex, I suppose—and fortunately I was so weak that he knocked me right though the doorway and out onto the grass. The rags were already starting to smoke, so there wasn't really any hope, but I had started to get up when the blast knocked me over. I hope I'm never as near to one again! My ears are ringing and there were things flying in all directions. Luckily I found myself rolling from the force of the explosion, so I didn't get nicked by the flames."

He looked up, saw the horror in Annis' face, and gave the hand he was holding a squeeze. "I'm not sure that it wasn't for the best anyway," he said softly. "I don't know what his poor father would have done if he had been brought up on charges." He paused and reflected for a moment. "You know, it's odd. His father did as much for him as any man alive could have done, but it was never enough for Davies. He thought he was justified in breaking all the rules, yet I've known men in the same situation who have turned out quite differently."

The rain had finally stopped falling, and now, in the darkness, the clouds began to part.

Her expression was eloquent. "All that matters now is that I have you back and that I never intend to lose you—ever!"

He clasped her to him. "My word, Taggy, we've been through sheer hell, yet, you know, it was almost worth it to me. When Davies was preparing to shoot me and you tried to shield me—that was when I realized that somewhere down deep you still loved me, even though I thought I'd thrown it all away."

She searched his face. "But you seemed to know it that first night, before everything went wrong."

He grimaced. "That was before your suitors started showing up and I learned of your engagement. Then you made it sound as if you'd engaged yourself to me only in order to escape Ambrose.''

''It was convenient,'' admitted Annis frankly. She lifted her eyes to his and searched them. ''But how ridiculous of you to think that, when you knew perfectly well that I had adored you ever since I was born!''

He shook his head. ''It was after my father's death—that visit—I knew the instant I saw you. It was as if I had been searching for something my whole life and you had been there right under my nose all along.''

''Oh, I wish you had told me,'' Annis said with a heartfelt sigh.

''I thought you knew,'' he said with some surprise.

Both felt a thousand regrets as they gazed into each other's eyes. It was not a time for looking backward, though, or for recrimination. ''We are the lucky ones,'' he said softly. ''We have been given the chance to begin anew.''

She smiled a little tearfully, and this time when they kissed it was as if they'd been doing it their whole lives. Their surroundings meant nothing to them, and it was with a rude shock that Annis heard her name being yelled loudly.

''Annis! Annis!'' She looked up and saw that in their preoccupation they had somehow missed the arrival of Laurie in Richard's curricle, accompanied by the groom. Laurie leapt down while the groom, wooden-faced, went to stand at the horses' heads.

''I like this!'' he snorted. ''Here I've been scouring the countryside, worried half out of my mind about you, and I find you making a public spectacle of yourself right out in an open field. I don't suppose you bothered to concern yourselves about my feelings for a minute, did you? No, you stopped to do a little sightseeing—'' His gaze was caught by the still-flaming wreck of the windmill, and he gave a low whistle. ''Phew! That must have been some fire. I wish I had seen it go up!''

Richard and Annis exchanged speaking glances, but Laurie was oblivious. He noticed the figure of the farmer and Tom beating out stray fires with their shovel and hoe and heaping wet dirt on glowing embers. ''Here those fellows are working their hearts out and you're just standing about useless.''

''Laurie,'' Richard said forcefully. ''I suggest you go and

help those fine fellows. Afterward you may ask them if they won't be kind enough to carry you to the next village, where you will find us staying at whatever passes for an inn. Brown, help Lady Burham into the carriage.''

''Very well,'' Laurie replied incuriously, adding, ''You do both look like the very devil. I mean to speak to you later about that pair of bays, though. One has a habit of kicking out—''

''Laurie,'' Richard responded in the same manner as before, ''you may share your observations with me later.''

''All right.'' Laurie shrugged. He had already stripped off his coat and now was hurrying forward to help the farmer and his son. Richard stepped up into the carriage and took the reins from the groom. Brown climbed up behind them.

''My dear?''

''Yes?''

''If your younger brother sees fit to disturb us with horse talk tonight, have I your permission to strangle him?''

''You would earn my undying gratitude,'' she replied seriously. Braving the groom's certain disapproval, she saluted her husband with tender haste on one cheek as they began the drive away from the burning ruins into the deepening peace of a starlit night.